ALL
SHALL
BE
WELL

Also by Deborah Crombie
in Thorndike Large Print®

A Share in Death

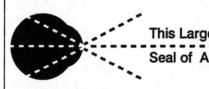

This Large Print Book carries the
Seal of Approval of N.A.V.H.

ALL SHALL BE WELL

DEBORAH CROMBIE

Thorndike Press • Thorndike, Maine

Published in 1994 by arrangement with Charles Scribner's Sons.

This is a work of fiction. Names, characters, places and incidents either are the product of the author's imagination or are used fictitiously. Any resemblance to actual events or persons, living or dead, is entirely coincidental.

Thorndike Large Print® Cloak & Dagger Series.

The tree indicium is a trademark of Thorndike Press.

The text of this Large Print edition is unabridged.
Other aspects of the book may vary from the original edition.

Set in 16 pt. News Plantin by Barbara Ingerson.

Printed in the United States on acid-free paper.

Library of Congress Cataloging in Publication Data

Crombie, Deborah.
    All shall be well / Deborah Crombie.
      p. cm.
    ISBN 0-7862-0298-X (alk. paper : lg. print)
    1. Police — England — London — Fiction. 2. Policewomen
— England — London — Fiction. 3. Assisted suicide —
England — London — Fiction. 4. London (England) —
Fiction. 5. Large type books. I. Title.
PS3553. R5378A771994
813'.54—dc20   94-19548

For Katie

It is sooth that sin is cause of all this
  pain,
But all shall be well and all shall be
  well and
all manner of things shall be well.

Juliana of Norwich, 15th century

ACKNOWLEDGEMENTS

As always, appreciation is due to The Every Other Tuesday Night Writers: Diane Sullivan, Dale Denton, Jim Evans, Viqui Litman, John Hardie, and Aaron Goldblatt, with special thanks to Terry Mayeux, who gave me much needed encouragement through the last chapters of this book.

I'd like to thank my editor, Susanne Kirk, and my agent, Nancy Yost, for their friendship as well as their professional expertise; and last but by no means least, my parents, Mary and Charlie Darden, for their unwavering support.

CHAPTER

1

Jasmine Dent let her head fall back against the pillows and closed her eyes. Morphine coats the mind like fuzz on a peach, she thought sleepily, and smiled a little at her metaphor. For a while she floated between sleeping and waking, aware of faint sounds drifting in through the open window, aware of the sunlight flowing across the foot of her bed, but unable to rouse herself.

Her earliest memories were of heat and dust, and the unseasonable warmth of the April afternoon conjured up smells and sounds that danced in her mind like long-forgotten wraiths. Jasmine wondered if the long, slow hours of her childhood lay buried somewhere in the cells of her brain, waiting to explode upon her consciousness with that particular lucidity attributed to the memories of the dying.

She was born in India, in Mayapore, a child of the dissolution of the Raj. Her father, a minor civil servant, had sat out the war in an obscure office. In 1947, he had chosen to stay on in India, scraping a living from his ICS pension.

Of her mother she had little recollection. Five years after Jasmine's birth, she had borne Theo and passed away, making as little fuss in dying as she had in living. She left behind only a faint scent of English roses that mingled in Jasmine's mind with the click of closing shutters and the sound of insects singing.

A soft thump on the bed jerked Jasmine's mind back to consciousness. She lifted her hand and buried her fingers in Sidhi's plush coat, opening her eyes to gaze at her fingers, the knobby joints held together by fragile bridges of skin and muscle. The cat's body, a black splash against the red-orange of the coverlet, vibrated against her hip.

After a few moments Jasmine gave the cat's sleek head one last stroke and maneuvered herself into a sitting position on the edge of the bed, her fingers automatically checking the catheter in her chest. Installing a hospital bed in the sitting room had eliminated the claustrophobia she'd felt as she became confined for longer periods to the small bedroom. Surrounded by her things, with the large windows open to the garden and the afternoon sun, the shrinking of her world seemed more bearable.

Tea first, then whatever she could manage of the dinner Meg left, and afterwards she could settle down for the evening with the telly. Plan in small increments, giving equal weight to each event — that was the technique she had adopted for getting through the day.

She levered herself up from the bed and shuffled toward the kitchen, wrapping about her the brilliant colors of an Indian silk caftan. No drab British flannels for her — only now the folds of the caftan hung on her like washing hung out on a line. Some accident of genetics had endowed her with an appearance more exotic than her English parentage warranted — the dark hair and eyes and delicate frame had made her an object of derision with the English schoolgirls remaining in Calcutta — but now, with the dark hair cropped short and the eyes enormous in her thin face, she looked elfin, and in spite of her illness, younger than her years.

She put the kettle on to boil and leaned against the kitchen windowsill, pushing the casement out and peering into the garden below.

She was not disappointed. The Major, clippers in hand, patrolled the postage-stamp garden in his uniform of baggy, gray cardigan and flannels, ready to pluck out any insubordinate sprig. He looked up and raised his clippers in salute. Jasmine mimed "Cup of tea?" When he nodded acceptance she returned to the hob and moved carefully through the ritual of making tea.

Jasmine carried the mugs out to the steps that led from her flat down to the garden. The Major had the basement flat and he considered the garden his territory. She and Duncan, in the flat above hers, were only privileged spectators. The planks of the top step grated against her bones as she eased into a sitting position.

The Major climbed the steps and sat beside her, accepting his cup with a grunt. "Lovely day," he said by way of thanks. "Like to think it would last." He sipped his tea, making a small swishing sound through his mustache. "You been keeping all right today?" He glanced at her for a second only, his attention drawn back to the rioting daffodils and tulips.

"Yes," Jasmine answered, smiling, for the Major was a man of few words under the best of circumstances. Those brief comments were his equivalent of a monologue, and his usual query was the only reference he ever made to her illness. They drank in silence, the tea warming them as much as the late afternoon sun soaking into their skins, until Jasmine spoke. "I don't think I've ever seen the garden look as lovely as it has this spring, Major. Is it just that I appreciate things more these days, or is it really more beautiful this year?"

"Hummff," he muttered into his cup, then cleared his throat for the difficult business of replying. "Could be. Weather's been bonny enough." He frowned and ran his fingers over the tips of his clippers, checking for rust. "Tulips're almost gone, though." The tulips wouldn't be allowed to linger past their prime. At the first fallen petal the Major would sever heads from stalks with a quick, merciful slash.

Jasmine's mouth twitched at the thought — too bad there was no one to perform such a service for her. She herself had failed in the final determination, whether from cowardice or courage, she couldn't say. And Meg . . . it had been too much to ask of Meg, she'd had no right to ask it of Meg. Jasmine wondered now how she had ever considered it.

Meg had arrived today looking even more untended than usual, her wide brow rumpled with distress. It took all Jasmine's strength to convince Meg that she'd changed her mind, and all the while the irony of it taunted her. It was she who was dying, after all, yet it was Meg who needed reassurance measured out in palliative doses.

She couldn't explain to Meg the reckoning

she had reached somewhere between last night's sleeping and this morning's waking. She knew only that she had crossed some meridian in her swift progress toward death. The pain held no more terror for her. With acceptance came the ability to hold and savor each moment, as well as a strange new contentment.

The sun dipped behind the square Victorian house across the garden, and its stone faded from gold to gray in an instant. The air felt chill against Jasmine's skin and she heard the faint bustle of traffic from Rosslyn Hill, evidence that life still eddied about her.

The Major stood, his knees creaking. "I'd best finish up. The light'll be gone soon." He reached down and hoisted Jasmine to her feet as easily as if she'd been a sack of potting soil. "In with you, now. Mustn't catch a chill."

Jasmine almost laughed at the absurdity of her catching a chill, as if an exterior circumstance could compare with the havoc her body had wreaked from within, but she let him help her inside and rinse the cups.

She locked the garden door after him and closed the casements, but hesitated a few minutes before drawing the blinds. The light was fading above the rooftops, and the leaves on the birch tree in the garden shivered in the evening breeze. From Duncan's terrace she might have watched the sun set over West London. For that privilege he paid dearly, and he had been kind enough to share it a few times before the stairs defeated her.

Duncan — now that was another thing she couldn't explain very well to Meg — at least not without hurting her feelings. She hadn't wanted Meg to meet him, had wanted to keep him separate from the rest of her existence, separate from her illness. Meg looked after her so zealously, tracking the progress of every symptom, monitoring her care and medication as if Jasmine's disease had become her personal responsibility. Duncan brought in the outside world, sharp and acid, and if he dealt with death it was at least far removed from hers.

As she sighed and lowered the blind, Sidhi rubbed against her ankles. The distinction between Duncan and Meg was all nonsense anyway — if Meg had immersed herself in her illness, her illness also made her a safe prospect for Duncan's friendship. No older woman-younger man scenario possible: dying made one acceptably non-threatening.

She found him a contradictory man, at once reserved and engaging, and she never quite knew what to expect. "Ice cream tonight?" she could hear him asking in one of his playful moods, a remnant of his Cheshire drawl surviving years in London. He'd jog up Rosslyn

15

Hill to the Häagen-Dazs shop and return panting and grinning like a six-year-old. Those nights he'd cajole her with games and conversation, rousing in her an energy she thought she no longer possessed.

Other evenings he seemed to draw into himself, content to sit quietly beside her in the flickering light of the telly, and she didn't dare breach his reserve. Nor did she dare depend too much on his companionship, or so she told herself often enough. It surprised her that he spent as much time with her as he did, but before her mind could wander down the path of analyzing his motivation she silenced it, fearing pity. She straightened as briskly as she was able and turned to the fridge.

The food Margaret left turned out to be a vegetable curry — Meg's idea of something nourishing. Jasmine managed a few bites, finding it easier to sniff and roll about on her tongue than to swallow, the smell and taste recalling her childhood as vividly as her afternoon dream. An accumulation of coincidence, she told herself, odd but meaningless.

She dozed in front of the television, half listening for Duncan's knock on the door. Sidhi narrowed his eyes against the blue-white glare and kneaded his paws against her thigh. What would happen to Sidhi? She'd made no provision for him, hadn't been able to face disposing of him like a piece of furniture. Her own brother Theo despised cats, the Major complained when Sidhi dug in his flower beds, Duncan treated him with polite indifference, Felicity pronounced him unsanitary, and Meg lived in a bed-sit in Kilburn with a landlady she described as ferocious — no good prospects there. Perhaps Sidhi would manage his next life without her intervention. He had certainly been fortunate enough in this one — she'd rescued him, a scrawny six-week-old kitten, from a rubbish bin.

She drifted off again, waking with a start to find the program she'd been watching finished. She wondered if, as her morphine dosage increased, her awareness would fade in and out like the reception on a poor telly. She wondered if she would mind.

Jasmine wondered, as the night drew in, if she had made the right decision after all, yet she knew somehow that once she had crossed that invisible line, there could be no going back.

Duncan Kincaid emerged from the bowels of Hampstead tube station and blinked in the brilliant light. He turned the corner into the High and the colors jostled before him with an almost physical force. All Hampstead seemed to have turned out in its shirt sleeves to greet the spring morning. Shoppers bumped and smiled instead of snarling, restaurants set up impromptu sidewalk cafes, and the smell of fresh coffee mingled with exhaust fumes.

Kincaid plunged down the hill, untempted by the effervescent atmosphere. Coffee didn't appeal to him — his mouth tasted like dirty washing-up water from drinking endless, stale cups, his eyes stung from other people's cigarette smoke, and having solved the case offered little solace for a long and dismal night's work. The body of a child found in a nearby field, the crime traced to a neighbor who, when confronted, sobbingly confessed he couldn't help himself, hadn't meant to hurt her.

Kincaid wanted merely to wash his face and collapse head first into bed.

By the time he reached Rosslyn Hill a little of the seasonal mood had infected him, and the sight of the flower seller at the corner of Pilgrim's Lane brought him up with a start. Jasmine. He'd meant to stop in and see her last night — he usually did if he could — but the relationship wasn't intimate enough for calling with excuses, and she would never mention that he hadn't come.

He bought freesias, because he remembered that Jasmine loved their heady perfume.

The silence in Carlingford Road seemed intense after the main thoroughfares, and the air in the shadow of his building still held the night's chill. Kincaid passed the Major coming up the steps from his basement entrance, and received the expected "Harummf. Mornin'." and a sharp nod of the head in response to his greeting. After several months of nodding acquaintance, Kincaid, intrigued by the brass nameplate on the Major's door, ventured a query regarding the 'H.' before 'Keith'. The Major had looked sideways, looked over Kincaid's head, groomed his mustache, and finally grumbled "Harley". The matter was never referred to again.

He heard the knocking as soon as he entered the stairwell. First a gentle tapping, then a more urgent tattoo. A woman — tall, with expensively bobbed, red-gold hair graying at the temples, and wearing a well-cut, dark suit — turned to him as he topped the landing before Jasmine's flat. He would have taken her for a solicitor if it hadn't been for the bag she carried.

"Is she not in?" Kincaid asked as he came up to her.

"She must be. She's too weak to be out on her own." The woman considered Kincaid and seemed to decide he looked useful. She stuck out her hand and pumped his crisply. "I'm Felicity Howarth, the home-help nurse. I

19

come about this time every day. Are you a neighbor?"

Kincaid nodded. "Upstairs. Could she be having a bath?"

"No. I help her with it."

They looked at one another for a moment, and a spark of fear jumped between them. Kincaid turned and pounded on the door, calling, "Jasmine! Open up!" He listened, ear to the door, then turned to Felicity. "Have you a key?"

"No. She still gets herself up in the morning and lets me in. Have you?"

Kincaid shook his head, thinking. The lock mechanism was simple enough, a cheap standard pushbutton, but he knew Jasmine had a chain and deadbolt. Were they fastened? "Have you a hairpin? A paperclip?"

Felicity dug in her bag, came up with a sheaf of papers clipped together. "This do?"

He thrust the bouquet into her hands in exchange for the clip, twisting the ends out as he turned to the door. The lock clicked after a few seconds probing, a burglar's dream. Kincaid twisted the knob and the door swung easily open.

The only light in the room filtered through the white rice-paper shades drawn over the windows. The flat was silent, except for a faint humming sound coming from the vicinity of

Jasmine's bed. Kincaid and Felicity Howarth stepped forward to the foot of the bed in an almost synchronized movement, not speaking, some quality in the room's silence sealing their tongues.

No movement came from the body lying swathed in the bed's swirl of colors, no breath gave rhythmic rise and fall to the chest on which the black cat crouched, purring.

The freesias fell, forgotten, scattering like pick-up sticks across the counterpane.

CHAPTER

2

"Stupid bloody cow." Roger's voice rose, echoing ominously in the small room. Margaret imagined the heavy clump of her landlady's feet mounting the stairs and reached toward him, as if her gesture might hush him. Mrs. Wilson had threatened more than once to evict Margaret if she caught Roger staying the night, and if she heard them quarrelling at half-past seven in the morning she wouldn't have much doubt about the circumstances.

"Roger, please, for heaven's sake. Mrs. Wilson'll hear you, and you know what she's like —"

"Heaven hasn't much to do with it, my dear Meg, except for the fact that your friend Jasmine's no nearer to it today than she was yesterday, thanks to you." The opportunity for sarcasm kept his volume down, but Margaret felt the coffee she'd gulped rise sourly in her throat.

"Roger, you can't mean that — have you gone mad? I told you she changed her mind. I'm glad she changed her mind —"

"So you can spend every spare second of your time fussing and cooing over her like some dumpy Florence Nightingale? It makes me sick. Why should I hang around? Tell me that, Meg, dear —"

"Shut up, Roger. I've told you not —"

"— To call you that. It's her pet name for you. How sweet." He took a step closer and grabbed her elbow, squeezing it between his fingers. Margaret could smell her soap on his skin, and the herbal shampoo he used on his hair, and see the light glinting off the red-brown patch of stubble he'd missed on his jaw. "Tell me why I should stick around, Margaret," he spoke softly now, almost whispering, "when you haven't any time for me, and she could hang on for months?"

Margaret jerked her arm free. "Why don't you go, then," she hissed at him, and she felt a distant surprise, as if the words came from somewhere outside herself. "Just bloody well bugger off, all right?"

They faced each other in silence for a long moment, the sound of their breathing audible over the background noise of Radio Four, and then Roger laughed. He lifted his hand and cupped it under Margaret's chin, tilting her head back. "Is that what you want, love?" Roger leaned closer, his mouth inches from hers. "Because you won't get it. I'll leave when I'm good and ready, not before, and don't you even think about clearing out on me."

The number eighty-nine bus bounced and rattled its way up the hill through Camden Town. Margaret Bellamy sat in the forward seat on the upper deck, her bulging shopping bag placed beside her as a bastion against intruders.

She needn't have worried. The only other occupant to venture climbing the stairs was a toothless old man absorbed in a racing paper. The seat's cracked upholstery stank of cigarette smoke and exhaust fumes, but Margaret found the familiar odor comforting. She gnawed her knuckle, the latest in a series of displacement behaviors designed to prevent her from biting her nails. An infantile habit, Jasmine called it. Jasmine . . .

Margaret's thoughts veered away, jumping to another track like a needle skipping on an old phonograph. She'd had to get out of the office, even if Mrs. Washburn had given her that fishy-eyed stare and said "Dentist again?"

"Bitch," Margaret said aloud, then looked

around to see if the smelly old man had heard her. And what if he had, she asked herself? It seemed like she'd spent her whole life trying not to offend anybody, and it had landed her in an awful bloody mess.

She should have told Jasmine about Roger, that was her first mistake. But when he'd first started asking her out she hadn't quite believed it herself, and didn't want to risk the humiliation if he dropped her as quickly as he'd picked her up. Afterwards, the right moment never seemed to materialize, and the guilt she felt for keeping it secret compounded her embarrassment. She rehearsed all sorts of "There's something I've been meaning to tell you" scenarios, and finally remained silent.

Actually, Roger hadn't really taken her out. Looking back on it, she saw that he merely had provided his presence and attention while she paid for almost everything. A small price it seemed at the time, to bask in the glow of Roger's looks, his connections, his air of knowing all the right people and the right places.

Still, it had been a small error of vanity, a forgivable mistake. The ones she had made since were not dismissed so easily. She never should have told Roger what Jasmine had asked her to do. And she never should have told him about the money.

The bus shuddered to a stop at South End Green. Balancing her bag against her hip, Margaret picked her way down the stairs and came blinking out into the sunshine. The huge, old plane trees and willows of the South Heath marched away to her right as she started up the hill. Sun sparkled on the waters of the ponds, and people flowed around her with that festive air that an unexpectedly warm spring day gives the English.

The unsettled feeling that had been nagging her since last night coiled more tightly in the pit of her stomach.

From Willow Road she turned away from the Heath and trudged up Pilgrim's Lane. Just as she reached Carlingford Road she looked up and saw the rear of an ambulance disappear as it turned left into Rosslyn Hill. Margaret's stomach spasmed and her knees threatened to give way beneath her.

Felicity stripped the bed, then straightened the spread over the bare mattress, tucking the corners with precision. Kincaid, having raised the blinds, stood staring down into the patch of garden. After a moment he shook himself and ran his fingers through his hair, then turned to face her. "Who's next of kin, do you know?"

"A brother, I think, called Theo," Felicity

answered, giving the spread a final smoothing across the pillow. She surveyed the bed for a moment, gave a satisfied nod and turned to the sink. "Although I'm not sure they got on well," she continued over her shoulder as she washed her hands before filling the copper kettle from the tap. "She mentioned him several times. He lives in Surrey, or Sussex, but I never met him." Felicity nodded toward the small, inlaid secretary Jasmine had used for her papers. "I imagine you'll find his number and address in that lot."

Kincaid was a bit taken aback by her assumption that he would be responsible for notifying Jasmine's relatives, but he had no idea who else might perform the unpleasant task. He didn't relish the prospect.

"It does take them like that sometimes — suddenly, you know." Felicity turned and examined him with concern, and Kincaid marveled at the speed with which she had regained her equilibrium. A few seconds shock — eyes closed, face wiped blank — then she had taken over with brisk professional competency. A common enough occurrence for her, he supposed, the loss of a patient.

"But she didn't seem —"

"No. I'd have given her another month or two, at the least, but we're not God . . . our predictions aren't infallible." The kettle whistled and Felicity turned away, scooping mugs off a rack and pouring boiling water over tea bags in one smooth motion. The dark, business-like suit seemed at odds with such household proficiency, and Felicity herself, soberly neat against the welter of Jasmine's exotic belongings, reminded Kincaid of a hawk among peacocks.

"She never spoke about it . . . her illness, I mean," Kincaid said. "I didn't realize it was so far —"

The front door swung open and bounced against the wall. Kincaid and Felicity Howarth spun around, startled. A woman stood framed in the doorway, clutching a shopping bag to her breast.

"Where is she? Where have they taken her?" She took in the neatly made bed and their arrested postures, and the bag slipped as she swayed.

Felicity was quicker off the mark than Kincaid. She had the bag safely on the floor and her hand under the woman's elbow before Kincaid reached them.

They guided her toward a chair and she slumped into it, unresisting. Not yet thirty, Kincaid judged her, a trifle plump, with wayward brown hair and painfully fair skin, and a round face now crumpled with distress.

"Margaret? It is Margaret, isn't it?" Felicity

asked gently. She glanced at Kincaid and explained, "She's a friend of Jasmine's."

"Tell me where they've taken her. She won't want to be alone. Oh, I knew I shouldn't have left her last night —" The sentence disintegrated into a wail and she turned her head from side to side as if searching for Jasmine in the flat, her hands twisting in her lap. Kincaid and Felicity looked at one another over Margaret's head.

Felicity knelt and took Margaret's hands in hers. "Margaret, look at me. Jasmine's dead. She died in her sleep last night. I'm sorry."

"No." Margaret looked at Felicity in appeal. "She can't be. She promised."

The words struck an odd note and Kincaid felt a prickle of alarm. He dropped down on one knee beside Felicity. "Promised? What did Jasmine promise, Margaret?"

Margaret focused on Kincaid for the first time. "She changed her mind. I was so relieved. I didn't think I could go through —" a hiccupping sob interrupted her and she shivered. "Jasmine wouldn't go back on a promise. She always kept her word."

Felicity had let go Margaret's hands and they moved restlessly again in her lap. Kincaid captured one and held it between his own. "Margaret. What exactly did Jasmine want you to do?"

She went still and blinked at him, puzzled. "She wanted me to help her kill herself, of course." She blinked again and the tears spilled over, and the words came so softly Kincaid had to strain to hear them. "Whatever will I do now?"

Felicity rose, fetched a mug of luke-warm tea from the kitchen, stirred in some sugar, and carefully wrapped both Margaret's hands around the cup. "Drink up, love. You'll feel more yourself." Margaret drank greedily until the cup was empty, unmindful of the tears slipping down her face.

Kincaid pulled up a dining chair and sat facing her, waiting as she fished a wad of tissue from her skirt pocket and mopped at her eyes. Her pale eyelashes gave her a defenseless look, like a rabbit caught in a lamp. "Tell me exactly what happened, please, Margaret. I'd like to know."

"I know who you are," she said, sniffing, studying him. "Duncan. You're much better —" Then red blotches stained her fair skin and she looked down at her hands. "I mean . . ."

"Did Jasmine tell you about me, then?" Jasmine had been very good at keeping her life compartmentalized, thought Kincaid. She had never mentioned Margaret to him.

"Just that you lived upstairs, and came to

visit her sometimes. I used to say she'd made you up, like a child's imaginary friend, because I'd never —" the word ended on a sob and the tissues came up again, "seen you."

"Margaret." Kincaid leaned forward and touched her arm, bringing her attention back to his face. "Are you sure that Jasmine meant to kill herself? She might have just been whistling in the wind, talking about it to make herself feel she had an option."

"Oh, no." Margaret shook her head and hiccupped. "As soon as the reports came back that her therapy wasn't successful, she wrote to Exit. She said she couldn't face the feeding tube — all pipes and plugs, she called it — said she wouldn't feel human any—" Margaret screwed up her face and pressed her fingers to her lips with the effort of holding back tears.

Kincaid leaned forward encouragingly. "It's okay. Go on."

"They sent all the information and we planned it out — how much she should take, exactly what she should do. Last night. It was to be last night."

"But she changed her mind?" Kincaid prompted when she didn't continue.

"I came as soon as I could get off work. I'd screwed myself up to tell her I couldn't go through with it, but she didn't even let me finish. 'It's all right, Meg,' she said, 'Don't worry. I've changed my mind, too.' She looked . . . different somehow . . . happy." Margaret looked at him with entreaty. "I believed her. I'd never have left her if I hadn't."

Kincaid turned to Felicity. "Is it possible? Would she have been able to manage it herself?"

"Of course, with these self-medicating patients it's always a possibility," she answered matter-of-factly. "That's one of the risks you take with home care."

No one spoke for a moment. Margaret sat with her shoulders slumped, red-eyed and spent. Kincaid sighed and rubbed his face, debating. If he alone had heard Margaret's disclosure, he might have ignored it, let Jasmine go unquestioned and undisturbed. But Felicity Howarth's presence complicated matters. She would be as aware of correct procedure as he, and to ignore indications of suspicious death smacked of collusion. And although his own grief and exhaustion kept him from isolating it, a sense of unease still hovered at the edge of his consciousness.

He looked up and found Felicity watching him. "I suppose," he said reluctantly, "I had better order a post mortem."

"You?" Felicity said, her brows drawing together, and Kincaid realized what he hadn't told her.

"Sorry. I'm a policeman. Detective Superintendent, Scotland Yard." Watching Felicity, Kincaid had the same fleeting impression he'd had when they found Jasmine's body. Her face went smooth and blank, as if she'd scrubbed it free of emotion.

"Unless you'd rather do the honors?" he asked, thinking he might have offended her by usurping her authority.

Felicity's attention came back to him, and she shook her head. "No. I think it's best if you take care of it." She nodded toward Margaret, who still sat unresponsive. "I've other matters to see to." She went to Margaret and touched her shoulder. "I'll see you home, love. My car's just outside."

Margaret followed her without protest, taking the shopping bag Felicity gathered up for her and cradling it against her chest. At the door, she turned back to Kincaid. "She shouldn't have been alone," she whispered, and the words seemed almost an accusation, as if he, too, were somehow responsible.

The door closed behind them. Kincaid stood in the silent flat, suddenly remembering that he hadn't slept for almost forty-eight hours. A thread of a cry broke the stillness and he spun around, heart jumping.

The cat, of course. He had forgotten all about the cat. He dropped to his knees beside the bed and peered underneath. Green eyes shone back at him.

"Here kitty, kitty," he called coaxingly. The cat blinked, and he saw a movement which might have been a twitch of its tail. "Here kitty. Good kitty." No response. Kincaid felt like an idiot. He brushed himself off and rooted around in the kitchen until he found a tin of catfood and a tin opener. He spooned the revolting stuff into a bowl and set it on the floor. "Okay, cat. You'll have to shift for yourself. I'm going home."

Exhaustion swept over him again, but he had a few more things to do. He checked the fridge, finding two nearly-full vials of morphine. Then he pulled the rubbish bin from under the sink and sifted through it. No empties.

He found Jasmine's address book easily enough, however, neatly stowed in a slot in the secretary. Her brother was listed with a phone number and address in Surrey. He had pocketed the book and put a hand on the doorknob when a thought brought him up short.

Jasmine had been a very methodical person. Whenever he'd visited her he always heard her draw the bolt and put up the chain behind him. Would she have lain quietly down to die without securing her door? Consideration for those entering the next day, perhaps? He shook his head. Access would have been easy enough through the garden door. And yet, if she'd died naturally in her sleep she would have locked up as usual the evening before.

The doubt irritated him, and he stepped into the hall and closed the door more smartly than it warranted. It was then he realized he'd forgotten to look for a key.

CHAPTER

3

The midday sun poured through the uncurtained southern windows of Kincaid's flat, creating a stifling greenhouse effect. He pushed open the casements and the balcony door, shedding his jacket and tossing it over the back of the armchair in the process. Sweat broke out under his arms and beaded his upper lip, and the telephone receiver felt slippery in his fingers as he dialed the coroner's office.

Kincaid identified himself and explained the situation. Yes, the body had been sent to hospital as there was no doctor in attendance to certify death. No, he'd not questioned the cause of death at the time, but had since learned something that made it suspicious. Would the coroner ask the hospital histopathologist to do a post mortem? Yes, he supposed it was an official request. Would they please let him know the results as soon as possible?

He thanked them and hung up, satisfied that he had at least started proceedings. The paperwork could wait until tomorrow. He stood looking irresolutely around the flat, dreading the call to Jasmine's brother.

Days-old dirty dishes cluttered the kitchen sink, cups containing sticky dregs smudged the dust on the coffee table while books and clothes littered the furniture. Kincaid sighed and sank into a chair, rubbing his face absentmindedly. Even his skin felt rubbery and slack with exhaustion. Leaning back and closing his eyes, he felt a hard lump beneath his shoulder blade — his jacket, Jasmine's address book in the breast pocket. He pulled the slender book out and sat studying it. It suited Jasmine, he thought — emerald green leather stamped with small, gold dragons, elegant and a little exotic. It crossed his mind that he must ask her where she got it, then he shook his head. He had yet to accept it.

The gilt-edged pages of the small book fluttered through his fingers like butterflies' wings and he caught glimpses of Jasmine's tiny italic script. Names jumped out at him. Margaret Bellamy, with an address in Kilburn. Felicity Howarth, Highgate. Theo he discovered under the T's, simply the first name and phone number.

He punched the numbers in more slowly

this time. The repeated burring of the phone sounded tinny and distant, and he had almost given up when a man's voice said "Trifles."

"I beg your pardon?" Kincaid answered, startled.

"Trifles. Can I help you?" The voice sounded a little peevish this time.

Kincaid collected himself. "Mr. Dent?"

"Yes. What can I do for you?" Peevishness became definite annoyance.

"Mr. Dent, my name is Duncan Kincaid. I live in the same building as your sister, Jasmine. I'm sorry to have to tell you that she died last night." The hollow silence on the other end of the line lasted so long that Kincaid wondered if the man were still there. "Mr. Dent?"

"Jasmine? Are you sure?" Theo Dent sounded bewildered. "Of course, you're sure," he continued with a little more strength. "What an idiotic question. It's just that . . . I didn't expect —"

"I don't think anyone —"

"Was she . . . I mean, did she . . ."

Kincaid answered gently. "She seemed very peaceful. Mr. Dent, I'm afraid you'll have to come and make arrangements."

"Oh, of course." A plan of action seemed to galvanize him into disjointed efficiency. "Where have they . . . where is she? I can't come until this evening. I'll have to close the shop. I don't drive, you see. I'll have to get the train in —"

Kincaid interrupted him. "I could meet you if you like, here at the flat, and give you the details then." He didn't want to explain over the telephone why the funeral arrangements might be delayed.

Theo gave an audible sigh of relief. "Could you? That's very kind of you. I'll get the five o'clock train up. Are you upstairs or down? Jasmine never —"

"Up." Theo's ignorance didn't surprise Kincaid — after all, he hadn't even known that Jasmine had a brother.

They rang off and Kincaid closed his eyes for a moment, the worst of his immediate responsibilities finished. It hadn't been as bad as he'd expected. Jasmine's brother sounded more bewildered than grief-stricken. Perhaps they hadn't been close, although he was finding that Jasmine's silence on a subject was not necessarily indicative. Feeling too fuzzy to think clearly about it, he wandered into the kitchen and peered into the refrigerator — eggs, a shriveled tomato, a suspicious bit of cheese, a few cans of beer. He popped open a beer and took a sip, grimaced and set it down again.

He had his shirt half unbuttoned and had

reached the bedroom door when the knock came — sharply official, two raps. Kincaid opened his front door and blinked. He didn't often see Major Keith dressed in anything except his gardening gear, and today he looked particularly natty — tweed suit with regimental tie, shoes polished to a looking-glass shine, neatly creased trilby in his hand, and an anxious expression puckering his round face.

"Major?"

"I just spoke to the postman. He said he'd seen an ambulance pull away from the building when he came past earlier and I wondered — there was no answer when I knocked downstairs just now. Is she all right?"

Oh, lord! Kincaid sagged against the doorjamb. How could he have forgotten that the Major didn't know? And they were friends, not just passing acquaintances — her comfortable afternoon visits with the Major were one thing, at least, that Jasmine had discussed. "I'm not sure you'd call them 'chats'," she'd said, laughing. "Mostly we just sit, like two old dogs in the sun."

Kincaid pulled himself together, sure that his face was stamped with dismay. "Come in, Major, do." He ushered the Major in and waved vaguely in the direction of a chair, but the Major turned and stood quietly facing him,

40

waiting. His eyes were a surprisingly sharp, pale blue.

"You'd best tell me, then," he said, finally.

Kincaid sighed. "She didn't answer the door to her nurse this morning. I came along and forced the lock. We found her in bed. She seemed to have died peacefully in her sleep."

The Major nodded, and an expression flickered across his face that Kincaid couldn't quite place. "A good lass, in spite of —" He broke off and focused on Kincaid. "Well, never mind that now." The remnants of his Scots burr became more pronounced. "Will you be seeing to things, then?"

Another assumption of an intimacy with Jasmine he hadn't felt he merited, Kincaid thought curiously. "Temporarily, at least. Her brother's coming up tonight."

The Major merely nodded again and turned toward the door. "I'll leave you to get on with it."

"Major?" Kincaid stopped him as he reached the door. "Did Jasmine ever mention a brother to you?"

The Major turned in the act of jamming his hat over the thinning hair brushed across his skull. Thoughtfully, he fingered the gray bristles that lay on his upper lip like thatch on a cottage roof. "Well now, I can't say as she did. She never said much. Remarkable for

41

a female." The blue eyes crinkled at the corners.

After watching the Major descend the stairs, Kincaid shut his door and leaned against the inside. Even working all night on a nasty case didn't account for the leaden feeling in his limbs and the cotton-wool in his head. Shock, he supposed, the mind's way of holding grief at bay.

He fastened the chain on the door, rammed home the bolt, and lifted the phone out of its cradle as he passed. Shedding clothes, he stumbled into the bedroom. Flies buzzed heavily in and out of the open window. A bar of sunlight lay diagonally across the bed, as substantial as stone. Kincaid fell into it and slept before his face touched the rumpled sheet.

The temperature dropped quickly as the sun set and Kincaid woke with the draft of cool air against his skin. The bit of southern sky he could see through the still-open window was charcoal tinged faintly with pink. He rolled over and looked at the clock, swore, and stumbled out of bed in the direction of the shower.

Fifteen minutes later he'd managed to get himself into jeans and pullover and was dragging a comb through his damp hair when the bell rang. All his expectations of a male version of Jasmine Dent vanished when he opened the door.

"Mr. Kincaid?" The man's question was hesitant, as if he were afraid he might be rebuffed.

Kincaid examined him, taking in the oval face and small bone structure, but there any resemblance to Jasmine ended. Theo Dent wore an extra layer of padding on his small frame, had a halo of curly brown hair shot with gray, round John Lennon specs and eyes that were blue rather than brown.

"Mr. Dent." Kincaid held out his hand and Theo gave it a quick jerk. His palm felt damp and Kincaid had the impression that his hand trembled. "Do you have a key to your sister's flat, Mr. Dent?"

Theo shook his head. "No. No, I'm afraid not."

Kincaid thought for a moment. "You'd better come in while I hunt something up." He left Theo standing with his hands clasped in front of him, rocking on his heels, while he rooted around in the bedroom bureau drawer. When he'd worked Theft one of his regulars had given him a set of lockpicks which he had never had occasion to use.

He held up the ring of delicate wires as he returned to the sitting room, and Theo's eyebrows rose questioningly above the rims of his spectacles. "I didn't think to look for a key when I locked up again earlier," Kincaid said in explanation. "These ought to do the trick."

"But how . . . I mean, it was you that found . . ."

"Yes. I picked it a little less elegantly this morning, I'm afraid. With a paperclip." If Theo Dent wondered how Kincaid came by a set of lockpicks, he didn't ask.

They descended the stairs and Kincaid made short work of the cheap lock. As he opened the door and stepped aside, his arm brushed against Theo's and he felt the tremor running through it. He paused and touched Theo's shoulder. "Listen. It's all right, you know. There's nothing to see. You don't even have to go in if you'd rather not. I just thought you might need to look through her papers."

Theo looked up at him, his blue eyes blinking earnestly. "No, I want to go in. I must. Forgive my being silly." He stepped past Kincaid into Jasmine's flat. His momentum carried him to the center of the sitting room, where he came to a halt, his arms hanging at his sides. He gazed at his sister's things, the jade and brass, the brightly colored silk hangings, and the neatly tucked hospital bed taking up more than its share of space.

To Kincaid's consternation tears began to slip beneath the gold spectacles and run unchecked down Theo's face. Standing among his sister's belongings he looked both pathetic and incongruous — the tweedy jacket over the pinstriped shirt and red braces seemed almost a parody of Englishness. He reminded Kincaid of the dressed-up teddy bears in shop windows.

"Here." He took Theo's arm and guided his unresisting body over to a dining chair. "Sit down." Kincaid hunted for some tissues on the table by the bed, and the sight of Jasmine's book and reading glasses sitting tidily next to the tissue box made him feel rather hollow himself. "Jasmine kept some whiskey in the cupboard," he said as he handed Theo the tissues. "We could both use something to drink."

Theo shook his head. "I'm not much of a drinker." He sniffed, took off his spectacles and wiped his face, then blew his nose. "But I suppose just a small one won't hurt."

Kincaid splashed a half-inch of whiskey in two glasses and handed one to Theo. "Cheers."

"Thanks. And please call me Theo. Under the circumstances anything else is rather absurd." They drank in silence for a few minutes, some of Theo's color returning. He buried his face in the tissues and blew, then pulled a rumpled handkerchief from his pocket and gently patted the tip of his nose.

"It's just that I didn't quite believe it," Theo spoke suddenly, as if continuing a conversation Kincaid hadn't begun, "until I came in and saw the flat empty, and the bed here in the sitting room. I didn't know about the bed."

Kincaid frowned. Jasmine had ordered the hospital bed several months ago. "How long since you'd seen your sister, Theo?"

Theo took another sip of the whiskey and contemplated the question. "Six months, I think. About that." He saw Kincaid's look of surprise. "Please don't get the wrong impression — what did you say your name was? I wasn't quite taking things in when you phoned."

"Duncan."

Theo nodded a little owlishly, and Kincaid thought he had not exaggerated his low tolerance for alcohol. "It's not that I didn't want to see my sister, Duncan, but that she didn't want to see me. Or rather," he leaned forward and waved his glass at Kincaid in emphasis, "she didn't want me to see her. After she knew she was ill she didn't encourage me to visit." Theo leaned back in his chair and sighed. "God! She could be so stubborn. I rang up

46

every week. Once, when I phoned and begged her to let me come she said, 'Theo, I'm losing my hair. I don't want you to see me.' I can't imagine her without it. Was she —"

"She did lose her hair, but it grew in again when they stopped the treatments. Quite thick and dark, like a boy's."

Theo considered this, nodded. "She always wore it long, since she was a girl. She was quite proud of it." He fell silent and closed his eyes for so long that Kincaid began to think he had dozed off. Kincaid had reached over to take the tilting glass from Theo's hand when he opened his eyes and continued as if he hadn't paused.

"Jasmine always looked after me, you see. Our mother died when I was born, our father when I was ten and Jasmine fifteen. But Father wasn't much use. It was always just the two of us, really." Theo took another sip of his drink and patted his nose again with the handkerchief. "She told me that the treatments had helped, that she was doing all right. I should have known better." He leaned back and closed his eyes again for a moment. When he opened them and spoke, his words were surprisingly bitter. "I think she couldn't bear to be at a disadvantage, couldn't bear not to be in charge. She robbed me of my only chance to repay her, to look after her the way she looked after me."

"Surely she didn't want to distress you," Kincaid suggested gently.

Theo sniffed. "Perhaps. But it would have been easier than this . . . this leaving things unfinished."

Deciding it unwise to offer a refill, Kincaid gathered up Theo's empty glass along with his own and washed them out in the sink. He felt unexpectedly light-headed himself, and remembered that the last thing he'd eaten had been stale sandwiches at his desk in the early morning hours. Theo's voice interrupted his thoughts before they wandered too far in the direction of food.

"The really odd thing is that she phoned me yesterday — that was odd in itself as she almost always waited for me to ring her — and said she wanted to see me this weekend. I thought she must be improving. She really sounded quite well. We made arrangements for Sunday, as I couldn't close the shop on Saturday."

A cruel trick to play on her brother, Kincaid thought, if Jasmine had intended to kill herself. He hadn't thought her capable of malice. Still, what did he know of the relationship between them, or about Theo, for that matter? He turned around and leaned against the sink, folding his arms across his

48

chest. "What do you sell, Theo? Jasmine never said."

Theo smiled. "Junk, really. As in j-u-n-q-u-e. Things not quite old enough to be considered antiques and not expensive enough to be considered much else. Anything from buttons to butter dishes." His face fell. "Jasmine helped set me up." He stood and began walking restlessly about the room, touching things. "I don't know what I shall do now." He shook his head, then turned and faced Kincaid again, holding a small porcelain elephant from Jasmine's writing desk. "What's to be done, about Jasmine, I mean? There will have to be arrangements made . . . I'm afraid I don't know where to start. Do you know what she wanted?" Theo's brow creased and he continued before Kincaid could speak. "Were you a close friend of my sister? I'm sorry — I've been so caught up in myself — I ought to have realized. It must have been very difficult for you."

Kincaid hadn't been prepared for sympathy. "Yes," he said, answering both question and statement, then took a breath and straightened up. It couldn't be put off indefinitely. "I was a friend of Jasmine's, but I'm also a policeman. When Jasmine's nurse and I found her this morning we assumed she had died of natural causes. Then Jasmine's friend Margaret arrived and told us that she had agreed to help Jasmine commit suicide."

Theo's pacing had taken him back to the dining chair. He collapsed in it as suddenly as if his legs had been cut from under him. "Suicide?"

"Margaret said that yesterday Jasmine told her she'd changed her mind, but now she thinks Jasmine just intended releasing her from her obligation."

"But why? Why would she kill herself?"

"Perhaps she didn't want to become too dependent on anyone, or suffer any more than necessary."

"Of course. Stupid of me." Theo's eyes had lost their focus, and he absently stroked the porcelain elephant he still held. "That would be like her."

"Theo, I had the coroner's office request a post mortem." Seeing Theo's look of incomprehension, Kincaid continued. "In a situation like this it's necessary to find out exactly what did happen."

"Is it?" Theo asked, still sounding puzzled.

"Well, it's the usual procedure if there's any uncertainty as to cause of death." It seemed to Kincaid that the second shock had rendered Theo unable to cope, and the whiskey probably hadn't improved matters. "I'm afraid the funeral arrangements will have to wait until afterwards. Perhaps you could get in touch with her solicitor?" Theo looked at him blankly. "Do you know her solicitor's name?" Kincaid asked.

Theo made an effort to collect himself. "Thomas . . . Thompson . . . I'm not sure." He stood up, still clutching the elephant. "Look. You've been very kind. Would you mind looking after things here a bit longer? I think I'd like to go home."

Kincaid wondered if he would make it. "Shall I walk with you to the tube station?"

Theo shook his head. "No. I'm fine, really." He stood up, and only as he held out his hand to Kincaid did he seem to realize he still held the small elephant. "It was mine as a child," he said in answer to Kincaid's questioning look. "I gave it to Jasmine when I moved into my first digs. Didn't think it fashionable, or grown-up, I suppose." He gave a self-deprecating snort and placed the elephant very carefully back in its position on Jasmine's desk. "You'll let me know?" he asked, turning to Kincaid and shaking his hand.

"Yes. As soon as I hear."

Theo turned and let himself out, leaving Kincaid in doubtful possession of Jasmine's flat.

Kincaid stood for a moment organizing his

thoughts, determined to ignore the rumblings of his stomach a bit longer. Theo Dent's revelation that Jasmine had arranged to see him this weekend, after a six month hiatus, made Kincaid feel even more uneasy about the whole business. Had Jasmine lied to both Margaret and Theo? In Margaret's case it might have been motivated by kindness, but surely not in Theo's.

Kincaid stuck his hands in his pockets and sighed as he looked around the familiar room. It seemed to him that Jasmine's quiet presence had provided an anchor in more than one life — both Margaret and Theo had wailed "What shall I do now?", as bereft as abandoned children, yet he had no idea what Jasmine had felt for them, or anyone else, for that matter. Her presence was already as elusive as smoke, and he thought he had known her quite well.

He went to the kitchen sink, intending to dry and put away the whiskey tumblers. His foot nudged something and he looked down curiously. It was the bowl of food he had put out that morning for the cat — untouched, dried and crusted over. "Damn and blast," Kincaid swore. He had forgotten about the cat. He'd meant to speak to Theo about it, hoping Theo would take the beast home, or make arrangements for it.

He knelt and peered under Jasmine's bed.

The dark, hunched shape of the cat remained exactly where he had seen it last, and he wondered if it had moved at all. "Kitty, kitty, kitty," he coaxed, which elicited as little response as before. Returning to the sink, Kincaid scraped the dried food into the bin and refilled the bowl. He shoved this offering as far under the bed as he could reach, then stayed down on knees and elbows, contemplating the cat. He felt guilty as well as helpless in the face of the animal's grief, and he had no experience with cats.

"Look," he addressed the cat, "that's all I can do for now. Whether or not you eat is up to you. I can't go on calling you 'kitty', and I'm not going to call you 'Sidhi' or anything equally absurd." The cat closed its eyes, whether from relaxation or boredom Kincaid couldn't guess. "Sid. From now on you're just plain Sid, okay?" He took silence as assent and got up, dusting off his knees.

He must find a key if he were to continue looking after the cat — he couldn't go on playing the amateur burglar. Where had Jasmine kept her keys? He thought she hadn't often used them since she became ill, but they must have been easily accessible. The small secretary seemed the obvious choice, and his search did not take more than a few minutes. He found a single key on a monogrammed brass key ring, tucked away in a wooden catch-all box on the desk's surface.

As he turned away a flash of color in one of the secretary's slots caught his attention. It was a weekly engagement calendar of the type sold by museum shops — each week's page accompanied by a Constable painting. He flipped through the last few months, finding visits to the clinic, birthdays, and his own name entered with increasing regularity. In the weeks of March he began to see botanical notations; the blooming of the japonica and forsythia, the daffodils, and as he turned to April, the flowering of the pears and plums, and the first tulip in the garden. All were things visible from the windows of the flat, and Kincaid felt that this had not been Jasmine's yearly ritual, but rather a cataloging of a last spring. In yesterday's space, opposite Constable's "View from Hampstead Heath", she had written 'Theo — Sunday?', and then, in very careful script 'my fiftieth birthday'.

He hadn't known.

CHAPTER
4

Kincaid woke slowly on Saturday morning, feeling drowsy and content until memory returned. The sense of loss descended heavily, weighing on his chest. He pulled himself up, shaking his head like a swimmer emerging from deep water.

If he had dreamed he had no recollection of it, but his mind was clear and he found he had come to a decision in his sleep. If the pathologist reported that Jasmine had indeed died of natural causes, then he would gladly lay aside his suspicions. But if not, he felt a need to be better prepared. Suicide was the obvious assumption — he had no concrete reason for feeling uncomfortable with it, yet he did. Perhaps he was guilty of bringing his job home, of attributing violence to the natural and peaceful death of a friend. Or perhaps he was resisting the idea of suicide because it made him feel culpable, as if he had failed her. But whatever the source of his unease, Kincaid had learned from experience to trust his instincts, and something about Jasmine's death didn't feel right.

The weekend would give him a grace period. He was off duty, and Jasmine's flat would be the logical place to start. He found, however, that the idea of going through Jasmine's personal effects alone depressed him. Even though Theo had pretty well given him carte blanche, he felt an uncomfortable sense of invading her privacy.

His sergeant's open, freckled face sprang easily to his mind. She was also off duty this weekend. He'd give her a ring and ask for her help. His snooping would seem less personal, and Gemma's brisk good sense would keep him from thinking too much. He rolled over in bed and reached for the phone.

Gemma sounded uncharacteristically cross until she recognized his voice. Even then she hesitated after he explained what he wanted, but he put it down to concern about her small son and assured her she could bring him along.

Satisfied with the arrangement, he got up and headed toward the kitchen and coffee. The sight of his sitting room jolted him to a stop, arousing something akin to panic. Although Gemma had dropped him off or picked him up on occasion, she had never been up to his flat. She'd think him an absolute slob if she saw this shambles. A major tidying-up was definitely in the offing.

Gemma James pulled her Ford Escort into a space before Kincaid's building by mid-morning. She killed the engine and sat for a moment, listening. The silence in Carlingford Road always surprised her. At her own house in Leyton, the traffic noise from Lea Bridge Road never dropped below a muted roar. It must be the Victorians' solid construction, she thought, looking up at the still shadowed faces of the flats. They were all red brick, rescued from severity by white trim on the windows and from conformity by the brightly colored ground-floor doors.

Toby began squirming in his car seat and she moved a little reluctantly, unbuckling him and wincing as he climbed across her and began bouncing on her lap. "Oof!" she said, and he giggled with delight. "You'll soon be too heavy to get in Mummy's lap at all. I'll have to stop feeding you." She tickled him until he squealed, then slipped her arms around his chubby body and nuzzled his straight, fair hair. At two, he was already looking more like a little boy than a baby and she begrudged any infringement on her time with him.

Her earlier annoyance flooded back. Did Detective Superintendent Duncan Kincaid think she had nothing better to do with her Saturday than help him with some vague personal problem? Then she frowned, admitting to herself that her reluctance had more to do with her own discomfort at crossing the carefully drawn line between her personal and professional lives than with his presumption. She had come because she was flattered that he had thought of her, and because she was curious.

Kincaid opened his door and stared at her, appreciation lighting his face.

"You said personal," she reminded him sharply, looking down at her burnt-orange T-shirt which she had fancied made her hair look more copper than ginger, then at the printed-cotton skirt and sandals.

"I'm glad I did. Gemma unstarched." He grinned at her, then swung Toby up in the air.

"You're not exactly a picture of sartorial elegance yourself," she added, looking pointedly at his faded jeans and Phantom T-shirt.

"Granted. Been tidying in your honor." He stepped back and waved her into the flat with a mock flourish.

"It's lovely," Gemma said, and heard the echo of surprise in her voice. Walls painted white to make the most of the southern light, blond Danish furniture with colorful cotton covers, one wall lined with books and another holding stereo equipment and framed London Transport posters — the overall effect was bright and comfortable and spoke of a man confident in his own taste.

"What were you expecting, squalid bachelor digs furnished with jumble-sale castoffs?" Kincaid sounded pleased.

"I suppose so. My ex-husband's idea of designer decorating was leaving the labels on the orange crates," Gemma said a little absently, her attention on the room's real draw — the view of North London's rooftops from the balcony doors. She crossed the room as if pulled by an invisible string, and Kincaid quickly opened the door for her. They stepped out together, Gemma unconsciously hooking a hand through Toby's braces.

Her delight and envy must have shown on her face because Kincaid said contritely, "I should have invited you up before now."

Gemma judged the balcony Toby-proof and let him go, then leaned against the rail with her eyes closed and her face turned up to the sun. She felt a sense of peace here, of retreat, that she never found at home. She didn't wonder that he guarded it jealously. Sighing, she turned to face him and found him watching

59

her. "You didn't ring me just so that I could admire the scenery. What's up?"

Kincaid explained the circumstances of Jasmine's death, and more hesitantly, his doubts. As he spoke he watched Toby digging happily with a stick in his sole pot of pansies. "Stupid of me, I suppose, but I feel somehow responsible, as if I let her down without knowing it."

In the clear light Gemma saw the shadows under his eyes and new lines framing his mouth. She looked out across the rooftops again, thinking. "You were close friends?"

"Yes. At least I thought so."

"Well," Gemma turned reluctantly from the view, "let's go have a look then, shall we?"

"Afterwards, I'll take you and Toby for lunch at the pub, and then maybe a walk on the Heath?" His tone was light but Gemma sensed entreaty, and it occurred to her that her usually self-contained superior dreaded spending the day alone.

"A bribe?"

He smiled. "If you like."

The first thing Gemma noticed about Jasmine Dent's flat was the smell — faintly elusive, sweet and spicy at once. She wrinkled her nose, trying to place it, then her face cleared. "It's incense. I haven't smelled incense since I left school."

Kincaid looked blank. "What?"

"You don't smell it?"

He sniffed, shook his head. "Must be used to it, I suppose."

Gemma squelched an illogical flare of jealousy that he had spent so many hours in this flat, with this woman she'd known nothing about. It was none of her business how he spent his time.

She looked around, while keeping a wary eye on Toby. A lifetime's accumulation, she thought, of a woman who had cared about things — things loved for their color and texture and their associations rather than their material value.

One wall held prints and Gemma went closer to study them. The center of the grouping was a sepia-tinted photograph of Edward VIII as a young man in Scouting uniform, smiling and handsome, long before the cares of Mrs. Simpson and abdication. A memento of Jasmine's parents, perhaps? Beside it a delicate, gold-washed print portrayed two turbaned Indian princes on elephants charging one another, their armies ranged behind them. The artist apparently had no knowledge of perspective and the elephants appeared to be floating in mid-air, giving the whole composition a stylized and whimsical air.

Gemma moved to the sitting room window and ran her fingers lightly over the carved wooden elephants parading across the sill. "Aren't elephants supposed to be lucky? Here, Toby, come and look. Aren't they lovely?" She turned to Kincaid and asked, "Do you think he might play with them? They seem sturdy enough."

"I don't see why not." He came across to her and lifted the window sash, and they leaned out and looked down into the garden together.

"Ohhh." Gemma exhaled the word as she took in the square of lawn, emerald green, smooth as a bowling green, bordered by ranks of multi-colored tulips, crowned with springing forsythia and the opening buds of the plum trees. "It is lovely." She thought of her shriveled patch of garden, usually more mud than grass, and looked at Toby intently lining the elephants up nose to tail. "Could he —"

"Better not." Kincaid shook his head. "Not until we can go down with him. If he trampled the tulips the Major might eat him." He grinned and ruffled Toby's fair hair. "Do you think we should divide up the —"

They both heard the mewing, faint even in the quiet flat. They turned and watched as the black cat crept from under Jasmine's bed and crouched, ready to retreat. "A cat! You

62

didn't tell me she had a cat."

"I keep forgetting," Kincaid said, a little shamefaced.

Gemma knelt and called to him. After a moment's hesitation he padded toward her and she scooped him up, holding him under her chin. "What's he called?"

"Sid. He wouldn't come for me." Kincaid sounded aggrieved.

"Maybe my voice reminded him of her," Gemma suggested.

Kincaid knelt and checked the food he'd left under the bed. "He's still not eating, though."

"No wonder." Gemma wrinkled her nose in disgust at the crusted food. "You'll have to do better than that." She put the cat down and rummaged through the kitchen cupboards until she found a tin of tuna. "This might do the trick." She opened the tin and spooned a little tuna into a clean dish, then set it before the cat. Sidhi sniffed and looked at her, then settled over the dish and took a tentative bite.

Kincaid had wandered back into the sitting room, touching objects absently before moving on to something else. "This won't do at all," Gemma said under her breath, remembering his normal assertiveness. "He couldn't find a haystack in the middle of the sitting room in this state, could he, Sid?" The cat ignored her, intent now on his food.

Kincaid stopped in front of the solid, oak bookcase and contemplated the spines as if they might reveal something if he stared long enough. Books were jammed in every which way, taking up every inch of available space. Gemma joined him and scanned the titles. Scott, Forster, Delderfield, Galsworthy, a much worn, leather set of Jane Austen. "There aren't any new ones," said Gemma, realizing what struck her as odd. "No paperbacks, no best sellers, no mysteries or romances."

"She reread these. Like old friends."

Gemma studied him as intently as he studied the books, deciding to take matters in hand. "Look. You start with the desk, all right? And I'll tackle the bedroom."

Kincaid nodded and crossed to the secretary. He sat in the chair, which looked much too delicate to bear his six-foot frame, and gingerly opened the top drawer.

Jasmine's small bedroom faced north, toward the street, and Gemma turned on the shaded dressing table lamp. The room held a narrow single bed with an old chenille spread stretched tightly over it, the dresser, a nightstand, and a heavy wardrobe — and unlike the sitting room, it reflected none of its owner's personality. Gemma sensed that the room had been used for sleeping and storage only, not inhabited in the same sense as the rest of the flat.

She started with the dressing table, working her way gently through layers of underclothes and bottles of half-empty cosmetics. Under slips and stockings in a bottom drawer lay a picture frame, face down. Gemma lifted it out and turned it over. A dark-eyed young woman stared back at her from a black-and-white studio photograph. Slipping the backing from the frame, she examined the back of the photograph itself. Neatly penciled letters read "Jasmine, 1962". Gemma turned the photo over again. The dark hair was long and straight, parted in the center, the face small and oval, the mouth held a hint of a smile at some secret not shared with the observer. In spite of the date on the back, the girl had an old-fashioned look — she might have modeled for a Renaissance Madonna.

Gemma opened her mouth to call Kincaid, hesitated, then carefully placed the photo back in the top of its drawer, face down.

She moved to the wardrobe and swung open the heavy doors. It held mostly good business suits, dresses and a few silk caftans. Gemma ran her hands appreciatively over the fabrics, then lifted the trousers and sweaters in the drawers.

The wardrobe's top shelf held rows of neatly stacked shoeboxes. Gemma slipped off her shoes, stepped up on the bottom shelf and lifted the top off a box, peering inside. Quickly she pulled the boxes off the shelves and laid them on the bed, removing the tops.

"Guv. You'd better come and look at these."

He came to the doorway, dusting off his hands. "What's up?"

"Composition books. Lots of them, all alike." Gemma opened one and showed him the pages covered with the same neat, italic script she'd seen on the back of the photo. She was suddenly very aware of his nearness in the small room, his quick breathing, the smell of aftershave and warm skin. She stepped back and said more loudly than she intended, "It looks like Jasmine kept a journal."

They sorted the boxes, checking the first page of each book for the date. "1952 is the earliest date I've found," Gemma said, rubbing her nose that itched from the dust. Her fingertips felt dry and papery.

Kincaid calculated a moment. "She would have been ten years old." They kept on in silence until Kincaid looked up and frowned. "The last entry seems to have been made a week ago."

"Did you find anything in the sitting room?" He shook his head. "No."

"Do you suppose she stopped writing because she knew she was dying?" Gemma ventured.

"Someone with a lifetime's habit of recording their thoughts? Doesn't seem likely."

"Or," Gemma continued slowly, "did it somehow go missing?"

They sat in the garden at the Freemason's Arms, eating brown bread with cheese and pickle, and drinking lager. They'd had to wait for one of the white plastic tables, but judged it worth it for the sun and the view across Willow Road to the Heath.

Toby, having mangled a soft cheese roll and most of the chips in his basket, sat in the grass at their feet. He was pulling things from Gemma's bag, muttering a running catalogue to himself — "keys, stick, Toby's horsey" — here he held a tattered stuffed horse up for their inspection. Kincaid thought blackly of the listing of a victim's effects, then pushed the thought away. He pulled a chip from Toby's basket and held it out to him. "Here, Toby. Feed the birds."

Toby looked from Kincaid to the house sparrows pecking in the grass. "Birdies?" he said, interested, then launched himself toward the sparrows, chip extended before him like a rapier. The birds took flight.

"Now look what you've done," said

Gemma, laughing. "He'll be frustrated."

"Good for his emotional development," Kincaid intoned with mock seriousness, then grinned at her. "Sorry." He liked seeing Gemma this way, relaxed and thoughtful. At work she was often too quick off the mark with assumptions, and he had more than once accused her of talking faster than she thought.

Good with Toby, too, he thought, attentive without fussing. He watched Gemma reel the toddler back in and plop him in the grass at her feet. She put a piece of her bread in the grass a few feet from Toby. "Here, lovey. Be very, very still and maybe they'll come to you." The sun had reddened the bridge of her nose and darkened the dusting of freckles on her pale skin. She became aware of Kincaid's scrutiny, looked up and flushed.

"You should wear a sun hat, you know, like a good Victorian girl."

"Ow. You sound just like my mum. 'You'll blister in that sun, Gem. You mark my words, you'll look like a navvy by the time you're thirty'," Gemma mimicked. "It can't last, anyway, this weather." She tilted her head and looked at the flat blue sky.

"No." No, but he could sure as hell sit here in the sun as long as it did, not thinking, listening to the sparrows and the hum of traffic from East Heath Road, watching the sun send golden flares from Gemma's hair.

"Duncan." Gemma's tone was unusually tentative. Kincaid sat up and squinted at her as he sipped from his pint. "Duncan, tell me why you don't think Jasmine committed suicide."

He looked away from her, then picked up a scrap of bread from his plate and began to shred it. "You think I'm manufacturing this to salve my wounded vanity. Maybe I am." He leaned forward and met her eyes again. "But I just can't believe she wouldn't have left something — some indication, some message."

"For you?"

"For me. Or for her friend Margaret. Or her brother." The doubt he saw in Gemma's hazel eyes made him defensive. "I knew her, damn it."

"She was ill, dying. People don't always behave rationally. Maybe she wanted you all to think it was natural."

Kincaid sat up, vehement. "She'd know Margaret wouldn't. Not after what passed between them."

"According to Margaret."

"Point taken." Kincaid ran a hand through his already unruly hair. "But still —"

"Look," Gemma interrupted him, her face beginning to flush with her enthusiasm for playing devil's advocate, "you say you don't think she died naturally in her sleep because in that case she would have bolted the door. But what if she felt too ill, perhaps lay down thinking she'd have a rest first —"

"No. She was too . . . composed. Everything was just too bloody perfect."

"So why couldn't she have drifted off during the evening, lost consciousness before she realized what was happening?"

Kincaid shook his head. "No lights. No telly. No book open across her chest or fallen to the floor. No reading glasses. Gemma," he gave a sharp, uncomfortable shrug, "I think that's what bothered me from the first, even before Margaret came and threw a spanner in the works with the suicide pact. It was almost as if she'd been laid out." He uttered this last remark a little sheepishly, looking sideways at her to gauge her reaction. Finding no expression of ridicule, he added, "The bed-clothes weren't even rumpled a bit."

"That's all consistent with suicide," Gemma said, and her gentle tone made Kincaid suspect he was being humored.

"I suppose so." He stretched his legs out under the table and regarded her over the rim of his almost-empty pint. "I know you think I'm daft."

Gemma merely lifted an eyebrow. She

70

picked up Toby, who was getting restless, and jiggled him on her knee until he laughed. "So what if the p.m. findings are positive?" she said between bounces. "The coroner's sure to rule suicide. There's no evidence to support opening an investigation."

"Lack of written or verbal communication of intent?"

Gemma shrugged. "Very iffy. And Margaret's story would be used to support suicide, not vice versa."

Kincaid watched a kite hovering over the Heath and didn't answer. Margaret. Now there was a thing. Why should he take Margaret's story at face value? Yesterday he had been too shocked and exhausted to question anything, but it occurred to him now that Margaret couldn't have invented a better story if she'd wanted it thought that Jasmine committed suicide, and it also absolved her of any guilt in not intervening.

"You've got that look," Gemma said accusingly. "What are you hatching?"

"Right." Kincaid drained his pint and sat up. "I'd like to have a word with Jasmine's solicitor, but I haven't a hope of seeing him till Monday."

"What else?" Gemma said, and Kincaid thought she looked inexplicably pleased with herself.

"Talk to Margaret. Maybe talk to Theo again."

"And the books?"

For an instant asking Gemma to help him crossed Kincaid's mind, but he rejected it as quickly as it came. That was one task he couldn't share. "I'll make a start on them."

They walked slowly back to Carlingford Road, holding Toby's hands and swinging him over the curbs. "No walk on the Heath, then?" Kincaid asked, for he'd seen Gemma glance at her watch more than once.

Gemma shook her head. "I'd better not. I promised my mum we'd visit — she says we don't come often enough."

Kincaid heard something in her voice, a shade of worry or aggravation, and remembered how she'd sounded on the phone that morning. Probably some bloke, he thought, and realized how little he knew about Gemma's life. Only that she'd divorced shortly after Toby was born; she lived in a semi-detached house in Leyton; she'd grown up and gone to school in North London. That was all. He'd never even been to Leyton — she always picked him up or met him at the Yard.

Suddenly the extent of his own myopia astounded him. He thought of her as reliable, attractive, intelligent, and often opinionated, with a special gift for putting people at ease in an interview — he'd looked no further than the qualities that made her valuable as an assistant. Did she date (this with a twinge of unidentified irritation)? Did she get on with her parents? What were her friends like?

He studied her as she walked beside him. She brushed a wisp of red hair from her face as she bent her head to answer Toby, but her expression was abstracted. "Gemma," he said a little hesitantly, "is anything the matter?"

She looked up at him, startled, then smiled. "No, of course not. Everything's fine."

Somehow Kincaid felt unconvinced, but he let it go. Her manner didn't invite further probing.

The blossom-laden branches of a plum tree overhung the walk, and as they passed beneath petals showered them like confetti. They laughed, the momentary awkwardness dissolved, and then they were saying good-bye before the flat.

Kincaid climbed the stairs alone, feeling the afternoon stretching before him like a desert. The red light on his answering machine flashed a greeting as he entered the flat and his spirits wilted even further. "Great," he said under his breath, and punched playback.

The duty sergeant's voice demanded to know just what the hell he thought he was playing at — hospital had called about a post mortem he'd requested — and if he didn't put his paperwork through the proper channels there'd be hell to pay. The remainder of the message he added almost as an afterthought, before ringing off abruptly.

Jasmine Dent's system had contained a lethal amount of morphine.

CHAPTER

5

Kincaid unsnapped the Midget's tarp and folded it from front to back, then unlocked the boot and stowed it away. He accomplished the maneuver neatly and quickly, having perfected it with much practice. The car's red paintwork gleamed cheerily at him, inviting dalliance in the midafternoon sun, but Kincaid shook his head and slid into the driver's seat. An idle down country lanes was not what he had in mind, tourist-poster day or not. He fished his sunglasses out of the door pocket, and put the car in gear.

After he crossed Rosslyn Hill, Kincaid made his way through the back streets of South Hampstead until he came into Kilburn High Road, just north of Maida Vale. He found Margaret Bellamy's address without difficulty, a dingy, terraced house in a block that had avoided gentrification. The front door was the dark red-brown of dried blood, but its peeling paint showed blotches of brighter colors beneath — lime-green, yellow, royal-blue — testimony to previous owners with more cheerful dispositions. He rang the bell and waited, wrinkling his nose against the odor drifting up from the rubbish bins below the basement railing.

The woman who opened the door wore polyester trousers stretched precariously over her bulky thighs, and a shiny jersey endured equal punishment across her bosom. She eyed Kincaid disapprovingly.

"Margaret Bellamy?" Kincaid tried out his best smile, wondering if she could hear him over the canned laughter bellowing from the back of the house.

The woman studied him a bit longer, then jerked her head toward the stairs. "Top of the house. On the right."

Kincaid thanked her and started up the steps, feeling her eyes on his back until he rounded the first landing. The smell of grease and the raucous sounds of the television followed him up three more flights, where the stairs ended in a dim hallway with streakily distempered walls. The two doors were unmarked and he tapped lightly on the right-hand one.

The sound of the downstairs' television

switched off, and in the sudden silence Kincaid heard the creak of bedsprings. Margaret Bellamy opened the door with an expectant half-smile. "Oh. It's you," she said, disappointment evident in her swollen face. She made an effort to smile again. "You'd better come in." Jerking her head toward the hall as she drew him in, she added, "She's listening, the horrid old snoop. That's why she turned the telly off." Margaret closed the door and stood awkwardly, as if she didn't know what to do with Kincaid now that she'd shut him in. She looked round the small room and grimaced.

He took in the small bed with its rumpled covers sagging to the floor, a single, stained armchair, a wardrobe, and an old deal table which seemed to serve as desk, dresser and kitchen.

Margaret made a small, circular motion with her hand and said, "I'm sorry." Kincaid thought the apology covered both herself and the room.

He smiled at her. "I lived in a bedsit myself, when I was training at the Academy. It was pretty dreadful, though I don't think my landlady could've held a candle to yours." This brought an answering smile from Margaret, and she moved to clear the chair for him. As she bent to scoop up a pile of clothes, she staggered and had to steady herself against the chair back.

"Are you all right?" Kincaid asked, and studied her more carefully. Her soft, brown hair was matted, and her eyelids were puffy from weeping. She wore a large T-shirt which had a section of its tail bunched in the waistband of faded gray sweatpants — probably the result of pulling them on hastily when he knocked on the door.

"Have you been out today at all?" he asked.

Margaret shook her head.

"Eaten?"

"No."

"I thought as much. Have you anything here?"

Another negative shake. "Just some tea, really."

Kincaid thought for a moment, then said briskly, "You make us some tea. I'll go down and ask your landlady to put together some sandwiches."

Margaret looked horrified. "She'd never . . . She wouldn't —"

"She will." He stopped at the door. "Though if Saint George is going to conquer the dragon, he'd better know her name."

"Oh." A flicker of amusement lit Margaret's face. "It's Mrs. Wilson."

* ★ ★

The door from which Kincaid guessed Mrs. Wilson had emerged earlier stood slightly ajar. He tapped smartly. The television still played very faintly, and over it he heard the shuffle of slipper-clad feet. The door opened a moment later and Mrs. Wilson squinted at him through the cigarette smoke which trickled from her nostrils. A dragon indeed.

"Mrs. Wilson?"

She glared at him suspiciously. "What of it?"

"Can I talk to you for a minute?"

"Not if you're aimin' to sell me something." The door began to inch closed. "I don't hold with solicitation."

Kincaid wondered what she thought he could be selling. "No. It's about Margaret. Please."

She snorted with annoyance, but stepped back enough to let Kincaid into the room. He surveyed Mrs. Wilson's lair with interest. It apparently served as sitting room as well as kitchen — a small sofa was jammed between the fittings, and a large color television held pride of place next to the fridge.

Mrs. Wilson sat down at the Formica-topped table and picked up the cigarette which lay smoldering in the ashtray. An open tabloid and a half-drunk cup of tea were evidence of her afternoon's activity. She didn't invite Kincaid to sit down.

"She's all wet, that girl," Mrs. Wilson pronounced disgustedly. "What's up now? More trouble with the boyfriend?"

Boyfriend? That was a complication he somehow hadn't expected, but it explained Margaret's dashed hopes when she'd opened the door. Kincaid thought quickly. What story would satisfy this harridan? From the looks of the headline in her paper — "Eleven-year-old mum fights authorities for baby!" — Mrs. Wilson's sympathies were aroused by melodrama, but the truth seemed a betrayal of both Margaret and Jasmine.

He improvised. "It's her uncle. Died suddenly yesterday, and Margaret's not taken it well at all."

Mrs. Wilson's heavy face remained as unmoved as her stiffly permed hair. "Figures." She looked at Kincaid suspiciously. "What do you have to do with it, anyway?"

"I'm a friend of the family. Duncan Kincaid." He held out his hand and Mrs. Wilson condescended to touch her pudgy fingertips to his before retrieving her half-smoked cigarette.

"So what's it to me?"

"She's not eaten anything since yesterday. I thought you might make her up some sandwiches?" Kincaid made the last remark with a raised eyebrow and as much persuasion as he could muster.

Mrs. Wilson opened her mouth to refuse, then stopped and eyed Kincaid speculatively. Desire for gossip warred with her natural inclination to do as little for anyone as possible, and maliciousness triumphed over sloth. "Well, I suppose I could just put something together, but I don't want her getting any ideas, mind you." She levered herself out of the chair, then jerked her head toward the vacant seat. "You'd better sit down." She continued over her shoulder as she opened the fridge, "Would this be her mother's brother or her father's that passed away?"

"Her mother's youngest brother, not much older than Margaret, in fact," Kincaid said glibly. "They were very close."

Mrs. Wilson spoke with her back to Kincaid, slicing something he couldn't see. "No family's ever had anything to do with her since she came here. Might as well be an orphan."

"Well, at least she's had her boyfriend to look after her," Kincaid threw out.

"Him!" Mrs. Wilson turned around and fixed Kincaid with a beady stare. "That one never looked after anything but himself, I can tell you. Sponging, more like it." She turned back to her slicing. "Too pretty for his own good, and oily with it. What he sees in her," she lifted her head toward the ceiling, "I don't know." She wiped her hands on her apron and presented Kincaid with a plate of squashy, if edible looking, ham and tomato sandwiches. "That do?"

"Admirably, thanks."

Having finished her task, Mrs. Wilson seemed disinclined to let him go. She lit another cigarette and propped her hip up on the edge of the table. Kincaid looked away from the sight of her spreading thigh and settled his weight back into the chair.

Mrs. Wilson took up her train of thought again. "I've told her I don't want him hanging around here, nor spending the night. Gives my house a bad name, don't it?"

Kincaid assumed the question was rhetorical, but answered it placatingly anyway. "I'm sure no one would think such a thing, Mrs. Wilson."

Mrs. Wilson preened a bit at this, and leaned toward him conspiratorially. "She thinks I don't know what's going on, but I do. I hear him come padding down the stairs at all hours of the night, like a thief. And I hear the rows, too," a pause while she inhaled and sent a cloud of smoke in the direction of Kincaid's face, "mostly him shouting and her wailing like a lamb led to slaughter. Silly cow," Mrs. Wilson finished with a snort. "I imagine she puts up with it 'cause she thinks she won't do any better."

Charitable old bitch, Kincaid thought, and smiled at her. "Then I don't suppose he's much comfort to her, at a time like this?"

"Not been here to comfort, or for anything else. Not since . . ." Mrs. Wilson squinted and drew on the last of her cigarette, then ground it out in the cheap tin ashtray. "Oh, must have been Thursday tea-time. He stormed out of here in a terrible temper. Near ripped the door off its hinges. But then," she shifted her weight as she thought and the table creaked in protest, "Thursday night is Ladies' Night down the pub and I was out till closing. If he came back later they were quiet enough making it up."

Kincaid decided he'd exhausted Mrs. Wilson's information for the time being, as well as his patience. He stood up and retrieved the sandwiches. "I don't want these to go stale, and I'd better be seeing about Margaret. I'm sure she'll appreciate your help, Mrs. Wilson. You've been very kind."

"Ta," she said, and wiggled her fingers at him coquettishly.

"Success," Kincaid said when Margaret let

him in again. In his absence she had tidied the bed and the scattered clothing, brushed her hair, and put on some pale pink lipstick. Her smile was less tentative, and he thought the time spent alone had brought her some composure.

Margaret's eyes widened as she saw the plate of sandwiches. "I can't believe it! She's never so much as loaned me a tea bag."

"I appealed to her better instincts."

"Didn't know she had any," Margaret snorted, taking the plate from Kincaid. Then she froze, her face crumpling with distress. "You didn't tell her —"

"No." Kincaid rescued the tilting plate and set it on the table. "I told a pack of lies. You've just lost your favorite uncle, your mother's youngest brother, in case Mrs. W. asks."

"But she doesn't have —" Margaret's face cleared. "Oh. Sorry." She smiled at Kincaid. "I guess I'm a little dense today. Thanks."

"Partly hunger, I imagine. Let's get you fed." The electric kettle whistled. Two mugs with tea bags sat ready beside it. Kincaid poured the tea and settled Margaret in the armchair, then pulled up the sash of the single window and leaned against the sill. As Margaret started on a sandwich, he said, "You'd better tell me about your family, after all the terrible things I made up."

"Woking," said Margaret, through a mouthful of ham and tomato. She swallowed and tried again. "Dorking. Sorry. I didn't realize I was so hungry." She took a smaller bite and chewed a moment before continuing. "I'm from Dorking. My dad owns a garage. I kept his books for him, looked after things."

Kincaid could easily imagine her managing a smaller, more familiar world, where here in London she seemed so vulnerable. "What happened?"

Margaret shrugged and wiped the corner of her mouth with a finger. "Nothing ever changed. I could see myself doing the same thing in twenty years, living bits and pieces of other people's lives. My dad's business, my sister's kids —"

"How did they take it?"

Margaret smiled, mocking herself. "I'm the plain one, so they never expected me to want anything different. I should have been content to have Dad's customers pat me and pay me stupid compliments, to be Aunt Meg and look after Kath's kids whenever she had something better to do."

"They were furious." Kincaid grinned and Margaret smiled back a little unwillingly.

"Yes."

"How long has it been?"

Margaret finished the last sandwich and

licked the tips of her fingers, then rubbed them dry on her sweatpants. "Eighteen months now."

"And no one's been to see you in all that time?"

She flushed and said hotly, "That malicious old biddy. I'd swear she keeps a list of anyone who —" Margaret dropped her head into her hands and leaned forward. "Oh Christ, what difference does it make? I feel sick."

Too much food, thought Kincaid, eaten too quickly on an empty stomach. "Keep your head down. It'll pass." He spied a worn face flannel and towel, folded on a shelf above the bed. "Where's the loo?" he asked Margaret.

"Next landing," she said indistinctly, her face now pressed against her knees.

Kincaid took the flannel downstairs and soaked it in cold water, and when he returned Margaret raised her head just long enough to press the cloth against her face. He moved restlessly to the window, wishing he had Gemma's skill at offering practical comfort.

The view — a small, weedy garden with an enormous pair of overalls swinging on the line — didn't hold his attention for long. Turning back to the room, Kincaid took note of Margaret's few possessions. The table held a handful of cheap jewelry in a dish, and a few cosmetic and lotion bottles. Next to the gas ring were a chipped plate and bowl, a saucepan and some cutlery. All the utensils were jumble sale quality, the cheapest necessities for a first move from home. The shelf above the bed held a radio, some dog-eared paperbacks and a framed photograph.

Kincaid stepped closer to study it. An older man, balding and hearty-looking in a tweed jacket, arm around his wife's slender shoulders, the three grown children grouped before them. A brother and sister, blond, good-looking, both radiating assurance, and between them Margaret, hair askew, smile lopsided.

"Mum and Dad, Kathleen, and my brother, Tommy."

Kincaid made an effort to wipe any sympathy from his face before he turned. Margaret watched him, waiting, he sensed, for some expected comment. Instead, he sat down on the bed and said, "It must have been tough, those first few months on your own."

"It was." Margaret looked down at the damp flannel in her hands and began folding it into smaller and smaller squares. "There wasn't anyone until I met Jasmine. I got a job in the typing pool in the Planning Office. When I did work for her she was always kind to me, but not" — a pause while she thought — "familiar, if you know what I mean." She looked up at Kincaid for assent, and he nodded. "A little distant. But then she got ill. She took leave for treatment, and when she came back you could tell she'd gone down, but no one spoke to her about it. They all acted like her illness didn't exist." Margaret looked up at him through her pale lashes and smiled a little at her own nerve. "So I asked her. Every day I'd say 'How are you?' or 'What are they giving you now?', and after a while she began to tell me."

"And when she left work?" Kincaid prompted.

"I went to see her. Every day if I could. No one else did." Margaret sounded indignant even now. "Oh, they'd club together on cards or a basket, but no one ever put themselves out to visit her."

"Did Jasmine mind?"

Margaret's wide brow creased as she thought about it. "I don't think so. She didn't seem to have any really close friends at work. No one disliked her, but they weren't chummy either." Margaret smiled at Kincaid a bit ironically. "She talked about you most often."

Kincaid stood up and took the few steps to the window. He had put off telling her the p.m. results long enough, and he tried to frame a gentle way to tell her that Jasmine had not died quietly in her sleep.

"Look," Margaret's voice came from behind him, "I know you didn't come here just to look after me. Jasmine didn't keep her promise, did she?"

Kincaid thought Margaret might have read his mind. He sat down opposite her again and searched her face. "I don't know. Her system contained a massive amount of morphine."

Margaret slumped back in the chair and closed her eyes. Tears welled from beneath her eyelids and ran down the sides of her nose. After a moment she leaned forward and rubbed her face with the crumpled flannel. "I should never have believed her." She barely whispered the words as she rocked her body backwards and forwards.

"Look, Meg. If Jasmine were determined to kill herself, there's no way you could have prevented her. Oh, for one night, maybe, but not indefinitely." When Margaret continued rocking, eyes closed, he leaned closer. "Listen, Meg. There are some things I need to know, and you're the only one who can help me."

The rocking slowed, then stopped. Margaret opened her eyes but stayed hunched over, arms crossed protectively over her stomach.

"Tell me why Jasmine needed your help."

"She didn't —" Margaret's voice caught. She reached for the cold dregs of her tea and swallowed convulsively, then tried again. "She didn't. Not really. I helped her figure the dosage — she was morphine dependent so we knew it would take a lot — but she could have done it herself. There was enough morphine, because she'd been maintaining the level she actually used while telling the nurse she needed her dosage increased. And the catheter would have held traces anyway."

"Then why?" Kincaid asked again, holding her gaze with his.

"I don't know. I suppose she just didn't want to be alone at the last."

Had Jasmine given in to weakness by asking Margaret's help, wondered Kincaid, and then found unexpected strength? He shook his head. It was possible, probable, logical, and yet he still couldn't believe it.

"What is it?" asked Margaret, sitting up a bit.

"Did Jasmine have —" Kincaid stopped as the door opened soundlessly. A man stepped into the room, regarding Kincaid and Margaret with an expression of amused contempt. Margaret, sitting with her back to the door, frowned at Kincaid in bewilderment and said, "What's the —"

"Well." The man spoke, the single syllable dripping with unsavory implications.

Margaret jerked at the sound of his voice and leapt to her feet, her face flushing an unbecoming, splotchy scarlet. "Rog—"

"Don't get up, Meg. I didn't expect you to be entertaining." Apart from a brief glance in Margaret's direction, all his attention was fixed on Kincaid.

Returning the scrutiny with interest and an immediate dislike, Kincaid saw a slender man of middle height, in perhaps his late twenties, wearing designer jeans and an expensive white cotton shirt open part way down the chest, cuffs turned back. He wore his light red-brown hair pulled back in a ponytail and his features were clearly cut. He was, Kincaid thought wryly, smashingly good-looking.

Margaret stood rigidly, gripping the back of her chair, and when she spoke her voice was high and uncontrolled. "Roger, where have you been? I've been wait—"

"Why the panic, Meg?" Roger didn't move from his slouching stance in the middle of the room, and made no effort to touch or comfort Margaret. "Don't you think introductions are in order?"

Kincaid took the initiative before Margaret could blurt anything out. "My name's Kincaid." He stood and held his hand out to Roger, who shook it with no great enthusiasm. "I'm a neighbor of Margaret's friend Jasmine Dent."

"Jasmine's dead, Rog. She died on Thursday night. I couldn't reach you anywhere."

Margaret trembled visibly.

Roger's eyebrows lifted. "Is that so? And you came to tell Margaret?"

"I came to see how she was getting on," Kincaid said mildly, leaning back against the edge of the table and folding his arms.

"How kind of you." Roger's public-school accent expressed sarcasm well. "Poor Meg." For the first time he took a step toward her, reaching out and pulling her stiff body to him in a brief embrace. He swiveled her around toward Kincaid again and rested a hand lightly on the back of her neck. "It must have been a shock, her going sooner than anyone expected."

"It wasn't like that. Jasmine died from an overdose of morphine," Margaret said, watching Kincaid's face as she spoke, seeking support. Roger let her go abruptly and she moved away from him.

"That's too bad, Meg. I'm sorry she —"

"Duncan knows about the suicide," she jerked her head toward Kincaid, "so don't bother to say you're sorry, Rog. I know you're not. No need for you to worry now."

"Worry? Don't be absurd, Meg."

Roger's voice was light, almost playful, but Kincaid sensed wariness replacing the nonchalance. "There is another possibility, you know," Kincaid said into the tension that vibrated in the room. Both faces turned toward him, Meg's bewildered, Roger's alert. "Someone might have given Jasmine help she didn't want."

"I don't . . ." Margaret began, then looked at Roger who, Kincaid thought, understood all too well.

The silence lengthened, until Kincaid straightened up and stretched. "I'm afraid I never caught your last name," he said to Roger.

Roger hesitated, then volunteered grudgingly, "It's Leveson-Gower." He pronounced it "Loos-n-gor".

How fittingly posh, Kincaid thought. He moved toward the door, then turned back to Margaret. "I'll be off, then. Are you sure you'll be all right, Meg?"

Margaret nodded uncertainly. Roger wrapped an arm around her waist, and with the other ran his fingernails slowly up her bare arm. Kincaid saw her nipples grow hard under her thin cotton shirt. She looked away from him, flushing.

"Meg will be just fine, won't you, love?" said Roger.

Kincaid turned back to them as he opened the door. "By the way, Roger, where were you on Thursday night?"

Roger still held Margaret before him, part

shield, part possession. "What's it to you?"

"I've a bad habit of liking people to account for themselves. I'm a copper." Kincaid smiled at them both and let himself out.

CHAPTER
6

The east side of Carlingford Road lay in deep shadow when Kincaid drew the Midget up to the curb. He rolled up the windows and snapped the soft top shut, then stood for a moment looking up at his building. It seemed unnaturally still and silent, the windows showing no light or signs of movement. Kincaid shrugged and put it down to his own skewed perception, but halfway up the stairs to his flat he realized he hadn't seen the Major since yesterday evening.

His heart gave a little lurch of alarm and he told himself not to be an ass — there was no reason anything should have happened to the Major. Death hadn't stayed lurking in the building like some gothic specter. Nevertheless, he found himself back downstairs, knocking on the Major's door.

No answer. Kincaid turned back to the

street, thinking to go through Jasmine's flat to check the garden, when he saw the Major turn the corner into the road. He walked slowly, hampered by the two shrubs he carried, a plastic tub tucked under each arm.

Kincaid went quickly to meet him. "Thought you might need some help."

"Much obliged."

Kincaid, accepting one of the five-gallon tubs, heard the breath whistling through the Major's nostrils.

"Long pull uphill from the bus."

"What are they?" Kincaid asked, shortening his stride to match his step to the Major's.

"Roses. Antiques. From a nursery in Bucks."

"Today?" Kincaid asked in some surprise. "You've carried these from Buckinghamshire on the bus?"

They had reached the steps leading down to the Major's door. Setting down his tub, the Major pulled off his cap and wiped his perspiring head with a handkerchief. "Only place to get 'em. Himalayan Musk, they're called."

As he set down his own tub, Kincaid looked doubtfully at the bare, thorny stems. "But couldn't —"

The Major shook his head vigorously. "Wrong time of year, of course. But it had to be something special." At Kincaid's even more perplexed expression, he wiped his face and continued, "For Jasmine. It's the scent, you see, not like those modern hybrid teas. She loved the scented flowers, said she didn't care what they looked like. These bloom once, late in spring. Masses of pale pink blooms, smell like heaven."

It took Kincaid a moment to respond, never having heard the Major make such a long speech, nor say anything remotely poetic. "Yes, you're right. I think she would have liked them."

The Major unlocked his door and stooped for the tubs. "Let me give you a hand," Kincaid said, lifting one easily.

The Major opened his mouth to refuse, hesitated, then said, "Right. Thanks."

Kincaid followed him through the door of the flat. His first impression was of unrelieved brown. The Major flipped on a light switch and the impression expanded into neat, clean and brown. A faded floral wallpaper in tints of rose and brown, brown carpet, brown covers on the inexpensive settee and armchair. No paintings, no photographs, no books that Kincaid could see as he followed the Major through the sitting room. The only splash of bright color came from the gardening magazines and catalogs stacked tidily on the pine coffee table.

The Major led Kincaid through the kitchen and opened a door into the concreted area which ran beneath the steps descending from Jasmine's flat. To the right, in the corner formed by the fence and the wall of the building, the Major had built a covered potting area. Kincaid stuck his head in the door and was rewarded with a rich, humic smell so strong it caught in his throat.

The Major climbed the steps to lawn level and put down his tub. Kincaid did the same and stood looking at the garden, struck by the contrast between the Major's flat and this small oasis of color and perfection. He wondered what sustained the Major during the winter months when nothing grew except a few sturdy perennials.

After a moment in which the Major seemed lost in contemplation as well, Kincaid asked, "Where are you going to put them?"

"There, I think." He pointed at the brick wall at the rear of the garden, the only unoccupied territory that Kincaid could see. "They're climbers. They'll take it over."

"Let me help." Kincaid was suddenly moved by a desire to participate in this memorial, more fitting than any service spoken by a stranger.

The Major hesitated before replying, a habit, Kincaid began to think, when anyone threatened to disrupt his solitary routine. "Oh, aye. There's another old spade in the shed."

Kincaid moved the tubs to the back of the garden, and when the Major returned with the spades and pointed out a spot among the pansies and snapdragons, he started to dig. They worked in silence as the shadows moved along the garden.

When the Major judged the holes deep enough, they placed the roses carefully, filling in around them and tamping down the earth with their hands. After years of living in city flats, Kincaid felt a grubby satisfaction he hadn't experienced since making mud forts in his Cheshire childhood.

The Major stood leaning on his spade, surveying their handiwork with satisfaction. "That's done, and done well. She'd be pleased, I'll wager."

Kincaid nodded, looking up at the darkened windows of Jasmine's flat. A level above, the sun flashed off his own. "I'm famished. Come out with me and have something to eat," he said impulsively, telling himself he was taking advantage of an opportunity to question the Major, and not influenced by the thought of his empty flat. He waited patiently now for the Major's reply, counting the seconds to himself.

The Major looked all around the garden,

consulting the tulips and forsythia. "Aye. We'd best wash up, then."

They chose the coffee bar around the corner on Rosslyn Hill, settling in to the vinyl booth and ordering omelets with chips and salad. The Major had brushed his sparse hair until his scalp shone as pink as his face, and Kincaid marveled at the generation which still put on a tie for a casual Saturday night meal. He himself had swapped his cotton shirt for a long-sleeved rugby shirt, his concession to the cooling temperature.

When their beer arrived and they had drunk the top off, the Major wiped the foam from his mustache and asked, "Did the brother come and take charge of the arrangements, for the funeral and such?"

"The brother came, all right, but he didn't feel up to taking over much of anything. And there won't be a funeral just yet."

The Major's pale blue eyes widened in surprise. "No funeral? Why ever not?"

"Because I ordered a post mortem, Major. There were indications that Jasmine might have committed suicide."

The Major stared at him for a heartbeat of shocked silence, then thumped his glass down so hard beer sloshed over the lip. "Why couldn't you just let her go in peace, man?

What difference did it make to anybody if the poor wee soul made things a bit easier for herself?"

Kincaid shrugged. "None, Major, and I would have let it go, if that were all there was to it. But some things weren't consistent with suicide, and I'm sure now that her death wasn't natural. I've had the p.m. report."

"What things?" asked the Major, fastening on the pertinent statement.

"Jasmine did intend suicide, we know that. She asked her friend Margaret to help her, but then she told Margaret she felt differently and had changed her mind. She left no note, no explanation. Surely she would have done that for Margaret. And," Kincaid paused long enough to sip from his pint, "she made arrangements to see her brother, whom she hadn't seen in six months, tomorrow."

The Major nodded along with every point, but when Kincaid finished said, "I canna believe someone would've harmed the poor lassie. She wouldn't have hung on much longer anyway." His blue eyes were surprisingly sharp in his round face.

The waitress arrived bearing their plates, giving Kincaid a reprieve. The Major doused his chips in vinegar, then poured HP sauce on his omelet. Kincaid wrinkled his nose as the vinegar fumes reached him. Bachelor habits, he thought. He'd be doing that himself in a few years.

"What do you think, Major? You knew her, maybe better than I did."

The Major speared a bite of egg with his fork and swabbed it through the pool of brown sauce on his plate. "Canna say I knew her well, not really. We only talked about," he forked egg and chips into his mouth and continued, "everyday things. The garden, the telly. Now Margaret I never met, but I'd see her coming and going, and sometimes she'd come out to the steps and wave at me when I was in the garden. A friendly lass. Not like Jasmine. I don't mean," he corrected himself "to say that Jasmine was unfriendly, just that she kept herself to herself, if you know what I mean." As if surprised by his own garrulity, the Major looked away from Kincaid and concentrated on his dinner.

The espresso machine hissed and gurgled like some subterranean monster as Kincaid took a bite of his own omelet. "Did you ever see anyone come with Margaret? A boyfriend?"

The Major frowned and shook his head. "Canna say as I did."

Kincaid felt sure he would have remembered Roger. "Did you ever meet Theo, her brother?"

"Not that I recall. She didn't have much in the way of visitors, except that nurse the last few months. Now that," he leaned forward confidentially as he scooped up the last of his egg and chips, "is one fine-looking woman."

Kincaid noted with amusement that the Major's passion for things vegetable didn't extend to the edible — most of his watercress and cucumber garnish lay limply abandoned on the side of his plate. "What about Thursday night? Did you see anyone visit then?"

"Not in. Never in on a Thursday. Choir."

"You sing?" Kincaid asked. He pushed his empty plate away and leaned forward, elbows on the table.

"Since I was a boy. Won prizes as a tenor, before my voice changed."

Kincaid thought the Major's complexion looked even more florid than usual. So that was the other sustaining passion. "I wouldn't have guessed. Where do you sing?"

The Major finished his beer and patted his mustache with his napkin. "St. John's. Sunday services. Wednesday Evensong. Practice on Thursdays."

"Were you back late on Thursday?"

"No. Tenish, if I remember."

"And you didn't see or hear anything unusual?"

Kincaid didn't hold his breath in expectation. It was the kind of question he had to ask, but fate was not usually generous in replying. If people saw something really unusual they spoke up right away, minor discrepancies would come back to them only when something jogged their memories.

The Major shook his head. " 'Fraid not."

The waitress whisked away Kincaid's empty plate and returned a moment later with their checks. The noise level in the cafe had risen steadily. Kincaid looked around and saw every table full and prospective customers standing in the doorway — fine weather combining with Saturday night to bring out the crowds. He drained the last of his pint reluctantly. "I guess we'd better make way for the mob."

As they reached the turning into Pilgrims Lane, the shadow of Hampstead Police Station loomed over them. Kincaid found it rather ironic that he had chosen to live a few short blocks from that most evocative of buildings, designed by J. Dixon Butler, the architect who collaborated with Norman Shaw on New Scotland Yard. In Kincaid's imagination fog always swirled around its Queen Anne gables, and Victorian bobbies marched briskly to the rescue.

When they reached Carlingford Road the Major spoke, breaking the silence that had fallen between them. "And what about the wee moggie? Have you made provision for it?"

"Moggie?" Kincaid said blankly. "Oh, the cat. No. No, I haven't. I don't suppose you'd —"

The Major was already shaking his head. "Canna abide the beasts in the house. Make me sneeze. And wouldn't have it digging in my flower beds." His mustache bristled in distaste. "But somethin' should be done."

Kincaid sighed. "I know. I'll see to it. Goodnight, Major."

"Mr. Kincaid." The words stopped Kincaid as he mounted the steps to the front door. "I think you'll do more harm than good digging into this business. Some things are best left alone."

Kincaid paced restlessly around the sitting room of his flat. It was still early, not yet nine o'clock, and he felt tired but edgy, unable to settle to anything. He flipped through the channels on the telly, then switched it off in disgust. None of his usual tapes or CD's appealed to him, nor any of the books he hadn't found time to read.

When he found himself studying the photographs on his walls, he turned and faced the brown cardboard box on his coffee table squarely. Classic avoidance, refusal to face a disagreeable task. Or to be more honest, he thought, he was afraid that Jasmine would jump out of the pages of her journals, fresh and painfully real.

Kincaid allowed himself one more small delay — time enough to make a cup of coffee. Carrying the mug back to the sitting room, he settled himself on the sofa in the pool of light cast by the reading lamp. He pulled the cardboard box a little nearer and ran his fingers across the neat blue spines of the composition books. They came away streaked with a fine, dry dust.

If he must do it, then he would start chronologically — in the earlier books the Jasmine he knew would be less immediate, and he'd already glanced briefly through the last book and found nothing immediately useful. He pulled the most faded book from the back of the box and opened it. The pages were yellow and crackly and smelled a bit musty. Kincaid stifled a sneeze.

The entries began in 1951. Jasmine's ten-year-old handwriting was small and carefully looped, the entries trite and equally self-conscious: Theo's accomplishments (the proprietary interest already evident), prizes won at school, a tennis lesson, a ride on a neighbor's horse.

Kincaid flipped easily through the pages of one book, a second, a third. As the years

106

flowed by the writing changed, developing into Jasmine's recognizable idiosyncratic script. Sometimes entries skipped weeks, sometimes months, and although they became more natural, they remained emotionally unrevealing. He'd started the fourth book when an entry dated in March, 1956, brought him up short. He went back to the beginning and began to read more carefully.

March 9

Theo's tenth birthday. The usual celebration. Same as last year and all the years before. The three of us round the dining table in our best clothes, stifling with the shutters closed, no one speaking at all. Cook made his idea of an English birthday cake. Awful (it's always awful), but father just sat there looking like doom and Theo didn't even snicker. I could've screamed.

Father gave Theo a model airplane kit which, of course, Theo doesn't care about at all. I'll end up helping him put it together, can't hurt Father's feelings. Exercised Mrs. bloody Savarkar's horse for a month to earn enough to buy Theo a new tennis racket. Not that I minded the horse, but Mrs. S. is a bitch, always lording it over us just because we're "poor English".

Do I really remember the night Theo was

born, or have I just heard the ayah's stories so many times I can't tell where her stories leave off and my memories begin. I remember shouting and smoke and the smell of burning, but I think that this all happened later and is somehow confused in my mind with the doctor pounding on the door and my mother's screams.

May 22

Mr. Patel pinched my arm again in class. He walks up and down the rows, making a dry-leaf rustly noise, looking over our shoulders while we're working. I can feel him coming up behind me, the back of my neck gets hot.

Today he grabbed my arm just below the shoulder and dug his fingers in, squeezing until I bit my lip to keep from crying out. He said I hadn't done my assignment properly, but it's just an excuse to keep me after and everyone knows it. I could hear the other girls sniggering behind my back.

"Jasssmine," he said when he'd let everyone else go, hissing the 's' in my name until my skin crawls. "Do you remember your English mother, Jasmine? You need someone to teach you things, Jasmine." He moved around his desk and I backed up against the doorframe, holding my books against my chest so he couldn't look there. "You know you shouldn't go out in the sun, don't you? It makes you

look like a native girl." He smiled at me then. He looked like a bald tortoise, with his stringy neck quivering and his eyes blinking. I ran before he could touch me again, ran all the way home and threw up. I wish I could kill him.

The finger marks on my arm turned purple by the time I got home. I changed into a long-sleeved blouse before Theo or Father could see. No point in telling Father. I tried once before. He just got that vague look of his like he wishes he were somewhere else, and said my imagination was running away with me.

I know why Mr. Patel asked me about Mummy. They think I'm half-caste, because of my coloring, and that Mummy wasn't English at all.

I remember my mother. I remember the slippery feel of her dresses and the way she smelled of roses. I remember the dolls she had sent to me from England and the stories we made up about them. "Grow up to be a proper English girl, Jasmine," she'd say, "so you'll know how things are done when we go home." That was all she talked about, going home. She must have hated it here. Is it possible for someone to die of homesickness?

June 5
Theo, the little toad, told father I stayed

out of school while he was away. Father put on his miserable face and said I was just trying to make life difficult for him, and now he'll have to speak to the head.

June 30
Father died yesterday. The doctor said it was his heart, something to do with the fevers he had when he first came out.

He was just reading the newspaper at dinner. Said he didn't feel well, in a surprised sort of way, then slumped over the table.

I can't believe it. What will become of Theo and me?

CHAPTER

7

Gemma sat at the kitchen table, huddled in Rob's old terrycloth dressing gown. It was his color, not hers — the deep wine shade turned her hair ginger. She knew she should throw it out, or give it to Oxfam, along with all the other odds and ends of her married life that cluttered the house. But sometimes, if she pressed the dressing gown's nubby fabric to her face, she imagined it still smelled of Rob.

"Silly cow," she said aloud. What had Rob left her that she should want any reminders of him? It surprised her that she still missed his physical presence. Not just sex (although that had been scarce enough since that day two years ago when she'd come home to find Rob's things gone and a note on the kitchen table), but the quick touch, the hand on her hair, having something other than a hot-water bottle to warm her feet against at night. Work and looking after Toby left not much time for becoming reacquainted with dating.

The thought of Toby brought her attention back to the untidy pile of bills before her on the kitchen table. Gemma got up and poured herself more coffee, wrapping her hands around the chipped Thistle mug (a souvenir of her honeymoon in Inverness.) Nearly nine o'clock on Sunday morning and Toby not up yet — last night's visit to her mum and dad's had exhausted him. Her sister's three wild ones had wound him to a fever pitch and Gemma had carried him kicking and screaming to the car, only to have him fall asleep in mid-shriek a few minutes later.

She contemplated the bills again, then carried her mug to the back door and stood looking out into the garden. Toby's plastic tricycle lay overturned in a muddy patch. Rob hadn't sent his support check for three months now, and the fees for Toby's day care were becoming more than she could manage. The mortgage on the house was steep, and she paid a sitter for Toby when she worked overtime as well. Rob's last phone had been disconnected, and when Gemma checked his flat she found he'd moved and left no forwarding address. The car dealership where he'd worked as a salesman gave her the same story, he'd given notice and disappeared.

Gemma felt panic hovering at the edge of her thoughts, waiting to pounce when she let her guard down. She'd taken such pride in her self-sufficiency, ignoring the importance of Rob's help because it didn't fit with the super-mum image she'd built for herself. Now she was reaping the consequences. Be practical, she told herself, look at your options. Selling the house and finding less expensive care for Toby didn't mean the end of the world, yet she still felt the weight of failure like a stone on her chest.

The loud burring of the kitchen phone jerked her out of the doldrums. She set her coffee on the countertop and grabbed the receiver off the extension, hoping not to wake Toby.

"Gemma? I'm sure ringing you two mornings in a row is a right nuisance, but I wondered if you'd like to make a couple of visits with me today."

She found that another early morning call from Kincaid didn't surprise her, nor did his off-duty voice. It held a trace of hesitancy she never heard at work. "Still unofficial?" she asked.

"Um, until tomorrow, at least. But I've had the p.m. result. Morphine overdose."

Gemma retrieved her cup and took a sip of tepid coffee. So he had been right about that, at least, and she'd been wrong in thinking his closeness to the situation might have clouded his judgement.

"I know you still think I'm making mountains out of molehills," he said into her silence, and Gemma heard the trace of amusement in his voice.

"Who did you have in mind?"

"Felicity Howarth, Jasmine's nurse, in Kew. And brother Theo, down in Surrey. It's a lovely day for a run," he added, cajoling.

"Mummy." Toby had padded into the kitchen on bare feet and stood sleep-flushed and tousled, holding his blanket.

"Come here, love." Gemma knelt and hugged him.

"Sorry?" Kincaid said, sounding startled.

Gemma laughed. "It's Toby. He's just got up." This wouldn't be an expedition for Toby — she'd have to ask her mum to keep him, and then her overworked conscience would give her hell for neglecting him.

"Gemma?"

"I'd have to make arrangements for Toby."

"I'll pick you up. What time?"

"No." She'd never had Kincaid to her house, and after seeing his flat yesterday she felt even more reluctant. "I mean," she said, realizing how abrupt she'd sounded, "I'll have to run Toby to my mum's and then I might as well come to the flat."

They rang off, and Gemma lauded Kincaid's tact in not reminding her that running Toby up to Leyton High Street hardly made it necessary for her to drive to Hampstead.

It seemed that Kew had tempted a good portion of London's populace to initiate rites of spring. Gemma, sitting in the passenger seat of Kincaid's MG with her face turned up to the sun, included herself in the observation. She had to keep reminding herself that she hadn't come along for her own indulgence, and made an effort to keep her eyes on the road rather than Kincaid's profile. Normally she preferred to drive him, but when she'd reached the Hampstead flat he'd insisted she leave her car and had loaded her briskly into the Midget, saying, "Relax, Gemma. It's your day off, after all." She had given in without too much difficulty.

They circled Kew Green, jockeying for position in the traffic. The roads leading off to Kew Gardens and the river were chock-a-block with cars, but once they cleared the Green's south end they left some of the congestion behind. They wound their way south and east through the side streets toward Felicity Howarth's address, moving past large detached houses with gardens, then less el-

115

egant semi-detached, arriving finally in a cul-de-sac of terraced houses. Uncollected litter cluttered the sidewalks, and the houses had an air of mean shabbiness, as if their owners had given up making an effort.

Gemma looked at Kincaid in surprise. "She's a private nurse? Have you got the right address?"

He raised his eyebrows and shrugged. "Let's give it a try."

Felicity Howarth's basement flat, unlike most of its neighbors, showed signs of some attention. The steps were swept, the door painted a glossy, dark green and the brass knocker polished. Kincaid rang the bell and after a few moments Felicity opened the door.

She stared at Kincaid as if she couldn't quite place him, then her face cleared. "Mr. Kincaid?"

Gemma, who from Kincaid's description had been expecting an elegant and uniformed model of starched efficiency, had her perceptions abruptly altered. Although Felicity Howarth's height and coloring might be striking under other circumstances, today found her not at her best. She wore faded sweats, no make-up, had a smudge of dirt across her forehead, and Gemma thought she looked tired and not overly pleased to see them.

"Doing a bit in the garden," she said apol-

ogetically, wiping more dirt across her forehead in an effort to rub off the smudge.

Kincaid introduced Gemma simply by her
name, then said, "I'd like to talk to you about
Jasmine."

"I guess you'd better come in." Felicity led
them into her sitting room, said, "Let me wash
up," then hesitated as she was turning away
and added, "Like some coffee? I was just about
to make some for myself."

Gemma and Kincaid took advantage of the
opportunity to look around the room. It was
neat and scrupulously clean, as Gemma could
testify after she surreptitiously ran a finger
along the edge of a bookshelf — it came away
without a smudge of dust. The furniture was
of good quality but not new, and the ornaments more likely to be family hand-me-
downs, it seemed to Gemma, than chosen with
a particular decorating scheme in mind. A
Sunday Observer lay scattered across the sofa,
the only evidence of untidy occupation.

Kincaid moved to the windows at the rear
of the room and stood looking into the brambly garden that lay at eye level. "She lives
alone?" Gemma asked softly as she joined him.

"Looks that way, doesn't it?"

Felicity returned, carrying coffee pot and
china cups on a tray. Setting the tray down
on the coffee table, she scooped the offending

newspaper from the sofa and tucked it out of sight beneath an end table. She seemed to have regained authority along with clean face and hands, directing Gemma and Kincaid to sit on the sofa while she poured for them, then pulling up a straight-backed chair for herself. The sofa was squashy in the center and Gemma found herself sinking, trying to keep her thigh from brushing against Kincaid's, and looking up at Felicity perched commandingly on her hard chair. She saw the corner of Kincaid's mouth twitch with amusement at her predicament. Felicity had performed a clever and practiced maneuver, thought Gemma, and was not a bit surprised when she took charge of the interview.

"You've had your post mortem results, then?" Felicity said to Kincaid, crossing her legs and balancing her cup on her knee.

"The pathologist found considerably more morphine than her prescribed pain dosage would have allowed. Could she —"

"Look," Felicity interrupted, leaning toward him, "I know how you must be feeling about this. You're shocked because you weren't expecting it, but I see this all the time. It's not unusual."

"Margaret believed —"

"You and I both know, Mr. Kincaid, that assisted suicide is a felony offense. I'm sure

118

Jasmine decided she couldn't risk implicating Margaret, and credited Margaret with enough sense to keep her mouth shut about their previous agreement. Jasmine didn't really need any help, not with access to liquid morphine."

Kincaid sat back and sipped his coffee, temporarily giving up the offensive and taking another tack. "Why liquid morphine rather than tablets?"

"Difficulty swallowing. The tumor pressed against the esophagus as it grew. Jasmine was managing very little soft food as it was, and if she'd gone on much longer a feeding tube would have become necessary." Felicity sighed and relaxed a little in her chair. "Her pain would have increased considerably, too, perhaps beyond manageability with drugs. I've seen similar tumors crack the patient's ribs."

"Did Jasmine know this?" Gemma asked, horrified by the description.

"I imagine so. Jasmine was an informed patient, she kept up with things." Felicity smiled and fell silent, and Gemma saw weariness beneath the crisp exterior.

"How can you bear to do what you do, to watch people suffer so?"

This time Felicity's shrug was almost Gallic in its eloquence. "Somebody has to. And I'm good at it. I make them comfortable, and I reassure them."

Kincaid finished his coffee, leaned forward and set his empty cup down deliberately on the table. "Felicity, how could Jasmine have accumulated enough morphine to kill herself? Didn't you supply the prescription for her?"

"She requested a dosage increase weeks ago. We don't make an effort to limit terminal patients' opiate consumption, we simply try to keep them comfortable. It's quite possible that she told me she needed more morphine and then maintained the same dosage." Felicity studied Kincaid. "That's all I can tell you, I'm afraid."

Felicity obviously intended this as a dismissal, but Kincaid crossed his ankle over his knee and smiled at her. "You say you met Margaret a few times. Did her boyfriend ever come around? His name's Roger — I'm sure you'd remember him."

"No, Margaret always came alone when I was there, and Jasmine never mentioned meeting any friend."

"Did Jasmine say anything to you about making arrangements to see her brother?"

Felicity shook her head and began stacking their coffee cups on the tray. "We never talked about personal matters. Some patients like to tell you their life story, but not Jasmine."

"Did anyone visit her at all? Or did you see anyone unfamiliar in the building recently?"

"No. I'm sorry."

Kincaid gave in gracefully. He stood up and shook Felicity's hand. "Thank you. You've been very helpful."

Gemma quickly followed suit. "Thanks for your time."

"It may be necessary for you to appear at the inquest," Kincaid added as an afterthought as they moved toward the door.

"All right. You'll notify me?"

Kincaid nodded and held the door open for Gemma. "Good-bye."

Gemma, turning back as the door closed to echo his farewell, had a last glimpse of Felicity Howarth standing alone in her sitting room.

They had joined the A24 toward Surrey before either of them spoke. Gemma glanced at Kincaid. He drove easily, hand resting lightly on the gear shift, his expression obscured by the sunglasses he'd pulled from the door pocket. "You're still not convinced, are you?" she asked.

He answered without taking his eyes from the road. "No. Perhaps I'm just being stubborn."

"You think she would have left a note for

Margaret or Theo," said Gemma, and added "or you," silently. She found herself increasingly curious about this woman who had occupied such a large portion of Kincaid's life, and of whom she had known nothing. He'd made some passing references to visiting a neighbor, but she had somehow assumed the neighbor to be male — a going-down-the-pub sort of thing. Just what had been his relationship with Jasmine Dent? Were they lovers, with Jasmine so ill with cancer?

Stealing a glance at Kincaid's abstracted face, Gemma was shocked to realize how little she knew of his personal life. It had seemed to her that he moved through life with a graceful ease which she both admired and resented. But perhaps not everything came as easily to him as she'd supposed — he was obviously suffering both grief and guilt over Jasmine's death.

Now that she thought about it, when had she ever given him much chance to talk about what he did away from work? She had nattered on about Toby, and Kincaid had listened as if the activities of a two-year-old were absolutely fascinating. That she would have to attribute to natural good manners, and resolved to be less obtuse in the future.

"Gemma?"

She focused on Kincaid and flushed, feeling

transparent. "Sorry?"

"You looked a bit glazed. I thought maybe my driving terrified you."

"No," Gemma answered, smiling. "I was just thinking," she scrambled for the first thing that popped into her head, "um, about Felicity. Wouldn't you think that if you spent your life caring for the dying, trying to offer some comfort, that you would need a very strong faith?"

"Possibly. Go on."

Gemma heard the frown she couldn't see behind Kincaid's sunglasses. "Eleven o'clock on a Sunday morning and Felicity was working in the garden — she hadn't been to church."

"Maybe she's R.C. and goes to early mass," Kincaid said, amused.

"No make-up," Gemma countered, "not even a trace of lipstick. Don't tell me a good-looking woman like Felicity gets up and goes to church on Sunday morning without a stitch of make-up."

"Very observant." Kincaid grinned at that, then sobered. "Maybe whatever faith sustains Felicity isn't the visible sort."

They were entering the outskirts of Dorking. Kincaid pulled a map from his door pocket and handed it to Gemma. "Make sure it's the A25 we want to Abinger Hammer, would you?" As Gemma rustled the map, he continued, "Meg comes from here. Says her father owns a garage. It's not far from London for her family to have cut her off so completely. You'd think —"

"Junction coming up," Gemma interrupted. "A25 west toward Guildford." After Kincaid navigated the roundabout she said, "Sorry. What were you saying?"

"Never mind. Let's think about lunch."

Abinger Hammer was more hamlet than village, a few shops, and a park with a stream running through it. Theo Dent's shop, Trifles, stood at the crook in the road, across from the tea room and the village clock with its distinctive wooden bell-ringer.

Gemma and Kincaid ate tomato and cheese sandwiches, sitting in the sun in the tea shop's tiny walled garden. The sandwiches came garnished with watercress, and were cheerfully delivered by a teenage waitress sporting pink hair and multiple earrings.

"Village punk," Kincaid said, tucking stray sprigs of cress into his mouth with a finger.

"Can't be much in the way of night life around here, surely?" Gemma hadn't conquered her Londoner's disdain for village life.

"Disco in the village hall, I imagine. Or video games in the pub for those old enough."

Gemma pulled a face. "Ugh!"

Kincaid laughed. "Think about it, Gemma. Isn't that just what you'd want for Toby when he's older? No trouble to get into?"

She shook her head. "I'm not willing to contemplate that yet." Gemma finished her sandwich and swatted at a fat bumblebee which was making bombing runs at their table. "Did you grow up in a place this small?"

"Not this small, no. Relatively civilized, by your standards. We had a coffee bar. No video games in those days, though, just darts." A flash of his grin told Gemma he was pulling her leg a bit. The persistent bee blundered into Kincaid's teacup. Kincaid dumped him out and stretched. "Let's go see what Theo Dent found to occupy himself last Thursday night."

Chimes rang somewhere in the back of the shop as Gemma and Kincaid stepped inside Trifles and closed the door behind them. The "Closed" sign hanging on the inside of the door bounced and swung rhythmically, a counterpoint to the fading bells.

It took a moment for their eyes to adjust after the brilliant sunlight outside. "Looks like we have the place to ourselves," Kincaid said softly as he looked around. "Not much trade for a Sunday afternoon."

"Too pretty outside," Gemma offered. The shop seemed unbearably warm and stuffy.

Sheets of light slanted in through the uncurtained front windows, illuminating dusty objects. Gemma turned, surveying shelves and cluttered tables which held, among other things, mismatched china tea sets, brass knick-knacks, faded hunting prints, and a glass case filled with antique buttons. "This stuff needs a rainy day for poking about in," she said, holding a willow-pattern butter dish up to the light and squinting at it. "Oh, it's cracked. Too bad."

They heard the thump of quick footsteps on stair treads and a door in the back of the shop flew open. "Sorry. I was just finishing my —" Theo Dent stopped in the act of pushing his spectacles up on the bridge of his nose, staring in bewilderment at Kincaid. "Mr. Kincaid? I didn't recognize . . . I wasn't expecting . . ."

"Hello, Theo. Didn't mean to startle you. Should have called first, I expect, but it was a nice day for a run."

Hogwash, thought Gemma, listening to Kincaid's disarming patter. She knew him well enough to be sure he'd had every intention of catching Theo off-guard. This might as yet be unofficial nosiness, but Kincaid's working techniques were in full play.

Kincaid introduced Gemma, again leaving their relationship open to the most likely assumption, and Theo shook her hand. Gemma studied him, seeing a small man with an oval face and a cap of brown, curly hair shot with gray, wearing gold-rimmed, round spectacles that gave him a dated look. His hand was small and softer than her own. "Nice to meet you. You've some lovely things here." Gemma gestured around the room, then picked up the first thing that came to hand, a small porcelain pot in the shape of a beehive.

"Do you really think so?" Theo sounded inordinately pleased. He beamed at Gemma, showing small, even, white teeth. "Do you like honey pots? Here, look at this one," he scooped a thatched porcelain cottage from a shelf, "and this," white porcelain this time, decorated with mice peeping from a tangle of brambles. "Did you know that the Egyptians believed honey came from the tears of the sun god Ra? No pharaoh was buried without a sealed honey —"

"Theo," Kincaid interrupted the enthusiastic monologue, "is there someplace we could talk?"

"Talk?" Theo sounded baffled. He looked hopefully around the shop, and when no chairs appeared, said, "Uh, sure. We could go upstairs, I guess." He turned and led the way, glancing back over his shoulder anxiously. "It's not much, you know . . . I hope you won't mind . . ."

The upstairs flat obviously served as both living quarters and office — the office consisting of a scarred wooden desk covered with scraps of paper and an old, black Bakelite telephone. Living quarters fared not much better, in Gemma's opinion. A day bed, hastily made, and a cracked leather easy-chair dominated the furnishings, both positioned with a good view of a new color television and VCR. A curtained alcove hid what Gemma assumed to be cooking and bathing facilities.

"Lunch," Theo said apologetically, scooping up a plate which held bread crusts and a paper instant-soup container, and placing it behind the curtain. He gestured Kincaid into the leather chair and pulled up the desk chair for Gemma. That left him standing awkwardly, until he spied an empty packing crate, turned it over and used it as an impromptu stool. Some of his anxious manner seemed to leave him and he smiled self-deprecatingly. "I don't do much entertaining, as you might have gathered. I would have tidied the place up a bit for Jasmine, if she had come." Theo took a deep breath. "Now, Mr. Kincaid, what did you want to see me about? You obviously didn't bring this pretty young lady to admire my stock." He nodded toward Gemma as he spoke, and, again, she had the impression of a slightly old-fashioned quality.

"I've heard your sister's post mortem results, Theo. She died from an overdose of morphine." Kincaid spoke softly, unemphatically.

Theo's eyes lost their focus and he sat so quietly that Gemma looked questioningly at Kincaid, but after a moment he sighed and spoke. "Thank you. It's what I've been expecting since you spoke to me about it on Friday night. It was kind of you to come all this way to tell me."

Gemma, knowing that kindness had not been his intention, saw Kincaid color faintly.

"Theo —"

"It was the shock that upset me so, you know. I've had a bit of time to get used to the idea now, and I see that it was just the sort of thing Jasmine would do. But what I still don't understand," Theo looked from Kincaid to Gemma, including her in the question, "is why she phoned and told me to visit her today."

"Theo," Kincaid tried again, "there is another possibility. The coroner will most likely return a verdict of suicide, unless we find evidence to the contrary."

"Contrary? What do you mean, contrary?" Theo's brows drew together over the gold rims of his spectacles.

Kincaid sat up and leaned toward Theo, speaking more urgently now. "Someone else could have given her the morphine, Theo. Maybe Jasmine told Margaret the truth — maybe she had changed her mind about suicide, and maybe someone didn't like that decision at all."

"You're not serious?" Theo searched Kincaid's expression for some hint of a joke, and finding none, turned to Gemma for confirmation.

She nodded. "I'm afraid he is."

"But why?" Theo's voice rose to a squeak. "Why would anybody want to kill Jasmine? She was dying, for Christ's sake! You said yourself she'd only a few months left." He took a breath and shoved his spectacles up on the bridge of his nose, then shook his finger accusingly at Kincaid. "And how could somebody give her that much morphine without her knowing?"

A good point, thought Gemma, and one that Kincaid hadn't tackled.

"I don't know, Theo. I'd assume it would have been someone she trusted. As to why," Kincaid's tone became less conciliatory, "someone could have been in a hurry for something. What do you know about Jasmine's estate, Theo?"

"Estate?" Theo's face was blank with incomprehension.

"Come on, man. Don't look so bloody baffled." Kincaid rose and paced the small room. "Surely you must have some idea how Jasmine intended to dispose of her property. She told me she'd made some good investments over the years, and she had a good bit of equity in the flat. Will it all come to you?"

"I don't know." Theo looked up at Kincaid, and it seemed to Gemma as if he had shrunk before her eyes. "She made the down payment on the mortgage here. I was broke, really down on my luck." He turned and spoke to Gemma, seeking understanding. "Some things hadn't worked out, you know? I never really thought about what would happen if she died."

Kincaid's eyebrows shot up in disbelief and he opened his mouth to protest, then changed his tack. "What were you doing on Thursday evening?"

"Thursday?"

"The night Jasmine died, Theo," Kincaid prompted.

"I was here, of course. Where else would I be?" Theo sounded thoroughly frightened now, near to tears.

"Start at the beginning," said Gemma, moved to bail Theo out. "What time do you close the shop?"

"About half-five, usually."

"So you closed up that day about half-past five? And then what did you do?"

"Well, I tidied up a bit and locked the till, and then I went across the road for my supper." Theo, visibly relaxing, looked expectantly to Gemma for his catechism. Kincaid had moved to the window and stood gazing down into the street.

"Across the street? I don't remember seeing a restaurant —"

"No, no. There's only the pub at night. The tea shop closes at five. I always go across to the pub for my supper. Good food and I can't cook much here," he gestured toward the curtain, "just a hot-plate, really."

"I thought you said you didn't drink much," said Kincaid from the window.

Theo flushed. "I don't. Just the odd half-pint of sweet cider."

Gemma took charge again. "What did you do when you finished your meal? Have you a car?"

The question seemed to anger Theo. "No, I don't have a bloody car, if it's anyone else's business. I came back here. There's not much else to do in Abinger Hammer. And besides," he smiled at Gemma, his brief spurt of temper evaporating, and nodded toward the VCR, "I had a new film. Arrived at the shop that afternoon. *Random Harvest*, 1942. Ronald Coleman and Greer Garson. Great stuff. There's this shell-shocked World War I officer and he's saved from spending his life in an asylum by this music-hall sing— never mind.

"That's it. I watched the film. I read a bit, then I went to sleep." He looked at Kincaid, who had come back to perch on the arm of the easy-chair. "Satisfied?"

"Sorry," said Kincaid, standing and holding out his hand to Theo, "I just like to get things straight. I'm afraid you'll have to appear at the inquest. I'll let you know the details."

"It was nice to meet you, Theo. I'm sorry about your sister." Gemma took Theo's hand, surprised to find it ice-cold in the overheated room.

Theo followed them down the steep stairs, and Gemma had a last glance at the brambly honey pot before Theo shut the shop door behind them.

They left the shop without speaking and started down the footpath toward the river. Kincaid walked with his shoulders hunched and his hands in his pockets, not looking at Gemma.

"You suckered me into playing good cop-bad cop with that poor man. And after he was so touchingly grateful to you. Is that what you had in mind when you asked me to come?" Gemma stopped, forcing him to turn and meet her eyes.

"No. Partly habit, I suppose. I feel like I've beaten a child. But Christ, Gemma. How could anyone really be so bloody gormless? You can't believe he never gave a thought to what would happen to Jasmine's money."

"Oh, I don't think he's stupid, Duncan." Gemma started walking again and Kincaid followed. "Innocent, maybe, and a bit fragile. Surely you can't think Theo had anything to do with Jasmine's death?"

"It's that helpless quality of his," Kincaid said with the beginning of a grin. "It's aroused your protective instincts. Somebody probably felt the same way about Crippen."

"You've no reason not to believe him," Gemma countered, stung. "Do you think about what would happen to your parents' money, or your sister's, if they were to die suddenly?"

"No. But they've not been ill, and they don't support me. It looks to me like Theo still needs all the help he can get. His business doesn't exactly seem to be flourishing."

They turned now and followed the watercourse toward the bridge at the village end. Cress, dappled green in the sunlight, grew thickly in the stream's running water. The children's play equipment stood deserted in the meadow, an empty swing moving gently in the breeze, and Gemma found herself wishing intensely that the afternoon had held no motive more sinister than a walk by the water's edge.

"It's nearly three o'clock, and by my count that's the only pub in the village." Kincaid pointed toward the low, white-washed building standing at the T-junction on the other side of the bridge. "I guess that qualifies as across the road. If we want to have a friendly chat with the landlord of the Bull and Whistle before closing time, we'd better get to it. And," the grin was back in full force, "I'll buy you a sweet cider."

The affable landlord of the Bull and Whistle confirmed that Theo had indeed eaten his supper there on Thursday evening. "Comes in every evening, about the same time. More likely I'd notice if he weren't here than if he were. Vegetarian lasagna on Thursday, I remember he looked pleased as punch when he saw the board." The publican replaced Gemma's coaster and eyed her appreciatively. "Anything else, Miss?"

"This is fine, thanks."

Gemma had ordered a dry cider with a quelling look at Kincaid, from which he deduced she was fed up with being teased about her preference for sweet drinks. She sat next to him at the bar, her expression inscrutable, looking crisp and as cool as her coloring would allow in pale trousers and a cinnamon cotton shirt. Looking at her, Kincaid felt rather rumpled and worse for wear.

The blackboard above the bar bore nothing but a few chalky streaks. "Nothing on today?" asked Kincaid.

"Wife takes Sunday off. Just cold pies and sausage rolls, or scotch eggs, if you like."

Kincaid shook his head. "Can you remember what time Theo Dent left here on Thursday?"

The landlord scratched his head. " 'Bout half-past seven, I should think. Nothing special on that evening. Sometimes he'll have another half of cider if there's a darts match, or a good crowd."

"Gets on with the locals, does he?" asked Kincaid with some surprise.

"Well, I wouldn't exactly say that. But he's friendly enough. Shy, maybe. More likely to watch than to join in, if you know what I mean."

"Have any idea where he went when he left here?"

The landlord laughed. "In Abinger Hammer? There's not much choice, is there? And he's not got a car. Went home, as far as I know."

"Thanks." Kincaid drained his pint and

136

looked at Gemma.

"Satisfied?" she asked acidly.

Kincaid grinned. "Not yet. Let's do a recce at the video shop."

Shop turned out to be an exaggerated description. Newsagent, post office and video rental were squeezed into a space about the size of Kincaid's bathroom. The young woman behind the counter chewed her gum slowly while she considered Kincaid's query, contributing to a rather unfortunate bovine resemblance.

Carefully, she counted the days backwards on her fingers. "Yeah. It was Thursday *Random Harvest* came in. Special ordered it for him." She revolved her index finger around her ear. "Weird guy. Nutty about old films. I tried to turn him on to some really good stuff, you know *The Terminator*, *Lethal Weapon*, like that, but he wasn't having any. Only watches dusty old things. The week before he wanted, uh, what's it called with Cary Grant? Arsenic and Old Ladies?"

"*Arsenic and Old Lace*," Kincaid corrected, smothering a grin. "And did he return *Random Harvest* the next day?"

"First thing," the girl answered, puzzled. "Thanks."

"You wouldn't dare make anything of it." Gemma had glared at him as they got in the car. "Lots of people love that film and don't go about poisoning their relatives."

Kincaid had to admit he found it difficult to imagine that Theo had got himself inconspicuously to London, murdered his sister, and managed to return home in time to watch a much anticipated video. He mulled it over as he drove, playing out various unlikely scenarios.

By the time they reached Hampstead he'd come up with nothing more definite than a resolve to discover if Theo were really as unaware of Jasmine's affairs as he claimed. He'd see Jasmine's solicitor straight away.

Kincaid couldn't persuade Gemma to stay when they reached the Hampstead flat, not even by tempting her with an offer of a drink on the balcony. She'd been restive on the drive back from Surrey, checking her watch often. What had started as a pleasant day had gradually deteriorated, and Kincaid had the feeling he'd failed her in some unknown expectation.

Perhaps she was still cross with him for bullying Theo, and truthfully he couldn't blame her. He'd only intended to gather a little information, but the man's helplessness made him feel awkward and inadequate, and that in turn irritated him.

Kincaid opened Gemma's car door and closed it as she got in. He stood, resting his hands on the open windowsill, so that she had to tilt her head to look up at him. "Thanks for coming with me, Gemma."

"Not much help, I'm afraid." She smiled and turned the key in the ignition. "Mind now, don't forget to look after the cat," she said as she pulled away, but Kincaid thought both the smile and the admonition seemed absent-minded.

He took the reminder to heart. After retrieving a beer and a stack of blue journals from his flat, he quietly let himself in Jasmine's door. Sid, curled in the middle of the hospital bed, began a rumbly purr when Kincaid stepped into the room. "Actually glad to see me this time, are you?" Kincaid addressed him. "Or just hungry, more likely." He spooned some tinned food into a bowl and set it down. The cat unbent enough to allow Kincaid to scratch behind his ears before turning all his attention to the bowl.

Beer in hand and journals tucked under his arm, Kincaid opened the French doors and sat down on the top step overlooking the empty garden. Leaning against the rail, as Jasmine had so often done, he began to read.

September 22, 1957
It's cold here. Cold all the bloody time, even though Aunt May says it's a "fair autumn". My hands and feet hurt from the chill and these stupid woolen clothes itch. I've come up

in little red bumps all over. At least I'll never be as pale as these English, with their skin like raw potatoes, faces blank as shuttered windows, voices like rusty saws scraping.

May's given me a bed in the cottage attic, Theo the spare room. She says it's because he's the youngest, but she favors him. Me she disliked from the moment she set eyes on my face.

I lie in the little bed at night and listen to the sound the wind makes in the rafters, and think about going barefoot in the dust, about cool, cotton dresses, and coconut milk, and pomegranates, and passionfuit, and the way the sunlight came through the green bamboo blinds in the Mohur Street house and made my room look like it was under water.

She says I've got to stay in school till I'm sixteen, it's the law. The girls don't speak to me except to make rude remarks. The boys just look.

Theo's fared better. He goes out with some of the boys after school. He's even starting to sound a bit like them.

I'd leave here the day I'm sixteen but I can't leave Theo in May's clutches. She's got plans for him, she's already worried about his marks, filling his head with talk about university.

We did fine, Theo and I, without any interference from her, and we will again, I swear it.

CHAPTER
8

Monday dawned cold and blustery, ending the idyllic weather that had accompanied Jasmine's death. Kincaid knotted his tie and shrugged into a wool jacket with a sense of relief mingled with anticipation. He studied his reflection in the bathroom mirror, expecting to find some visible mark of the weekend's slow passage, but the blue eyes staring back at him looked ordinary and not quite awake. With a last pass of the hairbrush, he judged himself presentable. Pausing only to pick up keys and wallet and to dump his unfinished coffee in the sink, he left the flat.

He took the tube, and exited at St. James Park. A few minutes walk brought him into the cold shadow of the steel and concrete tower which housed New Scotland Yard. The pavements were deserted except for the uniformed guard standing sentinel before the glass doors.

Litter rattled as it blew in the gutter. Not exactly a comforting sight, the Yard, but then Kincaid didn't suppose the architects had succor in mind. He gave a casual wave to the guard and entered the building.

The short walk had given him time to marshal his arguments and he went straight to his Chief Superintendent's office. Denis Childs' secretary, a plump, dark-haired girl, looked up from her typing and beamed at him. "Morning, Mr. Kincaid. What can I do for you?"

The Chief Superintendeiit had a talent for choosing staff both good natured and efficient, and they kept his political machinery well-oiled. "Is he in, Holly?" Kincaid nodded toward the closed door of the inner office.

"Reading his reports, I should think. Nothing pressing on this morning. Just give the door a tap." She'd turned back to the keyboard before she finished her sentence, her fingers flying over the keys.

The Chief Superintendent had done his office in Scandinavian Modern, all blond wood, cane, and greenery, and Kincaid suspected his motivation was more a matter of playing against convention than strong preference.

Denis Childs reclined in the chair behind his desk, report propped on his crossed knee, cigarette smoldering in the ashtray on the desk's edge. Childs' bulk made the furniture seem insubstantial, the subtle color scheme paling to anemic against his dark hair and lively brown eyes.

"What's up, Duncan? Pull up a chair." He flicked over the last page of the report and tossed it into his out-tray, stubbed out the cigarette and folded his hands across his middle, preparing to listen, as he usually did, with his attention fully engaged.

After settling himself in the visitor's armchair, Kincaid recounted the details of Jasmine's death and his subsequent actions.

"I'd like to make an official inquiry," he concluded. "Shouldn't require much manpower, just Gemma and myself, really."

Childs considered a moment before he spoke, steepling his fingers over his belly. "Sounds like a fairly straightforward suicide. You know we usually look the other way in these cases — nothing to be gained by pursuing the matter, particularly for the family. However, if there is any direct evidence that the young woman — what was her name?"

"Margaret Bellamy."

"— that Margaret Bellamy was present and physically assisted your friend's suicide in any way, we would have to press charges."

"I can't rule that out. She says she wasn't there that evening, but she has no corroboration." Kincaid shifted in his seat and the chair creaked alarmingly. "But that doesn't make any sense. Why mention the suicide pact? She need never have said anything, and I doubt I would have felt uneasy enough to order an autopsy."

"Shock?" Childs suggested, lighting a Player's from the pack on his desk and squinting at Kincaid through the smoke.

Kincaid shrugged in irritation. "She was shocked, yes, and probably not emotionally competent at the best of times, but she's not stupid. She must know the law. And that," he sat forward in the chair and gripped the arms, "is what really bothers me. Jasmine would have known the risk involved for Meg. I've read Exit's literature —" Kincaid ignored his chief's raised eyebrows at that "— and they recommend most strongly that one let friends and family know one's intentions, and leave indemnifying documents in case of suspicion."

"Suicide note?"

"Not necessarily . . . not if she wanted it to be thought a natural death. But Exit suggests a detailed statement of intent, signed and dated, in case the death is questioned. We're not talking about a scrawled 'just can't cope anymore' note. Jasmine left not a shred that I've been able to find."

Childs sighed and gently swiveled his chair

back and forth. "And you feel that's not in character? When people are ill they don't always behave —"

"You're not the first to suggest that, but I doubt I ever met anyone more rational than Jasmine, and you could certainly consider suicide as a rational decision for someone terminally ill."

"Have you spoken to her solicitor? She might have left the indemnifying documents with him."

"First on my list," Kincaid said, relieved at the interview's direction. He knew how reluctantly his chief let go a problem once he started to worry at it.

"I'll authorize a warrant to access the solicitor's files. Anything left for the forensics lads?"

Kincaid snorted. "It'd take a miracle, would have even in the first place. The place is clean. There are a couple of nearly full vials of morphine in the fridge, very unlikely there's enough missing to account for Jasmine's death. I'll bring them in, but I doubt very much we'll find anyone's prints who didn't have normal access. If it was murder, it was done very carefully." He chewed his thumb for a moment while he thought. "If Jasmine killed herself what did she do with the empty morphine vial? I've done a fairly thorough search."

Childs tilted his chair forward and ground out the stub of his cigarette. "I can spare you a few days, if nothing major comes in. I'll put Sullivan on this morning's lot, he's due for a headache." The wickedly benign smile accompanying the last comment made Kincaid glad not to be in Bill Sullivan's shoes.

"Gemma?" Kincaid asked.

"The last time I assigned her to Sullivan I got a right bollicking. Two redheads do not a team make, at least not these two. You can have her for a couple of days, if she'll put up with you — and mind you, this is only as long as I can spare you."

"Right," Kincaid said, standing up to go. "Thanks, guv."

Kincaid found Gemma already in his office, ensconced in the chair behind his desk. When she started to rise, he waved her back into the chair and propped himself on the edge of his battered desk. His office decor had never progressed beyond functional — he never seemed to get around to requisitioning more than bookcases from the Yard.

Every available inch of space in the small cubicle housed books. His mother's book graveyard, Kincaid thought as he surveyed the volumes jammed into the shelves without rhyme or classification. They arrived regularly in the post from Cheshire, always something she had 'just happened to come across' in the shop. From do-it-yourself plumbing manuals to Russian sci-fi, they ran the gamut of his mother's enthusiasms. In her battle for his continuing education Kincaid saw his mother's disappointment in his refusal to attend university, and he could never quite bring himself to return the books or give them away. And although he teased his mum about her obsessions, one couldn't grow up with books as he had and not love them for their own sakes.

Gemma closed the folder she'd been scanning and handed it to Kincaid. "Jasmine's p.m. report. No evidence of puncture marks, so the morphine must have been administered through the catheter."

"No surprise there."

"And I've been on to the coroner's office. The inquest is set for Wednesday." Gemma stood up and brushed some crumbs off the blotter, then picked up a coffee mug bearing lipstick traces on its rim. She'd traded her usual tailored outfit for a long, navy cardigan and a printed skirt in some soft material.

"Quick off the mark this morning, aren't you?" Kincaid grinned at her. "Second breakfast?"

Gemma ignored the dig. "I heard you'd

gone straight in to see the boss. Did he okay it?"

Kincaid sobered. "We've a couple of days, if nothing comes in that Sullivan can't handle. The rest are up to their eyeballs." He went around the desk and took the chair Gemma had vacated, leaning back and ticking items off on his fingers. "Jasmine's solicitor first off — I'll take that one. I'd like you to go round the borough planning office where Meg and Jasmine worked and see Meg. Find out what Jasmine told her about the legality of assisted suicide. Then interview whoever else seems likely. But first I want you to trace the lovely Roger Leveson-Gower. See what you make of him." Smiling at the thought of pitting Gemma's temper against Leveson-Gower's snide sarcasm, Kincaid added, "Maybe he'll tell you where he was on Thursday evening. He bloody well won't tell me."

Kincaid found the Bayswater address, a ground floor flat in a once-residential town-house, without difficulty. To his surprise, the brass nameplate simply bore the legend 'Antony Thomas, Solicitor'. Somehow he'd expected a high-powered string of names.

The receptionist took Kincaid's name, her dark eyes widening as she looked at his warrant card. Very young, very pretty, very likely

Pakistani, Kincaid thought. She glanced at him nervously every so often as he waited patiently in the straight-backed chair. When her intercom buzzed she ushered him into the inner office with obvious relief.

"What can I do for you, Superintendent?" Antony Thomas greeted Kincaid with a smile and a handshake. "Do have a seat. Though if it's police business I can't imagine how I could help."

Kincaid sat in the wing chair angled comfortably in front of the desk and considered Thomas. Another preconception shattered, although why his knowledge of Jasmine should have led him to expect a gruff old family retainer, he didn't know. Antony Thomas was slender, middle-aged, with a fringe of dark hair surrounding a shiny, bald pate, and a trace of Welsh lilt in his voice.

"Not entirely official business, Mr. Thomas," Kincaid began, and proceeded to tell him the circumstances of Jasmine Dent's death.

Thomas absorbed the tale in silence, and when Kincaid had finished sat a few moments longer, pulling at his chin with his thumb and forefinger. When he spoke his voice was soft, the lilt more pronounced. "I'm very sorry to hear that, Mr. Kincaid. I knew her situation, of course, but still one is never quite prepared. Had you known Jasmine long?"

The question surprised Kincaid. "Not long, no. Just since her illness forced her to leave work."

Thomas sighed and looked down as he straightened the pens on his blotter. "I knew her a very long time, Mr. Kincaid. More than twenty years. My office was in the same street as the chartered accountant she worked for at the time — Jasmine always had a head for figures. She first came to me over the settlement of her aunt's estate. What a lovely girl she was then, you should have seen her." He raised his head, his brown eyes engaging Kincaid's. "I was already married, with two small children," he passed a hand over the top of his head and smiled, "and hair, if you can believe that, but I must admit I was sorely tempted. Not to give you the wrong impression — I'm sure the fantasy was strictly on my part. But we did become friends over the years."

"Did she talk to you about suicide, Mr. Thomas? Or give you any documents stating her intent to commit suicide?"

Thomas shook his head. "No, she did not. I would have been very distressed."

Kincaid crossed his foot over his knee and straightened the crease in his trouser leg, thinking how best to approach the next bit. "I know it's a delicate matter, Mr. Thomas,

150

but I need to know how Jasmine left her affairs, and if she carried any life insurance. I found no copy of a will or insurance policy in the flat." He pulled the warrant from his inside jacket pocket, unfolded it and handed it across the desk to Thomas. "I think you'll find everything in order."

Thomas scanned the paper, then pushed his intercom. "Hareem, bring in the files for Jasmine Dent, would you please." Clicking off, he spoke to Kincaid. "I don't like it, but I'll give you what I can."

Hareem came in with the file, giving Kincaid another curious glance from under her lashes before shutting the door.

Thomas shuffled through the papers, nodding as he found the familiar drafts, then looked up at Kincaid with an expression of surprise. "She's named you executor, Mr. Kincaid. I thought your name seemed familiar."

"Me?" Kincaid said more loudly than he intended. "But why —" He stopped himself. There had been no one else she had trusted as competent and impartial. "Didn't she have to inform me?"

"No. But you can refuse, if you want."

Kincaid shook his head. "No. I'll carry out her wishes, though it does complicate things a bit."

Antony Thomas smiled. "Good. Let me give it to you as simply as I can, then.

"Jasmine made a new will in the autumn. She arranged to pay off the mortgage on her brother's business. Except for a couple of small bequests, the remainder of her estate goes to Miss Margaret Bellamy."

"Is there quite a bit?" Kincaid asked, a little surprised.

"Well, as I said, Jasmine had a knack for these things. It includes stocks and shares and the equity in the Carlingford Road flat. She and her brother both received a tidy nest egg when their aunt died. Jasmine invested it well, and she made a good income from her work. I don't believe she spent much on herself — in fact, except for the disbursements to her brother, I don't think she spent much at all."

Kincaid sat up a little straighter in his chair. "You mean financing Theo's shop wasn't the first time she'd lent him money?"

Thomas shook his head emphatically. "Oh, no. Not by any means. In fact, after I had helped her settle her aunt's affairs, she retained me to salvage some of his investment in a psychedelic nightclub. In Chelsea, I think it was."

"Theo? A psychedelic club?" Kincaid said, astonished.

"Nineteen sixty-seven or sixty-eight, that would have been. I had very little success,

I'm afraid, and if I remember correctly, that was the last of a string of bad investments with his aunt's money." Thomas snapped his fingers. "All gone, and in a very short time, too. After that, Jasmine funded him in various schemes — he went to art school and she supported him for a while, but his painting wasn't terribly successful."

Kincaid found the idea of Theo painting less ludicrous than Theo running a trendy disco. "Have you ever met Theo?"

"A few times, when he came in with Jasmine to sign papers, but I haven't seen him in several years."

"Did Jasmine give you any idea how the shop was doing?"

Thomas shook his head, the corners of his mouth turning down. "I only saw her the one time after her illness was diagnosed, and she didn't stay longer than necessary. I found her very . . . reticent."

Not wanting to discuss her illness with an old friend, Kincaid wondered, or not wanting to explain the change in her will? "Did you not find it odd, Mr. Thomas, Jasmine not making better provision for Theo?"

"Well, yes, as a matter of fact. She did say something rather cryptic, now that I think about it. Something about it 'being a bit late to cut the strings, but necessary all the same'.

And then there was the life insur—"

"Jasmine carried life insurance?" Kincaid leaned forward, hands on the edge of the chair seat.

Shrinking back a bit, Thomas said, "Yes, she —"

"Theo the beneficiary?"

Thomas nodded. "But it wasn't all that much, Mr. Kincaid, only twenty thousand pounds."

Kincaid deliberately relaxed again, leaning back in the chair and resting his chin on his joined fingertips. "Mr. Thomas," he said carefully, "does that policy carry a suicide exclusion clause?"

Frowning, Thomas turned the pages in the folder. "Here it is." He read for a few minutes, then looked up at Kincaid. "Yes. A two-year exclusion clause. And the policy was issued two years ago last month."

They looked at each other in silence until Thomas spoke, distress in his voice. "Surely Jasmine can't have planned . . . she wouldn't have known she was ill . . ."

"Perhaps she felt something wasn't quite as it should be." The first nagging symptoms, Kincaid thought, and the fear of seeing a doctor. "Did Theo know about the policy?" And, Kincaid wondered, did he know it carried an exclusion clause?

CHAPTER

9

As a child, Gemma had been intrigued by the idea of St. John's Wood. Pop stars lived there, and television celebrities. The name itself had fairy-tale connotations, and made her think of dark, arching trees and hidden cottages.

The reality, as she discovered when she was a bit older, was quite a disappointment. Ordinary upper-middle-class homes in ordinary streets, rapidly encroached upon by complexes of luxury, high-rise flats. She found the address Kincaid had coaxed from Margaret Bellamy on the phone, and a not-too-distant parking space for her car.

The house, built of white stone with pseudo-Greek columns fronting it, looked expensive and not terribly well-kept. Close-up the whitewash revealed scaly, diseased patches and weeds flourished in the cracked walk. Gemma rang the bell and held her cardigan closed against the wind as she waited. The hollow echo of the bell died away and Gemma had raised her hand to ring again when she heard the staccato click of heels on a hard floor. The door flew open, revealing a thin woman with a helmet of bottle-blond hair. She wore a white denim jumpsuit, the front of which displayed a starburst pattern in gold brads.

"What is it?" The woman's foot, clad in a gold sandal with spike heels, began a furious tapping against the tile.

Gemma, thrusting away speculation as to how anyone could walk in stilts like that without permanent spinal damage, brought her eyes back to the woman's face and smiled as she flipped open her warrant card. "Police. I'd like to ask you a few questions." Kincaid had said that Roger Leveson-Gower lived with his mum. While the woman was opening her mouth to retort, Gemma continued. "Are you Mrs. Leveson-Gower?"

"Of course I am. Whatever it is you —"

"If I could just come in for a few minutes," Gemma had already inserted her navy pump into the hall, her body following smoothly, "I'm sure this won't take much of your time." She shut the door with a decisive click, thinking that if she ever decided to give up police work she'd have a hell of an edge selling vacuum cleaners.

Mrs. Leveson-Gower opened her mouth to protest, then shrugged. "All right, if you must. But make it quick — I've an appointment." She glanced pointedly at her watch as she led Gemma through an open door on the right.

White, white and more white — the room's mirrored walls reflected white, linen-covered furniture and white, plush carpet, a snow queen's lair, thought Gemma, suitable for a not-so-enchanted wood. Mrs. Leveson-Gower sank down on one of the white sofas, crossed her knees and propped a foot on the edge of a glass and chrome coffee table. She did not invite Gemma to sit.

Gemma perched on the edge of the opposite sofa and took notebook and pen from her handbag, refusing to be rushed by the woman's obvious impatience. "Mrs. Leveson-Gower," Gemma said, pronouncing it 'Loos-n-gor' as Kincaid had coached her. 'They'll sneer at you if you get it wrong,' he'd said, 'and you can't afford to let Roger have the upper hand'. "Does your son Roger live here with you?"

The scarlet toenails on Mrs. Leveson-Gower's sandaled foot began a rhythmic jiggling, but her tone remained belligerent. "Roger? Why on earth do you want to know?"

"Just a routine inquiry, Mrs. —"

"Inquiry into what, for heaven's sake?" The

errant foot stilled suddenly.

If not for the mask of irritation etched into her features, Mrs. Leveson-Gower would have been a strikingly beautiful woman. An extremely well-preserved late forties, Gemma guessed, and the tautness of the skin over the bones spoke of expensive lifts and tucks. "An acquaintance of your son's died in questionable circumstances last Thursday evening. We're simply corroborating statements. Is he at —"

"What station did you say you were from, Sergeant? Let me see your identification again."

Gemma obligingly pulled the folder from her bag and handed it across. "Not your local station, ma'am. New Scotland Yard."

"What division?"

Gemma hadn't expected such a knowledgeable question. "C1, homicide." Mrs. Leveson-Gower went very still, and Gemma could almost hear the gears clicking in her brain.

"You're not going to speak to my son without our solicitor present." She stood up and started toward the door, speaking over her shoulder. "You can call and make an appointment at his conven—"

"Making arrangements for me, Mummy? I'm sure it's not necessary."

The man entered the room with such

smooth timing that Gemma felt sure he had been listening outside the louvered doors. He smiled at Gemma, showing even, white teeth, then turned his attention back to his mother. They faced each other silently across the expanse of white carpet like participants in a duel, then Mrs. Leveson-Gower left the room, without word or look to Gemma.

Roger, for Gemma had no doubt as to his identity, crossed the room and stood looking casually down at Gemma. She closed her mouth with a snap. Kincaid might have warned her, the sod, before she made a ninny of herself. Roger Leveson-Gower was stunningly good-looking. She could see the resemblance to his mother in his coloring — his mother must have had the same tawny hair before she resorted to bleach — but in him every line and angle had combined to perfection.

"I'm sure it's not worth the bother of a solicitor, whatever it is, Constable." He sat on arm of the sofa facing Gemma, so that she still had to look up at him.

"Sergeant," she said sharply, dropping her eyes and flipping open her notebook in an effort to regain control of the interview. "Last Thursday evening, Mr. Leveson-Gower. Can you tell me where you were?"

"What's it in aid of?" Roger asked in a tone of mild interest.

"Jasmine Dent's death, and your friend Margaret Bellamy's involvement. Miss Bellamy says she agreed to help Jasmine commit suicide, but that Jasmine changed her mind and she didn't see her after late afternoon on Thursday. Can you confirm that?"

"Last Thursday?" Roger frowned in concentration. "No. I was on a job and then out with my mates. But Meg would never have gone through with it, you know. Hadn't the nerve."

"She discussed it with you?"

Roger smiled, including Gemma in the joke. "Noble as hell about it, too, worrying about her ethical duty to ease suffering."

"And that didn't worry you? You didn't try to talk her out of it? Assisted suicide is a criminal offence."

"It was all just talk, like I said, Sergeant. Meg couldn't kill a wounded bird. There's a yawning gap between planning and execution." He stood and gave a cat-like stretch, then settled again on the sofa arm.

"Just what is it you do in the evenings, Mr. Leveson-Gower?"

Roger gave a bark of laughter. "Good god, you make it sound like I'm a ponce. Why so indignant, Sergeant?"

Gemma felt her color rising. She sounded pompous even to herself, but the man made

160

her throw up a full battery of defenses. Taking a breath to focus on her interview technique, she smiled at him sweetly and put the emphasis on her first word. "Are you a ponce, Mr. Leveson-Gower?"

"Nothing so glamorous as that, Sergeant, more's the pity." He still sounded amused. "I set up for clubs and discos. Lights, sound equipment, you know the sort of thing. The hours suit me."

"And that's where you were on Thursday evening?"

"Yeah. Dive called The Blue Angel." Roger raised one eyebrow with much practiced ease. "I suppose you'll want the address? And the names of my mates?"

"If you wouldn't mind."

He gave her an address in Hammersmith, then added, "Jimmy Dawson you can find at the petrol station just off Shepherd's Bush roundabout. We hung around at the bar till the show finished."

"What time would that have been?" Gemma asked, pen ready.

Roger shrugged. "I've no idea. I'd had a few pints, and I don't wear a watch." His shirt cuffs were turned back to just below his elbow, and he held up a tanned, bare wrist for Gemma's examination.

"And then what?"

"I came home and put my head on the pillow, just like a good little boy."

Gemma allowed her skepticism to show. "Is that so? And can your mother vouch for you?"

"I am not in the habit of registering my comings and goings with my mother. And besides, if I remember correctly, she was out that evening."

Under the smooth and slightly condescending reply, Gemma sensed irritation — so he was sensitive about living in his mum's house. She pushed her advantage. "You didn't check in with Margaret either? Not even by phone?"

"No. We don't have that kind of relationship, Sergeant." Condescension triumphed over irritation. His tone implied Gemma was a fool for expecting him to be accountable to anyone. He stood with the same easy grace as before. "Is that it, Sergeant?"

Gemma remained planted on the sofa, notebook in hand, determined not to let him terminate the interview. "Are you sure, Mr. Leveson-Gower, that you didn't go to Carlingford Road when you left the club that night? That you didn't visit Jasmine yourself?"

Roger smiled and Gemma had the unpleasant feeling the joke was on her. "No. I've never been to the Carlingford Road flat. You see, Sergeant, I never met Jasmine Dent at all."

★ ★ ★

Jimmy Dawson wore his hair in a pony-tail and looked to be in his late twenties, but those were the only similarities immediately apparent between Dawson and his friend Roger Leveson-Gower. Dawson's accent made it obvious they hadn't gone to the same schools.

" 'Ere, wot's all this about?" he said warily, after Gemma had fished him from under a car in a service bay and identified herself.

"Roger Leveson-Gower."

"Oh, him," Dawson said dismissively, and Gemma saw the tension drain from him. He jerked his head toward the glass-enclosed office and she followed, thankful when the door muted the roar of Shepherd's Bush roundabout. Dawson gestured her into a cracked leather chair, wiped his hands on a greasy rag and lit a Marlboro from a pack in his shirt pocket. "What's 'e done, then?"

Gemma ignored the question. "Was he with you last Thursday evening, Mr. Dawson?"

Dawson leaned against the desk and exhaled smoke from his nose while he thought about it. "Aye. And I can tell you when he left, too, 'cause he buggered off when it was his turn to buy a round."

"What time was that?"

"Band took a break around nine . . . not long after that, I'd say."

"Did he say where he was going?" Gemma asked, but without much hope. Even on such brief acquaintance she didn't expect Roger to slip up so easily.

"Nah. We was takin' the mickey out of 'im about his bird, but 'e wasn't havin' any."

"You've met Margaret, then?" Gemma asked, surprised.

Dawson shrugged. "She's all right. He brings her around sometimes."

"How do you know him, Jimmy — can I call you Jimmy?" asked Gemma, finding the friendship more and more unlikely.

"I play in a band, see?" Dawson grinned, showing teeth already beginning to yellow with nicotine, and played a little air-guitar riff. "And he sets up for us at some of the clubs."

"So you're not really close mates?"

"Nah. He's just around, you know? Has a way of weaselin' out of things, our Roger, always talking about what 'e's going to do when he's flush."

"Flush?" repeated Gemma.

"Aye." Jimmy Dawson ground out the stub of his cigarette in the metal ashtray on the desk, and the metallic smell stung Gemma's nose. "When he comes into 'is money, like."

CHAPTER

10

The stale cheese roll sat heavily in the pit of Gemma's stomach. She'd returned to the Yard just long enough to exchange information with Kincaid and grab a snack in the canteen.

Now as she struggled to parallel park the Escort in a space a size too small, and a taxi missed removing her right front fender by centimeters, she regretted the sandwich. Visions of leisurely lunches in cheerful cafes ran through her mind as she killed the engine and took a breath. Her mother's voice spoke insistently in her ear. "Why don't you get a nice job, love? One with a bit of class. You could be a solicitor's assistant, or a hairdresser like your sister."

Gemma shook her head and got out of the car, slamming the door loudly enough to shut out any more imaginary admonitions. She'd settle for stale cheese rolls, thank you very

much. Dodging traffic a little more reck-
lessly than usual, she crossed the street and
studied the entrance to the borough planning office.

The location near Holland Park, scrubbed
white stone and a glossy black door gave the
building an image befitting its function.
Gemma adjusted her shoulder bag and opened
the door. She stood in the hallway a moment,
listening, sensing the threshold hum of a busy
office — the murmur of voices and the faint
tapping of fingers against keyboards. To her
right a door stood open. Light from the bay
window fronting the street illuminated the girl
behind the simple desk. Except for the telephone glued to her ear, the girl might have
stepped out of a Whistler portrait, dressed all
in white, hair dark against milk-white skin.
"Hang on a minute," she said, looking expectantly at Gemma but not bothering to re-
move the receiver from her ear.

"I'd like to speak to whoever's in charge
of the office." Gemma showed her warrant
card.

The girl shrugged and rolled her eyes.
"You'll be wanting Mrs. Washburn, I expect.
Up the stairs, first on the right," she said, and
went back to her interrupted conversation. As
Gemma reached the door she heard the girl
say with exaggerated weariness, "He could

go on all night, he could. I'm that worn out."

Poor thing, thought Gemma with a smile. And curiosity deficient, too — most people rated crime over sex.

She knocked on the indicated door and this time received a sharp reply. "Yes? What is it?"

Gemma's first glance at Mrs. Washburn's irritated expression did not inspire confidence in an easy interview. The woman's heavy middle-aged features were made more forbidding by dark-framed spectacles and hennaed hair.

Smiling as pleasantly as she could manage, Gemma introduced herself while handing her identification across the desk, then pulled the visitor's chair to the edge of the desk and sat down, crossing her legs.

"What do you think you're —"

"I'd like to talk to you about Jasmine Dent, Mrs. Washburn."

Mrs. Washburn sat a moment with her mouth open, whatever grievance she'd been about to air forgotten.

Score one for me, Gemma said to herself, and continued before her adversary could recover. "I understand you worked quite closely with Miss Dent, Mrs. Washburn. I'm sure you'll be able to help me." She smiled in an encouraging manner, glancing at the brass name plate on the desk's edge. 'Beatrice Washburn' it stated in black, block letters. Gemma wondered if Jasmine had felt the need to demonstrate her importance in such a visible way, and if so, what had happened to it? In fact, what had happened to the personal effects Jasmine must have kept at the office?

"Well, I . . . Yes, of course I worked with Jasmine, such a tragedy, but I don't see how I can —"

"We have some questions regarding the circumstances of Miss Dent's death. As I'm sure you realize, interviewing friends and associates is routine procedure." Gemma leaned forward confidentially. "Since you assumed her position upon her death, Mrs. Washburn, I thought you would be most knowledgeable about Miss Dent's work and her personal relationships."

Denial carried too great a loss of face. Mrs. Washburn swallowed and took the bait. "I came here only a short time before Jasmine's illness forced her to resign, so I really didn't know her at all well."

"But she must have trained you?"

Mrs. Washburn puffed up with injured dignity. "I had considerable experience as a planning officer before I came here. I was with —"

"Surely there are always things to learn in

any new situation. Every office has its own special way of doing things, its own personality, and Miss Dent would have been most familiar with it."

"She was helpful, yes, but she didn't believe personal confidences had a place in the office, and I agreed with her."

Mrs. Washburn finished the sentence with such an acid expression that Gemma guessed she might have approached Jasmine, angling for gossip, and been rebuffed. "Did Miss Dent have a special relationship with anyone else in the office?"

"It doesn't do to socialize with the clerical staff. I'm sure Jasmine was aware of that."

The old trout, thought Gemma. She'd bet all the girls in the office made faces at her behind her back. "What about Margaret Bellamy?"

"Margaret?" Irritation creased Mrs. Washburn's heavy face. "I believe Margaret did visit her at home a few times after she retired, but I don't know that they were particularly friendly before then."

Gemma stood up. "I'd like to see Margaret, if you can spare her a few minutes?"

"You're welcome to her, if you can find her." Mrs. Washburn snorted in disgust and looked at her watch. "That girl can find more excuses for taking long lunches and coming late in to work. She's half-an-hour late again and I'll have her on the carpet for it. She'll not last much longer under me, I can tell you."

"I'll wait," said Gemma, when Mrs. Washburn didn't offer. She found it very odd indeed that Mrs. Washburn hadn't asked why the police were looking into Jasmine's death. Curiosity was a natural human condition, and, to Gemma, Beatrice Washburn's lack signalled either a secret or an absorbing self-interest. "Mrs. Washburn," Gemma turned back when she reached the door, "who informed the office of Jasmine's death?"

The heavy face remained blank. "I don't know. One of the typists buzzed up and told me. Carla. You'll have to ask her." She turned back to the file on her desk before Gemma shut the door.

Gemma followed the faint sound of voices to the end of the hall, then opened the door and stuck her head round it. The conversation stopped as if it had been sliced off. Two girls sat at computer terminals, their desks shoved together to make room for the jumble of filing cabinets and drafting tables in the room. A third desk, its chair empty, stood under the window.

The girls looked up at Gemma, their warily blank faces making it evident they knew who she was. So she'd underestimated the little receptionist — the office grapevine worked, after all. "I'm looking for Margaret Bellamy," she said innocently, stepping into the room and closing the door.

The nearest girl pushed her roller chair away from her desk and swiveled toward Gemma. "Not in." She smiled tentatively, showing a chipped tooth.

"Do you think she'll be back soon? I'll wait."

The girls exchanged glances, then the first one spoke again. "She'd better be. The old ba— Mrs. Washburn'll have her knickers as it is."

"Late, is she?" Gemma crossed to the first girl and held out her hand. "I'm Gemma James."

"I'm Carla. She's Jennifer." A nod toward the other girl, who had not yet spoken.

Carla had a mop of frizzed brown hair pulled up with a band, and a square-jawed, pleasant face. Her legs, very visible under a spandex mini-skirt, looked like tree trunks. The other girl, Jennifer, Gemma pegged as carrying what she called the perfection gene. Some women were born with it — if not, there was no point in trying to achieve it: Flawless skin, perfect features, fashion-model's body, hair that always did just what it was supposed to, clothes the latest trend. It would be nice if she could talk as well, thought Gemma, then chided herself for being catty.

"Have any idea where she might be?" Gemma propped a hip on a low filing cabinet and looked at her watch — nearly half-past one.

The girls looked at each other again, and this time an unspoken signal must have passed between them because Jennifer spoke. "Out with her boyfriend, maybe." Her soft voice held a trace of an accent Gemma thought might be West Country, and her blue eyes showed surprising intelligence. "She was awfully upset this morning. About Miss Dent. You're here about Miss Dent, aren't you?"

The grapevine not only worked, it worked wonders. "In a way," Gemma answered noncommittally. "Do you know Margaret's boyfriend?"

The girls smiled with shared amusement. "Roger?" said Jennifer. "We should be so lucky." She glanced at Carla, who pulled a face. "No, really," she continued, "I was with her when she met him."

Gemma folded her arms and tilted her head, looking as if she had all day. "Really? When was that?"

Jennifer thought about it, creasing her smooth brow and pulling her Cupid's-bow lips into a little moue. "About October, I think. I took her round the clubs with me one night. I felt a bit sorry for her, see," she flicked another look at Carla from under her lashes and Carla nodded agreement. "She never did anything but go home by herself to that dreadful bedsit. So I thought . . . well, you know."

"That was very kind of you, I'm sure." Gemma's voice was warm with approval. "So then what happened?"

Jennifer smiled at her, showing teeth as small and even as a child's. "Nothing. We sat at the bar in this place and nobody even talked to us. You'd have thought we had the plague or something. And then this gorgeous guy comes up. I mean really gorgeous, like a . . ." Jennifer ran her tongue around her lips while she struggled for a descriptive phrase. "Like an American telly star or something. I thought wow, get ready for this one," her shoulders gave a little wiggle, "and then he chats up Margaret." Remembered consternation puckered her face and she shook her head in disbelief.

Jennifer's remarks seemed bare of conceit in the usual sense, it was more as if her universe had simply stopped behaving in its expected way. Men looked at Jennifer — men did not look at Margaret, and you didn't mess about with the laws of physics.

"Just as well, as it turned out," said Carla. "Our Roger didn't turn out to be such a great prize."

"Why ever not?" asked Gemma.

This time Carla looked at her friend for encouragement, and Jennifer gave a tiny nod. Carla looked down at her lap, still hesitant, and stretched her skirt down a bit over her thighs. "Oh . . . he never takes her anywhere, never spends any money on her. He just goes to her bedsitter and . . . you know." Color flooded up to the roots of Carla's frizzy hair and she didn't meet Gemma's eyes.

"How do you know?" Gemma asked softly. She shifted her behind a little where it had gone numb against the filing cabinet. "Does Margaret confide in you?"

"No," Carla answered, the blush not receding. "Some days you can just . . . tell. Look, I shouldn't have said —"

"Never mind." Gemma cut her off, not wanting to let her dwell on what would feel to her like disloyalty. "About Miss Dent. Were she and Margaret special friends at work?"

Carla answered after a moment, when Jennifer didn't speak. "Not really. Miss Dent was always fair — not like some I could name," she shot a black look in the direction of Mrs. Washburn's office, "and friendly in a distant sort of way, but she didn't take her tea breaks

174

with us or anything like that. It was only after she left," Carla said slowly, thinking about it, "that Margaret started to visit her. 'I saw Jasmine yesterday' she'd say, all puffed up about it, like calling Miss Dent 'Jasmine' made her better than us."

"Was this before she met Roger, or after?"

The girls looked at each other, concentrating. "Before," said Jennifer, and Carla nodded.

"Yeah. That's right, 'cause Miss Dent left just before August Bank Holiday, and it wasn't long —"

The door opened and Carla stopped dead, flushing again. Jennifer merely assumed a blank expression and went back to her typing.

A woman stumbled breathlessly into the room, her fair skin pink with exertion, her fine, brown hair awry and the tail of her blouse slipping out of her skirt. "Sorry I'm late. I didn't mean —" The sheaf of papers she clutched in her hand slipped to the floor as she became aware of Gemma. Squatting, she shuffled the papers awkwardly into a stack, and kept her eyes cast down.

"You're Margaret," Gemma said, making it a statement. A flash of pale blue eyes through pale lashes, then Margaret bent her head again to her papers. The skin on the back of Gemma's neck tightened as she realized that

175

Margaret Bellamy was very frightened indeed. "I'm a friend of Duncan Kincaid's. Is there somewhere we could go and have a cup of tea?"

"Mrs. Washburn'll kill me. I'll lose my job." Margaret twisted nervously in the red plastic booth.

"It'll be all right. I'll square it with her, I promise." Gemma leaned across the table and touched Margaret's hand. A sturdy hand, Gemma saw, with short fingers, and nails bitten to the quick. It was also ice-cold and damp, and Gemma felt a faint trembling under her fingers.

A harried waitress slammed cups of industrial-strength tea on the Formica table, sloshing it into the saucers. Gemma had remembered passing the busy cafe around the corner from the planning office. The atmosphere was not exactly soothing, but Margaret seemed unaware of the noise and the sharp smell of hot grease drifting from the kitchen.

"Margaret —"

"I'm really in trouble, aren't I?" Margaret said, the words so near a whisper that Gemma had to lean forward again to catch them. "Roger says I could go to prison. And it's all my fault. I should never have said anything to your friend . . ."

"I think," Gemma paused, stirring generous helpings of milk and sugar into her tea in an effort to make it taste less like cleaning fluid, "that if you told the truth, you did exactly the right thing. Duncan just wants to be sure that it really was Jasmine's choice."

Margaret shook her head slowly from side to side, tracing her finger through the puddle of tea on the table. "I still can't believe she lied to me. I thought I'd accepted it, but I hadn't. That day . . . I was so relieved when she said she'd changed her mind —" she looked up at Gemma, "do you think I fooled myself into thinking she really meant it, just because that's what I wanted to hear?"

Out of the corner of her eye Gemma saw the waitress approaching with a couple of tattered plastic menus. Gemma raised her hand and waved the woman away without ever taking her eyes from Margaret's face. "If you were so frightened, why did you ever agree to help her?"

"Oh, it was different at first. I felt so special." Margaret sat up a bit straighter in the booth and smiled for the first time. "For someone to want to spend their last minutes on this earth with you, to trust you that much — especially Jasmine. She didn't get close to people very easily. Nobody had ever felt that way about me, you know?"

Gemma nodded but didn't speak.

"And it was exciting. Planning, organizing. Having a secret that nobody knew. Life and death." Margaret smiled again, remembering. "Sometimes I imagined telling everyone at work, but I knew I couldn't. It was too personal, just between Jasmine and me." She took a sip of the tea, then made a face as the tannic acid bit into her tongue and she looked into the cup for the first time.

"Then what happened?"

Margaret shrugged. "It got closer. And I got scared." She gave Gemma a look of entreaty. "She looked so good at first. Her hair had grown again from the treatments. I knew she tired easily, but she didn't really seem ill. Then her flesh just started to melt away from her bones. And every day she grew a little weaker, every day she'd ask me to do some little thing she'd been able to do for herself the day before. The chest catheter went in. She started liquid morphine, even though she never talked about the pain."

This time Gemma caught the waitress's eye and mouthed 'hot water'. The cafe was beginning to empty and the noise level had dropped enough that she could hear Margaret's soft voice without straining. When the steaming, tin pot arrived, Gemma poured hot water into Margaret's half-empty cup without asking, then settled back to wait.

"She never set a time," Margaret continued as if there'd been no interruption, eyes focused on the circle her hands made around the hot cup. "I started to dread it — every day when I'd visit her I'd think 'Is this the day'? Is she going to say 'I'm ready, Meg, let's do it now'? My stomach knotted up. I felt sick all the time. I started to think about having to put the plastic bag over her head if the morphine didn't work.

"One day she seemed very calm, less restless than usual. I wondered if she'd increased the morphine. Then 'I'll not see fifty, Meg,' she says. 'There's no point.' And I knew she'd made up her mind."

Gemma sipped her watered-down tea and waited. When Margaret didn't speak again, she asked gently, "Did she give you an exact date?"

"The day before her birthday. I'd lie awake nights and think about watching her die. How would she look? How would I know when it was over? I couldn't bear it. And I couldn't tell her."

When Margaret looked up, Gemma saw that her eyes looked bruised and swollen, as if she'd been weeping for days. "Did you tell her?"

"I thought that was the most terrible day I'd ever spent. I didn't know it could get worse." Margaret rubbed the back of her hand across her mouth. "Most of the day at work I spent throwing up in the loo. I worked myself up to tell her as soon as I walked in." Her lips twisted in a smile at the irony of it. "She didn't even let me finish. 'Don't worry, Meg,' she said. 'I don't know if I've found my courage or if I've lost it, but I'm going to stick it out.' "

"What made you believe her?" asked Gemma. "Why didn't you think she was just trying to let you off the hook?"

Margaret's wide brow creased as she thought about it. "I don't know if I can explain, exactly. There wasn't any . . . tension in her. No screwing herself up for something, no excitement. Do you see?"

Gemma considered. "Yes, I think I do. She didn't ask you to stay?"

"Just for a bit. I did all the things I usually did for her — fed the cat, tidied up. Then I walked down to the Indian take-away and got a curry for her supper. She couldn't eat much, really, but she still made the effort."

"Margaret," Gemma said, treading carefully now, "didn't Jasmine ever talk to you about the legal implications of assisted suicide?"

Margaret nodded eagerly. "She said as long as I didn't actually touch her or give her anything, I'd be all right. And we didn't think anyone would ever know. Jasmine said we'd make sure it looked natural — she didn't want complications."

Had Jasmine simply made things easy for Margaret? Had her calm that day come from resolution rather than acceptance? Was she such a skilled actress that she had lied easily to the people who knew her best? And if so, why? Gemma thought of the girl in the photograph, with her delicate beauty and her closed, almost secretive, expression. A clever woman, an organizer, a planner — had her request to see Theo on Sunday been just an unnecessary bit of stage management? Gemma shook her head. She couldn't see Jasmine elaborating just for the sake of it.

And there was one question she hadn't asked Margaret. "Jasmine left a will, Meg." Gemma used the diminutive Jasmine had chosen. "Did she tell you about it?"

Margaret stared into her empty teacup as if the answer might lie in the tea leaves' random design.

Gemma waited, not offering any encouragement, not breaking the tension that grew in the silence.

"We argued." The tips of Margaret's fingers turned white as she pressed them against the cup. "I told her it was terribly unfair, but she wouldn't listen — she said she'd done all she could for Theo. I didn't want to benefit from her death. It made me feel awful, like I'd loved her for a price." She looked up at Gemma, her eyes reddening and glazing with tears. "You do understand, don't you?"

Reaching across the table and laying her fingers on the back of Margaret's hand, Gemma said, "Did you tell anybody else about the will, Meg, anyone at all?"

Margaret jerked her hand away from Gemma's and the empty cup rocked in its saucer. "No! Of course not. I didn't tell anybody."

Gathering up her handbag and cardigan, Margaret pushed her cup away, and after a moment Gemma caught the sharp, acrid odor of fear.

CHAPTER 11

"Cut and dried."

"All right. Justify it." Kincaid pushed his chair away from his desk and propped his feet up on the open bottom drawer. He'd gone bleary-eyed from an afternoon's paperwork when Gemma, smelling of cold air and crackling with excitement, had charged back into the office.

"She's bloody terrified, poor little rabbit." Gemma stopped pacing and sat on the arm of the visitor's chair, hands beneath her bottom. "I don't mean I think she knew beforehand, but she let that boyfriend in on the will, and now she's sweating it." She leaned forward for emphasis, reaching up with quick fingers to tuck back hair that the wind had teased from the clip at the nape of her neck. "Let's say Roger was waiting for Margaret that afternoon when she left Jasmine's,

183

and she told him Jasmine had changed her mind. They have a row, and Roger goes off to do his set-up. Later on he makes some excuse to push off early, then pops round to Jasmine's flat."

"I thought he said he'd never been there."

Shoulders lifting in a tiny shrug, Gemma said, "So maybe he lied. Who's going to contradict him? Margaret?" She paused for a moment, then continued more thoughtfully. "Or maybe he told the truth. That wouldn't have stopped him showing up at her door, making some kind of excuse. He could be very . . . plausible, I think."

Kincaid leaned back in his chair, hands clasped behind his head, and grinned. "Not immune to our Roger, then?"

Gemma shivered. "Like being locked up with a snake. Gave me the creeps, he did. I'd not put anything past him. What if," she stood and began pacing the small confines of the office again, "somehow he found out about Jasmine's will before he ever met Margaret? Why else would he chat up Margaret in the first place? He must have women queuing up to go out with him. And don't tell me," she added, coloring as she saw Kincaid smile, "that he sees the purity of her soul or something, because I don't believe it."

"I don't either, but it may not be that simple, all the same." Kincaid remembered the scene he'd witnessed in Margaret's room — Roger enjoyed displaying his sexual hold over her, and that was probably only the tip of the iceberg. "Just suppose you're right, Gemma, far-fetched as it is, how could Roger have known about Jasmine?"

"Bribed her solicitor?"

Kincaid shook his head, thinking of Antony Thomas's gentle outrage. "Not likely. But what if you're right about the first part and Roger did go to Jasmine's flat that night? He's never met her, he makes some excuse for coming, and then what? Does he say 'Excuse me, let me give you an overdose of morphine?' " He jabbed a finger at Gemma. "I'd swear there was no struggle."

"Maybe he told her Margaret had just been using her, and then Jasmine decided to kill herself after all."

"All he had to do was wait. Why would he risk the final outcome?"

"Perhaps he thought he was losing his hold over Margaret, and made one last-ditch attempt," said Gemma, settling back into the chair and crossing her legs.

They looked at each other a moment, speculating, then Kincaid straightened up his chair and kicked his desk drawer shut. "No evidence, Gemma. Not a shred. I'll admit Roger looks a likely suspect, but we'll have to keep digging. And I'm not at all happy about Theo." He looked at his watch and stretched, then pulled down the knot on his tie and unbuttoned his collar. "Let's call it a day. I'm knackered. Fancy a drink before you go home?"

Gemma hesitated, then made a face. "Better not. I've played truant enough lately. See you tomorrow." She went out with a wave, then stuck her head round the door again. "Don't forget to look after the cat, now."

The weather change had driven the weekend hordes from Hampstead Heath. Spring had flaunted her true colors and driven them scurrying back into pubs and parlors, except for a few solitary dog-walkers and resolute joggers. Litter left behind from the warm-weather festivities blew fitfully across the grass. Stopping at the flat only long enough to change into jeans and anorak, Kincaid crossed East Heath Road at the bottom of Worsley and plunged onto the Heath itself near the Mixed Bathing Pond. He felt a need to work the kinks out of mind and body. Running required too much focus, or at least that's what he told himself, so he turned north and walked, letting his thoughts wander where they would.

Gemma's theories worried him more than he'd admitted. He trusted her instincts, and if she said Margaret Bellamy was dead scared, he believed her. But he couldn't make a logical construction out of the rest of it — there were just too many holes.

He smiled, thinking of Gemma's arguments. Sometimes her enthusiasm amused him, sometimes it irritated him, but that was one reason they worked well together — she charged into ideas headlong while he tended to worry at them, and often together they came to a satisfactory conclusion.

The path crossed the viaduct pond and he stopped a moment, hands in pockets, admiring the view. New-leafed branches formed mirror images of themselves in the water, and to the west the spire of Hampstead's Christ Church rose above the still-bare fingers of the taller trees. Gemma had been different at the weekend, some of the fiery energy banked down to a lazy contentment. Bright cotton clothes against skin faintly flushed from the sun, an elusive scent of peaches when he'd stood next to her in Theo's dusty shop — Kincaid blinked and shook himself like a dog coming out of water.

He started walking again, head down into the wind, beginning the long climb to the Heath-top. Somehow, in the course of the weekend, the atmosphere between them had shifted. Today they'd worked together in their usual way, and he'd begun to think he was imagining things, but then he sensed her uncharacteristic hesitation when he suggested they stop for an after-work drink. They often did that, talking over the day's progress and planning the next, and only now did he realize how much he looked forward to it. Maybe he demanded too much of her time, and she resented it. He'd be more careful in future.

Twigs of gorse, heavy with yellow blossom, scratched and snagged at his sleeve as he absentmindedly passed too near. Beautiful and irritatingly prickly, like Gemma — and like Gemma, it needed to be handled with caution. He smiled.

His path dead-ended at the top of Heath Street, just across from Jack Straw's Castle. The parking lot of the old pub was already full, and when the door swung open the wind carried a faint drift of music to Kincaid's ears. The boisterous crowd didn't appeal to him and he turned left down Heath Street, feeling the pull in his calf muscles as he made the steep descent. When he reached the tube station, an impulse sent him straight ahead rather than left into Hampstead High Street. Church Row came up shortly on his right, and he turned into the narrow lane, the spire of St.

John's leading him on like a compass needle.

Kincaid entered the churchyard through the massive wrought-iron gates. A drunk snored on a bench by the church door, disturbing the silence. Kincaid turned left, into the dim greenness of the tomb-covered hillside, which even in early spring was tangled and over-grown with vegetation. The path wound under the heavy boughs of evergreens, passing damp, gray stone slabs, splotched with lichens. He stopped at his favorite spot, just before the lower boundary wall.

"John Constable, Esq., R.A., 1837," read the carved inscription on the side of the tomb. Constable lay with his wife, Mary Elizabeth, and the marker also bore witness to the death of their son, John Charles, age twenty-three. Constable's name was associated with the history of almost every part of Hampstead, as he rented one house after another from 1819 until his death, and was said to have asked to 'take his everlasting rest' in the village he immortalized in his paintings.

Why Kincaid found the Victorian monument comforting he couldn't have said, but since he'd lived in Hampstead he had developed a habit of coming here to think when he couldn't quite sort something out. He sat on a rock and rubbed a twig between his fingers, crumbling the dry bark to dust. Frowning, he tried to clear his mind, concentrate. His gut-instinct told him that Meg really had loved Jasmine, would not have harmed her against her wishes. Roger, however, was a different kettle of fish, and a smelly one at that. Sex was a powerful and often twisted force, and he wasn't sure how blind an eye Meg might have persuaded herself to turn in order to preserve her relationship with Roger.

And Theo? Had Theo resented his sister more than he loved her? He certainly had reason to be grateful to her, but the contrariness of human nature could make gratitude a difficult burden to bear.

He began to see Jasmine sitting in the center of a radiating web of relationships, inviolate. What had she felt for anyone? Had she moved through her life untouched and untouching? She'd faced her illness with such equanimity. He couldn't reconcile the passionate girl in the journals with the woman he'd known — charming, witty, intelligent, and more guarded than he ever had imagined.

Kincaid sighed and stood up. The light was fast fading, the graves had no secrets to impart, and if he weren't careful he'd be blundering his way back up the hill. He realized that the wind had died, and beyond the boundary hedge the lights of the city glowed in the gathering dusk.

The drunk was gone when Kincaid reached the church again. From within the building, muffled by the heavy doors, voices sang in familiar cadence. "Evensong," Kincaid said aloud. When had he last heard an Evensong service? The sound took him back to the sturdy red-brick church of his Cheshire childhood. His parents had deemed the Evensong service the only compromise between their Anglican upbringing and their liberal philosophies, and while the family often attended Evensong, Kincaid could not remember being inside the church on a Sunday.

Inching open the scuffed, blue-leather-padded door and slipping through, Kincaid made his way to the last pew and eased into it. Only a few scattered forms filled the seats in front of him. He wondered that the service, so lightly attended, was held at all.

Voices rose, the sound filling the hollow space inside the church, and the notes of the massive organ vibrated through the pew into his bones. Kincaid relaxed, idly watching the choir director. The man used his hands like blunt instruments, chopping and jabbing his signals to the choir. He looked, in fact, more like a rugby forward than a choir director — well over six-feet tall, with massive shoulders under his surplice and a square, heavy-jawed head.

The director moved a step to the right and Kincaid caught a glimpse of a familiar face in the choir's back row. A fringe of gray hair around a balding head and a ruddy face, a clipped gray mustache — so accustomed was Kincaid to the Major's usual tweedy attire that the full, white fabric of the surplice had disoriented him for a moment. How could he have forgotten the Major telling him he sang with the St. John's choir? Kincaid watched, fascinated by the sight of his taciturn neighbor raising his voice in a joyous, open-mouthed bass.

The service drew to a close. The final 'amen' hung trembling, then the choir filed out. The other congregants passed Kincaid on their way to the door, smiling and glancing curiously at him. Regulars, he thought, wondering just who the hell he was. When the porch door closed on the last straggler, Kincaid stood and walked toward the altar.

"Excuse me."

The director had his hand on a door which Kincaid thought must lead to the vestry. He swung around, startled, his movements surprisingly graceful for such a large man. "Yes?"

"Could I speak to you for a minute? My name's Duncan Kincaid." Kincaid thought fast. He didn't want to make a professional inquiry of a friend and neighbor just yet, only set his own mind at ease. Perhaps his jeans, anorak and wind-blown hair weren't a disadvantage after all.

Hand outstretched, the choir director came toward Kincaid. "I'm Paul Grisham. What can I do for you?"

Kincaid heard in his voice a familiar lilt. "You're Welsh," he said, making it a statement. Paul Grisham's face broke into a grin, showing large, crooked teeth. His nose, Kincaid saw, had been broken, and probably more than once.

"That I am. From Llangynog." Grisham cocked his head, studying Kincaid. "And you?"

"A near neighbor, across the border. I grew up in Nantwich."

"Thought you didn't sound London born and bred."

"You play rugby?" Kincaid touched a finger to his own nose.

"I did, yes, when my bones knitted quicker. Wrexham Union."

Kincaid shifted a bit and leaned against the altar rail. He sensed Grisham waiting for him to get to the point, and said casually, "I just happened by, quite by accident. I'd no idea you had Evensong service." He nodded his head toward the choir stall behind Grisham. "Was that Major Keith I saw?"

Grisham smiled. "You know the Major?

One of our mainstays, he is, though you wouldn't think it to look at him, the crusty old devil. Regular as clockwork, never misses a practice."

"Twice a week?" Kincaid hazarded.

"Sunday and Thursday evenings."

"He's my downstairs neighbor. I'd no idea he sang, but I had wondered where he disappeared to so regularly. Figured he was off for a pint." Kincaid straightened up as Grisham hiked up his robe and fished a set of keys out of his trouser pocket. "I was just startled to see him, that's all."

"If you don't mind, I'll let you out the front before I lock up. Vandals, you know," he added apologetically.

"Not at all." Kincaid turned and together they walked up the aisle. "Didn't mean to take so much of your time."

When they reached the vestibule Grisham stopped and turned to face Kincaid, seeming to hesitate. In the dim light, Kincaid had to look up to read his expression. The man overreached him by a head — he must be nearly as big as the Super.

"You said you were his neighbor — the Major?"

Kincaid nodded. "Since I bought my flat, three years ago."

"Know him well?"

Shrugging, Kincaid answered, "Not really. I'm not sure anyone does." Jasmine came suddenly to mind, with her tales of afternoon tea with the Major, and he thought of the rosebushes planted in her memory. "I don't know. There was someone, perhaps. Our neighbor, but she died just last week."

Grisham reached for the heavy porch door, swinging it open as if it were cardboard. "That explains it, then. Last Thursday night he left practice early, said he felt ill. First time I've ever known him to do that, and I was a bit worried about him, living alone and all. But he's not the sort of person you could ask."

"No," Kincaid agreed, stepping out into the darkness. "I don't suppose you could. Thanks for your time. I'll come back," he said, meaning it, and as the door closed he saw a flash of Paul Grisham's white teeth.

What he didn't add was that Jasmine could not have accounted for the Major's sudden indisposition. He hadn't learned of her death until Kincaid told him, mid-day on Friday.

He stopped for a pie and a pint at the King George, halfway down the High. When he came out into the street again the still air felt damp against his skin. Rain tomorrow, or he'd be buggered. Turning up his collar and shoving his hands in his pockets against the chill, he walked home slowly, looking in the lighted windows of the empty shops.

His footsteps led him naturally to Jasmine's door, and he let himself in with the key he'd attached to his keyring. When Kincaid turned on the lamp Sid blinked at him from the center of the bed, then seemed to levitate himself into a stretch.

"Hullo, Sid. Glad to see me this time? Or just hungry?"

The cat followed him into the kitchen and sat watching expectantly as Kincaid rooted in the drawer for the tin opener. "Not going to wind about *my* ankles, are you, mate?" Kincaid said, thinking of how he'd seen the cat wrap himself around Jasmine's slender ankles at feeding time. As she grew more fragile he'd been afraid the cat would make her fall, but he hadn't said anything.

"Let's not get too familiar, okay?" He set the dish on the floor, then ran his fingers down Sid's smooth back as the cat came to the food. Remembering Gemma's instructions, he found the litter box tucked away under the bathroom sink, emptied it into the rubbish bin and refilled it from a sack he found in the cupboard. He lifted the rubbish bag free of the bin and tied it up for collection.

Feeling virtuous, he refilled Sid's water

bowl and stood watching the cat eat. "What's going to become of you, eh, mate?" As Sid polished the empty dish with his tongue, Kincaid added, "Looks like you've done the worst of your grieving." Human or animal, in most cases the body reasserted itself soon enough. You drank cups of tea, or whiskey. You ate what was put in front of you, and life went on. "See you tomorrow, mate."

He left a lamp lit for the cat and went upstairs to Jasmine's journals.

June 5th, 1963

All I can think about is how I feel when he touches me. My skin burns. I can't eat. I can't sleep. I feel a little sick with it all the time but I don't want it to stop, and there's this hard knot in my belly that aches and won't go away no matter what I do. I know what people say about him, but it's not true. He's different with me, gentle. They just don't understand him. He doesn't belong here, any more than I do. We're throwbacks, both of us, to something darker, less English. Aunt May says some of my mother's family were French and that's why I look the way I do, but you can tell from the way she says it that she despised my mum. "Rose Hollis," she says, "didn't have the sense God gave a child. I don't know what

197

your father was thinking of when he married her and took her to India." Poor mummy. He killed her, as surely as if he'd stuck a knife in her heart, and I'm afraid. I don't want the same thing to happen to me, but it's out of control already and I don't see any way to turn it back.

We'll go away, soon as I've saved enough working for old Mr. Rawlinson. London, where nobody will know us, where we can be together all the time. Get a flat somewhere. I know I promised I'd not go without Theo, but he can leave school after this year and maybe by that time I'll be able to look after him, too.

I dream about him when I can sleep. When I close my eyes I see his face against my eyelids. His dark hair lies like silk against my hand when I run my fingers through it. Last night we met behind the social club as soon as it was dark. It was bingo night, and I could hear them calling inside, numbers and letters. "Jasmine?" he says, in that questioning way, as if he can't quite believe in me, and then his mouth turns up at the corners when he smiles. But the light lasts longer every evening, and there's nowhere we can go to be alone, where he can kiss me, put his hands where I want him to touch me. Aunt May would kill me if she found out, and his old mum's even worse. Dry and shriveled as old prunes, both *of them, and sick with envy.*

I have an idea, though, and if I can carry it through, there won't be anything that can come between us.

CHAPTER
12

The previous evening's promise of rain fulfilled itself. Kincaid peered through the Midget's windscreen in the gray light, straining to see the road, while the wipers clicked monotonously back and forth, scrubbing at the drizzle. He'd left the M3 at Basingstoke, heading west on the two-lane A roads, toward Dorset.

The decision, made somewhere between finishing his coffee and leaving his flat for the Yard, had taken him by surprise. He'd dreamed of Jasmine — the fierce girl of the journals, not the Jasmine of unbreachable reserve, fragile from her illness — and awakened with an imprinted image of her scribbling in her tiny attic room.

There'd been a gap after the entry about the boy, and when she wrote again it was of living in London, finding a flat, adjusting to a new job. Compared to the earlier entries these were strangely emotionless, as if the journals had been relegated to trivial record keeping.

Kincaid had given up, exhausted, but found himself worrying at it again this morning. He'd done some quick arithmetic — Jasmine had been twenty-one at the time of that last entry, and to him she seemed oddly immature. If he hadn't grown accustomed to her taking charge of Theo and coping with whatever life threw her way, perhaps the fact that she'd survived her teens still sexually inexperienced wouldn't have struck him so forcibly. But the more he thought about it, the less surprising it seemed. Mature beyond her years in some ways, Jasmine had still been very much the outcast. She wouldn't have fit in comfortably with teen-age flirtations and rough camaraderie, and life in a small English village didn't leave much room for exploration.

Behind his unexpected pilgrimage lay the hope that he might find some answers in the hamlet of Briantspuddle — that some trace of Jasmine Dent's passage from childhood to adulthood remained.

The lane ran tunnel-like between the high hedges, dipping and twisting like a rabbit's burrow. Occasional gaps in the green walls revealed only muddy farmyards. Kincaid had rechecked his map when he'd stopped for a quick lunch in Blandford Forum, but he'd begun to wonder if he'd read the last signpost right when the lane crossed a stream, took a sudden right-angle turn and ejected him into a clearing. A string of white-washed cottages straddled the road and a signpost at the central fork proclaimed "Briantspuddle".

Kincaid stopped at the intersection. No church . . . no pub — not having either repository of village information would make his task more difficult. He took the west fork of the lane, hoping to find a likely source of gossip.

A few hundred yards farther on he came upon another smattering of cottages, even smaller than Briantspuddle. These cottages were washed in pale colors, rather than white, but except for wisps of smoke escaping from a few of the chimneys, the smaller hamlet appeared just as deserted. A stone cross, a carved madonna-like figure imprisoned within its stem, seemed to draw the surrounding cottages to it like congregants facing a preacher.

Kincaid stopped the car and got out. The rain had earlier diminished to a mist just fine enough to make his wipers squeak, and now he realized it had stopped. He walked around the cross, examining its unusual construction.

The design reminded him of a traditional market cross, but it was somehow very modern in feel. In the front, the Madonna crouched under a peaked roof at the bottom of the spire, while in the back a larger, unidentifiable figure seemed to float midway up the column. An inscription ran around the cross's square base, and Kincaid read as he circled the cross once again: *It is sooth that sin is cause of all this pain, But all shall be well and all shall be well and all manner of things shall be well.*

Kincaid returned to the car and headed back the way he'd come. When he reached Briantspuddle again he pulled the Midget onto the verge and killed the engine. Stretching, he levered himself up out of the car and felt the cool air settle on his skin like a cloak. He took a deep breath, invigorated by the clean, damp silence.

A faint rhythmic sound broke the quiet and Kincaid turned, searching for its source. Something moved behind the shrubby border of the best-kept cottage, beneath a row of flowering plums and brilliant yellow sprays of forsythia. He took a few steps closer and the movement resolved into the top of a gray head. Nearer still, an elderly woman kneeling, weeding her flower bed.

She looked up, unsurprised, and smiled at him. "Have to take advantage," she said, nodding at the low, gray clouds. "Won't hold off long." Her voice was cultured, with only a faint trace of Dorset burr.

Kincaid stuck his hands in his pockets and smiled his most charming smile. "Nice border." On closer inspection she looked quite frail, in her eighties, perhaps, and wore a tweed skirt and twin-set under an old, oiled jacket. Her thin gray hair was twisted into a neat knot on top of her head, and on her feet she sported, not the expected heavy leather brogues, but a pair of neon nylon trainers.

Frowning at him, she gave the comment serious consideration, and finally shook her head. "You've missed the rhododendrons, you see. Another month, that's when it's glorious. These," she gestured with her trowel toward the pansies and daffodils in the bed, "are just the opening act."

This time Kincaid grinned from pleasure, liking her grave humor. "A little soft shoe?"

"Exactly." She smiled back at him, resting her gloved hands on her knees, and Kincaid decided she had once been very beautiful. Her glance held curiosity now as she searched his face. "Are you passing through?" she asked, then added, "What a silly question. Briantspuddle isn't on the way to anywhere."

"No, not exactly. Have you lived here long?"

"Depends on what you call long. Since before the War. That was Briantspuddle's heyday, you know. Ernest Debenham, the department store magnate, decided to make it a model farming village. These cottages he either built or restored." She raised a coquettish eyebrow. "You do know which war I mean, young man?"

"You wouldn't have been around for the first one, much less remember it."

"Now you're flattering me." She brushed her gloved hands together and pushed herself up with a grimace. Kincaid stretched out a hand to her and she nodded her thanks.

"Would you remember a woman called May Dent, by any chance?"

Her face went blank with surprise. "May? Of course. We were neighbors for years. She lived just across the road, there." Kincaid turned and looked where she pointed. The cottage sat back from the road at the end of a shrub-bordered walk. No flowers brightened its black and white severity, and high windows peeking from beneath the thatched eaves gave it a secretive air.

Extracting his warrant card from his jacket pocket, he opened it to the woman's puzzled glance. "My name's Duncan Kincaid."

She looked from the card to his face, her brow furrowing. "You don't look like such a big cheese."

Kincaid laughed. "Thank you. I think."

Coloring, she said, "I'm making an idiot of myself. I never meant to be one of these tiresome old women who thinks anyone younger than sixty ought to be in nappies. I'm Alice Finney, by the way." She held out her hand to Kincaid and he took it, feeling the lightness of her bones between his fingers.

"Mrs. Finney, do you remember May Dent's niece and nephew, who came from India to live with her?"

She stared at him in consternation. "Of course I remember Jasmine and Theo, as well as I do my own name. But that's been thirty years if it's been a day. Why on earth would you want to know about them?"

Taking a breath, he tried to organize his approach. "It's about —"

Alice Finney shook her head. "No, no." She nodded toward the blank faces of the cottages. "I can tell this isn't going to be a 'middle-of-the-village' matter. You'd better come in. I'll make us some tea, and you can tell me properly, from the beginning."

"Yes, Mrs. Finney," Kincaid answered, meek as a schoolboy, and followed her up the walk.

Saucer balanced on his knee, Kincaid lifted a china cup so delicate he was afraid his breath might crack it. Outside the sitting room windows, mist had settled in again, fading the plum blossom to a pale wash of color. Alice Finney knelt at her grate, lighting a small, coal fire. When Kincaid moved to help her, she waved him back. "I've done it myself for nearly fifty years. No use being coddled now."

She sat down opposite him in a brocade armchair, its seatcover a bit shiny with wear. At Kincaid's inquisitive glance, she picked up her cup and continued. "My Jack and I would have been married fifty-five years this spring. He was a pilot, so he died a little more gloriously than some — in the air rather than the trenches. Not that it was much comfort to him, I imagine." She smiled at him, suddenly, impishly. "Don't look so properly funereal, Mr. Kincaid. To tell you the truth there are days I can't remember what he looked like, it's been so long ago. And at my age remembering is just a sentimental indulgence. Tell me about Jasmine and Theo Dent."

In the warmth and comfort of Alice Finney's faded sitting room, all of Kincaid's rehearsed introduction dissolved. "Jasmine Dent was my neighbor. And my friend. She was terminally ill with lung cancer, so when she died at first we assumed that the disease had progressed faster than expected."

Alice Finney listened intently, not taking her eyes from Kincaid's face even to sip her tea. At the mention of Jasmine's death she pinched her lips together in a small grimace.

"Then we discovered that Jasmine had asked a young friend to help her commit suicide, but had backed out at the last minute. I ordered an autopsy." Kincaid paused, but Alice didn't interrupt. "She died from a morphine overdose, and I don't believe it was self-administered."

"Why?"

He shrugged. "I could give you lots of logical reasons, but it's more gut-reaction than anything else, to tell you the truth. I just don't believe it."

"And it's brought you here." Alice leaned forward and lifted the teapot from the small, oval table, then refilled both their cups. "I'll tell you what I can." She sat quietly for a moment, her eyes unfocused as she gathered her thoughts, then she sighed. "It was a bad business from the very beginning. May Dent was never meant to have children. She hadn't the capacity to love them, though to give her credit, perhaps she tried with Theo. She was a bitter woman, one of those people who always feel life has short-changed them. Perhaps she loved her brother more than she should, though in those days," the corners of Alice's mouth turned up in amusement, "one didn't speculate about such things. Whatever the cause, she despised her sister-in-law, never had a good word to say about her."

"And Jasmine?" Kincaid got up, went to the grate and banked the settling fire.

"Jasmine must have reminded May of her mother. Whatever the cause, those two rubbed each other the wrong way from the moment they set eyes on one another. And Jasmine . . . Jasmine was difficult. I'd retired from teaching when they closed the village school — the children went to the nearest comprehensive — but I still had connections, privy to gossip, you might say."

"You were the village schoolmistress?" Kincaid was enchanted with a vision of a younger Alice, guiding her charges with the same gentle humor.

"I had two young children to raise by myself, and neither the luxury nor the inclination to be idle," she answered crisply. "Jasmine," she continued as if he hadn't interrupted, "was not liked. Not actively disliked, perhaps, but she didn't fit in, she made the other children uncomfortable." Alice paused, frowning. "Jasmine was a beautiful girl, but in a haunting sort of way. Different. They didn't know what to make of her. I tried to befriend her myself — I thought she might need someone to confide in, and it certainly wouldn't have been May — but she wasn't having any. There was a reserve about her, a secretiveness, that one couldn't penetrate."

Kincaid nodded. "What about Theo? Did he fit in any better?"

Alice leaned back in her chair and stretched her legs toward the fire. Kincaid noted that her ankles, above the padded tongues of the trainers, were still trim.

"I suppose you could say Theo adjusted more easily. He looked more English, for a start. He lost his colonial accent as quickly as he could. I don't imagine Jasmine ever did, completely?" Alice inquired of Kincaid. "She had that very precise enunciation, and a trace of the sing-song that comes from speaking the Hindustani dialects."

"No, she never lost it. And it grew more pronounced with her illness." Kincaid realized that Jasmine's voice had been one of the things that had attracted him to her — that, and her intelligence, and her sharp, dry humor.

"Theo did make friends with the local children, or was at least allowed to tag along. And May coddled him a bit in the beginning. He was only ten when they came, after all. Still practically an infant. But he always had this lost-puppy air about him, as if he might be kicked any minute."

"And as they got older?"

"What always surprised me," said Alice, "was that Jasmine stayed as long as she did. I imagine it was her sense of duty to Theo that kept her here. She was very protective of him, and very jealous of May. Especially when Theo began to get into trouble."

"Trouble? Theo?" Kincaid straightened up, his interest quickening.

Alice moderated her comment. "Well, I don't think Theo ever did anything wrong in a malicious sense. He was just one of those boys that attract bad luck, and unsavory friends, and it began to tell. Always in the wrong place at the wrong time, if you know what I mean."

Kincaid smiled. "I've heard that once or twice before. And how did May react to Theo's little escapades?"

"She defended him at first, but after Jasmine left, the escapades became more serious than setting pastures alight and joyriding in other people's autos." Leaning forward, Alice took a biscuit from the plate and nibbled at its edge. "Chocolate digestives. My one vice," she added apologetically. "May stopped talking about sending him to university. It was a pipe dream, anyway, he'd never done well enough at school to merit it."

"Do you know why Jasmine left?" Kincaid

211

asked, treading delicately now.

"No. But I always wondered. She just quit her job and disappeared. Literally here one day and gone the next. May was absolutely furious. Called her an ungrateful bitch, which was strong language for May. Of course, from the time Jasmine left school May had done nothing but complain about her, what a burden she was and how anxious she was to be rid of her — though I think Jasmine began paying her share of the housekeeping as soon as she found her first job. And it wasn't as if May couldn't afford to keep her."

"So you'd have thought May would have been thrilled."

"Exactly. But that was May for you. Never satisfied, especially when she got what she wanted." Alice stared into the fire, and Kincaid waited, not interrupting. "There was something, though . . . I would have put it down to malicious gossip and forgotten all about it, if Jasmine hadn't disappeared so soon afterwards."

"A rumor?"

"Yes — that Jasmine was going around with that boy from over in Bladen Valley, the one who wasn't quite right. Did you come through Bladen Valley?" She gestured to the west. "Another experiment, that. Built during the first War, though, to house the estate workers.

A fitting place, I suppose, for a war memorial."

"Is that what that is? The stone cross?"

Alice nodded. "Done by the sculptor Eric Gill. It's supposed to be one St. Juliana, a fifteenth-century mystic. What she had to do with war I never discovered."

"Mrs. Finney," Kincaid led her gently back, "what was wrong with the boy?"

"I'm not sure. Not retarded. More unbalanced, mentally ill, perhaps. Given to sudden fits of violence, if the stories were true, but it's been a very long time ago." She sighed.

"I've tired you," Kincaid said, instantly contrite. "I'm sorry."

"No, no, it's not that." Alice Finney straightened up, some of her crisp demeanor returning. "I'm aggravated with myself, if you must know, because I can't remember the boy's name. I don't like not being able to remember things — makes me feel old." She smiled. "Which I'm not, of course."

"Of course," Kincaid agreed.

"All his people are gone now, too, I think. The boy's mother had him institutionalized, not long after Jasmine left, I believe. And she's been dead for a good fifteen or twenty years now. There was no other family that I know of."

"What happened to Theo, after Jasmine left?"

"He did finish school, if I remember rightly, but couldn't seem to find his feet afterwards. Couldn't find work, got into a bit more trouble all the time. And then May died. Took pneumonia and was gone, just like that. Jasmine never came back, not even for the funeral, and after May's affairs were settled and the cottage sold, Theo disappeared, too. And I never heard another word of either of them, until this day."

"Did May leave them anything, do you know?"

"She must have had quite a tidy nest egg. Tight as an old trout, May was. Managed her inheritance a sight better than her brother managed his, apparently, but I've no idea how she divided it between the children — there was no other family. She could have left everything to a home for wayward cats, for all I know." She paused, her brows drawing together in concentration. "You might try the solicitor's office in Blandford Forum."

"The one where Jasmine worked? It's still there?"

"It was the only one at the time, so naturally they handled May's affairs. Old Mr. Rawlinson's dead, and the son may not remember Jasmine, but it might be worth a try."

Kincaid rose. "You've been a great help. I never meant to take so much of your time."

"Nonsense." She stood, shaking off Kincaid's proffered help. "Do you think I have better things to do than take tea with an attractive young man who's interested in everything I have to say? It's an old woman's dream, my dear."

Kincaid had the sudden urge to do something very improper, very un-English. Placing his fingertips on her shoulders, he said, "You're delightful. Your Jack was a very lucky man, and if I were a few years older, Alice Finney, I'd marry you myself." He leaned over and kissed her cheek, and her skin felt as soft as a young girl's lips.

Blandford Forum, Alice had informed him, had burned nearly to the ground in the summer of 1731. The fire had started in the tallow-chandler's house and spread quickly from one thatched roof to another. Tragic as the destruction must have seemed at the time, Blandford Forum had risen from its ashes as a Georgian gem. The offices of Rawlinson and Sons, Solicitors, had been housed in a Georgian building in the rebuilt Market Place as long as anyone could remember.

Peering through the frosted glass of the inside door, Kincaid could make out only fuzzy shapes. He pulled open the door and the lumps resolved themselves into ordinary waiting room furniture, a desk, and behind it, a receptionist.

She swiveled away from her typewriter and smiled at him. "Can I help you?"

"Uh, I'm not sure, to tell you the truth. Is Mr. Rawlinson in?"

"He's in court this afternoon." Glancing at her watch, she added, "I'm afraid he may be a while yet. Would you like to make an appointment?"

She diplomatically didn't add, thought Kincaid, that any self-respecting idiot would have made one in the first place. The nameplate on her desk read 'Carol White', a good, solid English name. It suited her. Middle-aged and well-built, with an open, friendly face and a glorious head of wavy, shoulder-length chestnut hair — in a few years she would begin the slide toward matronly, but she was still very attractive indeed.

"Would that be young Mr. Rawlinson?"

She stared at him, perplexed, but still polite. "Old Mr. Rawlinson passed away ten years ago. You're not from around here, then?"

"London, actually." Kincaid again fished his warrant card from his pocket, and extended it to her.

"Oh." Her eyes widened and she glanced up at his face, then back at the folder. "Fancy that. What would Scotland Yard want with us?"

Kincaid heard the sharp, little intake of breath — the ordinary citizen's response to the copper's unexpected appearance — and he hastened to reassure her. "Just some very dusty information. Is there any chance Mr. Rawlinson might remember a girl who worked here almost thirty years ago? Her name was Jasmine Dent."

Carol White stared at him, then said slowly, "No. Mr. Rawlinson would have still been away at school. But I do. I remember Jasmine."

Unasked, Kincaid picked up a visitor's chair and swung it around next to the desk, never taking his eyes from Carol White's face. "*You* do?"

Still hesitant, she continued. "I know it's a bit silly of me, but I hate to admit I've been here as long as I have. I came here straight from leaving school, same as Jasmine, but she was a couple of years older."

"Mr. Rawlinson needed two secretaries?"

"You could say that." She smiled, showing even, white teeth. "Mr. Rawlinson liked pretty young girls, and we were both that, if I do say it myself." Holding up a hand to forestall Kincaid interrupting, she added, "Oh, I don't mean he was a real dirty old

217

man — never tried anything on, as far as I know — he just fancied himself a bit of a rogue. And since he paid us the bare minimum in those days, I guess he could afford us."

Having moved around to the side of Carol's desk, Kincaid discovered that what he had thought to be a dress was actually a thigh-length tunic, beneath which she wore skin-tight, black, stretch trousers and high-heeled sandals. Following his appreciative gaze, she laughed. "Dressed courtesy of my teenage daughter, who can't stand for her old mum to go out looking like a frump." Then sobering, she said, "Truthfully, I think Mr. Rawlinson intended from the beginning to groom me as Jasmine's successor. She must have made it as clear to him as she did everyone else that she didn't intend to stay in this poky town any longer than she had to. Jasmine was ferociously ambitious, Mr. Kincaid. What became of her? Is she a great success? I could never see her as housewife and kids material."

"No, she never married. And she did quite well for herself. She was supervisor in a borough planning office."

"Was?" Carol White asked quietly. "Then she's —"

"She had cancer."

"Oh. I'm sorry." Her eyes filled with tears

and she shook her head. "God, how silly of me. It's not even as though we were great friends, haven't thought of her in years — it's just that whenever I hear of someone I knew growing up dying, it gets me right here." She thumped her chest with a fist, then reached in her desk drawer for a box of tissues and blew her nose. "A reminder of my own mortality, I guess. If it can happen to them, it can happen to you."

"I know exactly what you mean," Kincaid said, thinking of his own reaction, not only to the deaths of those he knew, but to the deaths of strangers — that aching sense of loss he never quite managed to control.

"But I don't understand." Giving her eyes one last wipe, Carol threw the tissues in the wastebin beneath her desk and collected herself. "Why are you asking about Jasmine?"

Kincaid gave her an answer even more brief than the one he'd given Alice Finney, but she nodded, apparently satisfied. Years of working in a solicitor's office would have taught her to be discreet.

"You said you weren't particularly close friends?"

"Oh, we talked, the way girls will in an office, about what was going on, and who's bum Mr. Rawlinson had patted most often that week. Just chatter, really. But if you ventured into anything too personal she'd snap shut like a clam." Carol paused, screwing up her face in earnest concentration. "Sometimes . . . sometimes I had the feeling Jasmine had never had a friend, didn't know what to do with one."

"Then what gave you the impression she was so ambitious?"

"London. That's all she talked about. And she pinched every penny, brought her dinner from home every day, even did child-minding in the evenings to make a bit extra. I remember that she didn't get on well with her old-maid aunt."

Kincaid smiled. "I think that's a safe assumption," he said, then returned to her earlier point. "Did Jasmine not go out, then, if she was so careful with her money? A pretty girl that age, you'd think there'd be plenty to do in a town this size."

Carol shook her head. "I even tried to fix her up a few times with a double-date, but she wasn't having any."

"Did she talk about men? I don't mean to sound like a chauvinist, but it does seem the natural thing."

"I'm sure that's all *I* talked about, night and day," Carol said, laughter in her voice. "Must have been bloody boring, now that I think about it. But Jasmine . . . no, not that

I remember." She stared into space for a moment, eyes unfocused, and Kincaid waited. "There was something, though. Those last couple of months before she left, she seemed different — had that 'cat-that-ate-the-canary' look about her. Sometimes I almost expected her to wash her whiskers."

"But she never confided in you?"

This time the shake of her head was wistful. "No. Sorry."

"What about when she left? Did she tell you anything beforehand?"

"I was just as shocked as anyone. She just came in that day, gave her notice, cleaned out her drawer and left. Mr. Rawlinson was dead chuffed, I can tell you."

"Did you hear from her after that?"

"Not a word. But she did take me aside and tell me good-bye that day. She wished me luck."

This time it was Kincaid who sat silently, thinking that this office had probably not changed much . . . imagining Jasmine sitting where Carol sat. Jasmine bent over the typewriter . . . Jasmine's dark head silhouetted against the faded cream wallpaper. What had made her take flight, abandoning her carefully made plans, and her brother?

"Did you ever meet her brother, Theo?" he asked, following his thought.

"Not until the old aunt died, and we handled her affairs." She shrugged, the movement flexing the fabric across her full breasts. "He wasn't up to much, was he? 'Course, he was just a kid, not more than seventeen or eighteen at the time. That probably explains it."

"Explains what?"

Carol White looked down at her intertwined fingers, the pink-varnished nails paired like lovers. "Oh, I've probably said more than I ought. It's been such a long time, and I'm not sure what I really remember. I think Mr. Rawlinson had to handle everything, the funeral arrangements, the sale of the cottage . . . Theo was so shattered. Almost hysterical. Only natural, I suppose, but at the time I thought his behavior rather odd — most young men who come into enough money to make them independent have to work at appearing grief-stricken."

"I didn't realize that May Dent had provided so well for Theo."

"Well enough, but I believe Jasmine held the money in trust until he came of age." She straightened and took a breath, the sudden sharpness of her movements signalling to Kincaid the end of the interview. "Mr. Rawlinson should be back soon. Do you want to wait?"

"No. I think you've been more help than

he possibly could." Kincaid stood and replaced his chair, lining the legs up precisely with the worn spots in the aging carpet. When he held out his hand, Carol White took it and said, "I'm sorry about Jasmine. Really."

"Thank you," he said gravely, and she smiled, some of the discomfort leaving her face.

"Mr. Kincaid," she called as he reached the door, and he turned back. "It's not true, what I said about not thinking of Jasmine all these years. I've envied her, thought about how glamorous her life must have been, while I stayed here and did all the expected things. I always felt a bit of a coward." Her shoulders lifted almost imperceptibly. "Maybe it wasn't such a bad choice, after all."

CHAPTER
13

Gemma left the car garaged at the Yard and took the tube to Tottenham Court Road. Driving in London was difficult enough, driving such a short distance in the rain was foolhardy.

The address Felicity Howarth had given for her employer was a street level door tucked between an Indian take-away and a dry cleaners. Gemma wrinkled her nose against the pungent smells coming from the take-away — her stomach already felt empty and it would be at least an hour before she could even consider it lunchtime. Turning her raincoat collar up against the drizzle, she squinted at the names next to the bell-pushes. A tattered business card taped next to the 2B buzzer read 'Home-Care, Inc.'

Having tried the front door and finding it unlocked, Gemma pushed it open and climbed the concrete stairs without pushing the buzzer. She knocked at 2B, and after a moment the door swung open.

"I told you I didn't —" Her mouth open, the woman stared at Gemma in surprise. Recovering enough to smile apologetically, she added, "Sorry. Thought you were my boyfriend come to finish a row. Can I help you?"

Through the open front door Gemma could see directly into the sitting room of the flat. One side of the room contained ordinary furnishings — sofa, chair, television — the other held a desk, filing cabinets and a computer terminal. "This is Home-Care?" What began as a statement ended as a tentative question.

"Oh." The woman sounded taken aback. "Yes, it is, but most of our business is done by phone, so I wasn't expecting . . . as you can see." She gestured at herself — jeans, faded pink T-shirt with the tail out, bare feet sporting scarlet toenail polish. Gemma judged her to be in her forties, a sturdy woman with a pleasant face and a shock of thick brown hair liberally sprinkled with gray.

"My name's Gemma James." Gemma took her warrant card from her bag and held it up for inspection. "We're making routine inquiries into the death of one of your patients. A Miss Jasmine Dent."

Color drained from the woman's face, and

her fingers tightened where she held the edge of the door. "Oh, Christ." She looked behind her, as if for support, then turned back to Gemma. "Felicity told me about the p.m. I suppose you'd better come in." She closed the door and waved Gemma toward the sofa, then added, "My name's Martha Trevellyan, by the way." While Gemma sat down on the sofa and pulled her notebook from her bag, Martha Trevellyan fished a packet of Player's from under the papers on her desk. She lit one, then said through the smoke as she shook out the match, "I know what you're thinking. Health-care professionals shouldn't smoke. Sets a bad example, right? Well, by my last count I've quit fifteen times, but it never seems to stick."

"Is Home-Care your business, Miss Trevellyan?"

"Yes." Martha Trevellyan sat down on the edge of the chair opposite Gemma. "Two years ago I decided to get out of nursing, try something that might not kill me before I reached fifty." She smiled a little ruefully at Gemma and tapped her cigarette on the coffee table ashtray. "Look, Sergeant — it is Sergeant, isn't it?" Gemma nodded. "What's this all about? I'm still operating on a shoestring, here. Any allegations of negligence could ruin me."

"Perhaps you could start by explaining how you operate." Gemma waved a finger toward the room's work area.

"Most of our business comes through referrals, even from the beginning. I'd done critical nursing and the doctors I'd worked with recommended me to their patients who needed in-home care." She settled back in her chair, looking more comfortable as she began to talk about a familiar subject. "I keep a list of nurses who can work for me full or part time. When we acquire a new patient, I match them with an available nurse, keep things coordinated as necessary. I bill the patients, then pay my nursing staff. Simple enough?"

"Beautifully," said Gemma.

"Except that good nurses demand high wages, and my profit margin is very, very slim." Martha leaned forward and crushed her cigarette out in the ashtray. "It's not exactly the Ritz around here. You might have noticed. I'll need a few more years of good luck and hard work if I want to provide comfortably for my old age." She smiled as she spoke, but it didn't conceal the worry in her eyes.

The flat, although small and cluttered, looked scrupulously clean, and the furnishings were of good quality if rather conventional taste. "It could be worse, as far as temporary situations go," said Gemma with an answering smile, and she felt Martha relax a little further. "Tell me, Miss Trevellyan —"

"Actually, it's Mrs. — I've been divorced for donkey's years. Raised two kids by myself, but now they're both out and educated I could afford to take a risk." She nodded toward her work area. "Call me Martha, why don't you. I'll feel less like I'm in the dock."

Gemma didn't mind conceding to her small request. It was common enough, and seemed to help close the gap people felt between themselves and the police. "How did you acquire Jasmine Dent as a patient, Martha?"

"Doctor's referral, if I remember correctly. I can check my files." Lighting another cigarette, she stood and went to one of the metal cabinets beside her desk. She pulled open a drawer and ran her fingers along the colored tabs before extracting a medical chart. "Dr. Gwilym, all right. Cancer specialist. He's sent quite a few my way."

"Was there anything unusual about Jasmine's case?"

Martha thought for a moment, then shook her head. "No, not really. By the time we get them, there's not usually much chance of remission. She was in good hands with Felicity." At Gemma's inquiring look, she continued. "Felicity Howarth's my best nurse. I pretty much let her pick and choose which cases she wants, according to her schedule and what's geographically convenient for her." Thoughtfully, she added, "And it's also a matter of personal preference. All nurses have them. Felicity does particularly well with cancer patients."

"Did Felicity Howarth choose Jasmine's case?"

"As far as I can remember. Felicity's been carrying an especially heavy caseload lately. I thought it might be a bit much for her, but she insisted. Said she needed the money."

"Do you know why?"

Hesitating, Martha stubbed out her cigarette before she answered. "I don't feel comfortable giving out personal details about my employees." Gemma waited in silence, and after a moment Martha sighed and said, "Well, I don't really see what harm it can do. I know Felicity has a son in a private nursing home, some sort of childhood injury. Maybe the fees have gone up. It must cost her a bundle anyway." Then she added a little combatively, "But I don't know that that's what she wanted the money for. She could be saving for a cruise, for all I know. I'm sure she deserves it."

Don't we all, thought Gemma, trying to ignore the growing hunger signals from her stomach. "One more thing, Martha. About the morphine. How easily could Jasmine have saved enough morphine to kill herself?"

Martha Trevellyan lit another cigarette, and Gemma saw the return of tension in the sharpness of her movements. "Look. You have to understand. When the doctor orders unlimited self-administered morphine for a terminal patient, we have no real way of monitoring how they use it. Miss Dent could have requested more morphine while actually keeping her dosage the same. It happens. More often, honestly, than any of us like to admit. What are you going to do, slap their hands? Most of them do it as insurance, in case the pain becomes more than they can bear. And in Jasmine's case, because of the position of the tumor, the pain probably would have been very bad indeed."

Martha Trevellyan's account of Jasmine's treatment and condition tallied with Felicity Howarth's, but Gemma still felt curious about Home-Care's system. "Who's responsible for acquiring drugs for the patients?"

"I am. I keep a log, and the staff sign it when they make a withdrawal. Then I do a regular cross-check between the patients' charts and the medication log."

"No discrepancies?" Gemma asked.

"None," Martha Trevellyan said flatly. She drew on her cigarette, then tapped it several times against the lip of the ashtray. "Just how far is this inquiry going to go, Sergeant? Are we accused of anything?"

"Felicity Howarth will have to appear at the inquest tomorrow and make a statement as to Jasmine Dent's treatment and state of mind. After that," Gemma shrugged, "it will depend on the coroner's ruling."

"She didn't tell me," Martha said, disconcerted. "But then that's Felicity for you — she wouldn't have wanted to worry me." She studied Gemma for a moment, squinting against the rising smoke as she ground her cigarette out in the ashtray. "There's one thing I don't understand. Why are you lot spending your time on a simple suicide? Surely you have more important things to do?"

"Felicity didn't tell you?"

"Tell me what?"

"There's a possibility the suicide may have been assisted, and that's a felony offence." Gemma made a silent wager on Kincaid's intuition. "Or it may not have been suicide at all, but murder."

There was no word from Kincaid when Gemma got back to the Yard. She shook her head as she thought about his morning call from the car. *Dorset?* He'd accused her of chasing after wild hares often enough, but she couldn't remember ever driving across three counties on a moment's whim.

It worried her, this obsession he seemed to be developing about Jasmine Dent's past. He'd not spoken to her about Jasmine's journals since she'd helped him carry them up to his flat. Had he found some clue in Jasmine's early life, or was it just morbid curiosity, an attempt to resurrect a girl he hadn't known? Remembering the photo she'd found facedown in Jasmine's bureau drawer, Gemma still couldn't say what had kept her from showing it to him. Had it been for his sake, or her own?

She'd taken refuge in Kincaid's empty office, and the silence gave her no answer.

Gemma sat up smartly in Kincaid's chair and shrugged off her uncharacteristic mood. It was probably just the curry she'd eaten on a too-empty stomach. She had problems enough without taking on his. She'd write up a report of the morning's interview, and if Kincaid hadn't called by the time she'd finished, she just might get away early.

After she picked up Toby at the sitter's in Hackney, Gemma headed east toward Leyton. Anxious as she had been to leave the Yard, the thought of the long evening at home suddenly palled.

Leyton High Street hadn't changed much

since her childhood. The red-brick shop-fronts had sprouted a few more wire safety-grills, the Chinese take-away had been replaced by a Greek gyros, a shop that Gemma remembered as selling knitted goods now displayed neon-sprayed T-shirts in its windows — but the basic character had remained the same. Once a village in its own right, Leyton had been absorbed by London long ago, and only the High Street served as a reminder of its former identity.

Her mum and dad had owned the bakery on the High since before Gemma was born, and she'd grown up in the rooms above the shop, smelling sausage rolls, and pork pies, and fresh bread even in her sleep. She'd worked in the shop after school, and even now she felt her father's disappointment that neither of his daughters had cared to stay in the business.

Gemma left the car in the public carpark and walked to the shop, Toby holding her hand and pretending to hop like a kangaroo every few feet. The day's persistent drizzle had stopped, and by the time Gemma reached the shop some of her earlier unease had lifted. It was a few minutes before closing time and her mum was still behind the counter, busy with last minute customers.

"Gemma! What a nice surprise. Toby, love,

give Granny a kiss, there's a good boy." Vi Walters wiped a hand across her perspiring brow and said to Gemma, "Could you give us a hand, love? It's a bit of a panic just now."

"Sure, Mum." Gemma always had to repress a smile at the thought of her grandparents' stubbornness in naming their carrot-haired daughter so inappropriately. Violet had become Vi as soon as she was old enough to express an opinion and had stayed so ever since, although the ginger curls were fading slowly into gray.

"Where's Dad?" Gemma asked as she came round the counter and tied on a white apron. Toby headed straight for the toy basket kept for the purpose of entertaining him and his two small cousins.

"In the back. Slicing bread for Mrs. Tibbit. You can stay for tea, can't you, love?"

Nodding yes, Gemma took the last customer's order. Her parents' routine never varied — close the shop, have tea as soon as her mum could get it on the table, then settle down for the evening in front of the telly. Gemma found it both irritating and comforting.

This evening was no exception, and half an hour after closing they sat at the red Formica table in the flat's kitchen, eating buttered toast, boiled eggs and jam-filled cake. Gemma had eaten her childhood meals at the same table, spilled her milk on the same lino floor.

All her mother's time and energy went into the shop, not into what she referred to as "tarting the place up". The bakery's reputation reflected her mother's care, and Gemma supposed she and her sister hadn't really suffered as a result. Her sister —

Gemma's thought came to a guilty halt. "How *is* Cyn?" she asked as she helped her mum with the washing up.

Her mother gave her that sideways look of disapproval that could still make her cringe. "You could pick up the phone and ring her yourself. I hadn't noticed your fingers were broken."

"I know, Mum." Gemma sighed. "Just tell me."

"You just missed her, you know. She was here last night with the little ones. That new salon seems to be working out a treat for her. She's already had a rise, and the manager says . . ."

Out of long habit, Gemma made interested noises in the proper places, her mind somewhere else altogether.

"Gemma, you've not listened to a word I've said." Her mother looked more carefully at her, concern replacing the exasperation in her expression. "You've been quiet as the tomb all evening, come to think of it. Are you all right, love?"

Gemma hesitated, torn between her need to confide and reluctance to give her mother ammunition. The fact that her marriage had failed while her sister's remained intact was a constant sore spot with her mum, although Gemma didn't see that her brother-in-law was such a prize — he was a lazy lout who spent more time on the dole than he did on the job.

Need won out. "I think Rob's skipped out on me, Mum. It's been months since he's sent any money for Toby, and I don't know how much longer I can manage things the way they are."

Instead of answering, Vi ran some water in the electric kettle and pulled two mugs off the shelf. "Sit down. We'll have another cup."

Gemma almost laughed. Tea, the universal problem solver. Her mother never dealt with anything unless fortified by strong, sweet tea. From the sitting room she heard her father's voice and Toby's giggle, then the opening music from *Coronation Street*. Her mum was making a real sacrifice.

"Have you looked for him?" asked Vi as she sat opposite Gemma and pushed her cup across to her.

"Of course I have. I tell you he's done a skip, Mum. Left his job, no forwarding address, no phone number. I've talked to everyone I can think of who knows him — nothing."

"His mum?"

"If she knows anything she's not telling me, and it's her grandchild that's going to suffer, for god's sake. How could he do this to us? The bastard." Gemma felt her throat tighten, heard the threat of tears in her voice. She gulped down tea so hot it scalded her mouth.

"Just how bad it is it, Gem?"

Gemma shrugged. "The mortgage is high, even if the place is a hole. One of Rob's great investment ideas — I'd lose everything if I had to sell it. But it's Toby's care that eats me up, not just regular days but nights and weekends when I have to work."

Vi took a sip of her tea. "Could you find something less expensive?"

Shaking her head vehemently, Gemma said, "No. It's not as good as it should be, even with what I'm paying."

"Gemma," Vi said slowly, "you know we'd look after him. You only have to ask."

She met her mother's eyes, then looked away. "I couldn't do that, Mum. I'd feel . . . I just couldn't."

"Think about it, anyway, love. Even as a temporary measure."

Temptation rose before Gemma. It would be an easy out, but it would mean a loss of independence that she didn't want to consider. She took a breath and smiled at her mother. "I'll keep it in mind, Mum. Thanks."

Twilight was falling as Kincaid joined the North Circular Road. The journey back from Dorset had seemed interminable, and after miles of listening to his own thoughts make the same repetitive loop, jockeying for position in London traffic came as a welcome antidote.

He escaped the main artery and crossed the relative quiet of Golders Green into North Hampstead. When he reached the junction of North End Way and Heath Street, he made an impulsive left turn. Spaniard's Road ran like a bridge across the top of the darkening Heath, isolated, empty of traffic. A white face flashed in his headlights — a solitary figure waiting at a bus stop — then the jut of the Bishop's tollgate into the road and he was negotiating the bustle of the Spaniards Inn carpark. As Kincaid pulled up the car, the door of the old pub opened, spilling a wave of light, warmth, and savory smells into the night.

A few minutes later, balancing a plate of sausage, chips and salad, and a pint, Kincaid squeezed his way into a seat at a single table. Back to the wall, he could watch the room as he ate. He was always more comfortable as observer rather than observed, and the mill of activity allowed his mind to wander.

Had today brought him any closer to finding the real Jasmine? Tantalizing disconnected images ran through his mind — Jasmine's face framed in the window of the Briantspuddle cottage; Jasmine's dark hair swinging to cover her face as she bent over the typewriter in Rawlinson's office; Jasmine propped up in bed in the Hampstead flat, laughing as he told her some exaggerated story from work. If he dug long enough and deep enough, would all the little pieces finally fit together to make a whole? Was there any such thing as a definitive person — could one ever say that *this* was Jasmine, and not *that?*

He realized that some of the melancholy restlessness that had been riding him since he left Dorset had to do with a growing reluctance to continue reading Jasmine's journals. Everything he learned increased his perception of her as an intensely private, even secretive person, and his sense of trespass became ever more pronounced.

He found himself staring absently at two girls ordering food at the counter. One had orange hair cropped almost to her skull, the other a straight fall of fair hair halfway down her back. Spandex minis left their legs bare from the buttocks down, in spite of the chill, damp evening. He supposed vanity provided them sufficient internal warmth — what bothered him was not the likelihood of their catching a chill, but that he'd no idea how long they'd stood there before he noticed them. He must be getting old.

The sight of the girl's long blond hair triggered the usual response — a déjà vu of pain shut off almost before it became conscious. Vic. How odd to have this insight into Jasmine's innermost thoughts, when he had never known what his own wife was thinking. His relationship with Jasmine had in some perverse way become more intimate than marriage.

Kincaid mopped up the last bit of chip and sausage with his fork. Reluctant or not, he would go home and pick up the journals where he had left off. It was impossible now to leave the job unfinished, the life not followed to its conclusion. A feeling of urgency, almost of necessity, compelled him.

For months after Jasmine's settling in London, the journal entries reminded Kincaid of the daybooks kept by Victorian wives. *Bought curtains for flat. Spent ten pounds to furnish kitchen with necessities. Enough left to pay rates?* Gaps appeared, then finally the entries began again, undated, sporadic and disconnected.

Kincaid skimmed the pages, stopping occasionally to read an entry more carefully.

May's dead, just like Father now. Should feel something, I suppose, but I don't. Just blank. Did she know she was dying? Was she frightened, or did she stay starched as a preacher's drawers even at the end? Did she think of me? Was she sorry?

Could I have loved her, if I had tried harder?

Won't go back, not even for Theo.

This city seems to breed solitude in its slick, wet streets, in the cold that inhabits the stones. You could pass your whole life here, faceless, unrecognized, unacknowledged. I walk the same way to work every day, stop in the same shops, but I'm still a stranger, just "Miss."

The flat welcomes me home with its stink of old grease and I feed just enough coins into the electric fire to keep from freezing. Sometimes when I fall asleep I dream of India, dream I'm in my bed in the Mohur Street house, and I hear the early morning peddlers singing below my window.

I never dreamed May had so much money. Or that she would divide it equally between us. *She did try to be fair, even though she didn't feel it. I have to give her that.*

Why did she squirrel it away all those years? She lived like she couldn't buy the next day's milk, bitched about how she couldn't afford to keep me even when I was paying my share of the housekeeping, and all the time she had thousands of pounds sitting in the bank. The old cow.

A new flat, a groundfloor in Bayswater. Small, but clean, with sunlight through the windows, and the tiny patch of back garden has a plum tree just beginning to bloom. Look forward to coming home to a simple meal I've made myself, a glass of wine, everything just the way I want it. Safe. For the first time I feel a sliver of hope that life here might not always be so dreary, then there's the nagging reminder that May's money made it possible. I used it for the down-payment, but I won't spend more. Determined to live off my wages, not use the principal. Theo's already asking for loans against his balance, can't say no to him. He seems so lost.

The dreams started again. Woke up sweating and sick, didn't sleep the rest of the night. Wrote his mum again last week. No answer. There's no one else I can ask. I shouldn't. I know I shouldn't. Shouldn't think, shouldn't remember, shouldn't write.

Sometimes it seems it all happened to someone else, it's so distant and distilled, then the dreams come.

A red-letter day today. My first day as junior assistant in the borough planning office. Pay's not much, but it's the first position with a chance for advancement.

This morning I got off the bus a stop early and walked through Holland Park. Gusts of wind scooped the leaves along the walks, people gripped their coats tighter and scurried with their heads down, but I felt exhilarated, as if I owned the park, owned the city, owned time even, and could stretch it as much as I wished.

Glorious as it was, at the same time I stood outside myself, aware of the experience, wondering if I could hold on to it, imprint it in my memory. Things fade so quickly. Already it's less intense, the edges are blurring, the joy bittersweet.

Everything he touches turns to disaster. A club this time, the latest everything, a sure success. Only it wasn't quite the right neighborhood, or there wasn't enough cash to keep it afloat through the critical period, or his partner raked the profit off the top. There's always something.

Am I to blame? If I hadn't left when I did . . . he wasn't strong enough to care for May when she got ill. She died in his arms. I didn't know. Theo said she looked so frightened. I couldn't have done anything for May, but I might have been some comfort to Theo.

Think Theo might be using drugs. What to say? Better or worse that I meddle? All his money's spent, trickled away like dust. Minimum wage work in the packing room of a Chelsea gallery — some friend took pity. He asks me for painting lessons. What can I do?

This is all there is. Told John to bugger off. Politely. Wasn't his fault. Nothing works. It's never the same.

CHAPTER
14

Dr. James Gordon opened his inquest into the death of Jasmine Dent at nine o'clock on Wednesday morning. The courtroom trapped the previous night's chill, and smelled faintly of stale cigarettes. Kincaid felt thankful that in London coroners were usually doctors with law qualifications and most of them could be counted on to conduct an inquest with dispatch. County coroners, often small-town solicitors with more knowledge of local politics than medical jurisprudence, were sometimes tempted to grandstand. Kincaid had dealt with Dr. Gordon before and knew him to be fair, conscientious, and more to the point, intelligent. Gordon's blue eyes, as faded in color as his thinning, sandy hair, were sharp with interest. He presided at a scarred oak table in the small room, facing Kincaid, Gemma, Margaret Bellamy and Felicity Howarth. All except Gemma had been called to give evidence, and no one else was in attendance.

They waited in silence as Gordon studied the papers spread in front of him. Kincaid glanced at the three women, thinking how clearly their postures reflected their personalities. Gemma looked both relaxed and alert, hands clasped loosely in her lap. In the gray light filtering through the courtroom's single window, her hair shone copper-bright against the dull olive of her jacket, and when she felt Kincaid's gaze, she looked up and smiled.

Margaret, although reasonably well-combed and groomed, twisted a quickly disintegrating tissue between her fingers. When she'd first walked into the room, Kincaid had noticed that her skirt hem drooped in places as if small boys had swung on it as it hung out to dry.

Felicity Howarth wore charcoal instead of navy, but was otherwise as neatly dressed as he'd first seen her the day of Jasmine's death. She sat finishing-school straight in the hard wooden chair, hands folded over her briefcase-like handbag. Her red-gold hair lacked some of its previous luster, however, and the lines around her eyes were more evident. Kincaid remembered Gemma telling him, when they had compared notes that morning, that Felicity was carrying a particularly heavy caseload just now.

"Mr. Kincaid."

Gordon's voice jerked Kincaid's attention back to the table. "Sir?"

"Mr. Kincaid, I understand it was you who requested the Coroner's Office to arrange an autopsy?"

"Yes, sir."

"Rather unusual circumstances, I should think, a senior officer with CID personally requesting an autopsy." Gordon's blue eyes searched Kincaid's face, but he continued before Kincaid could answer. "I assume you've sent the file to the Director of Public Prosecutions?"

Kincaid nodded. "Yes, sir."

"Grounds for bringing proceedings against anyone?"

"Not as yet, no."

Gordon sighed. "Well, there's not much I can do other than issue a burial order." He scanned their faces. "Next of kin here?" At Kincaid's negative shake of the head, Gordon raised his eyebrows, but said only, "I'll put the certificate of death in the post, then."

Kincaid sensed a sudden easing of the atmosphere in the room. He hadn't been aware of any previous tension, and even now couldn't pinpoint the source. Meg or Felicity? Because of the nature of her work, Felicity might very well have been called to give evidence before. Meg was the least likely to have been aware of the brevity of an opening inquest, or to have known that the coroner had no legal power to accuse anyone.

"But," Gordon said loudly, bringing all eyes back to his face, "I would like to clarify a few points to my own satisfaction."

Crafty old devil's playing it for all it's worth, thought Kincaid, and smiled.

"Mrs. Howarth," said Gordon, "you visited Miss Dent last Thursday, is that correct?"

Felicity nodded. "In the morning. I helped her with her bath, checked her catheter, just the usual things." She spread her hands in a helpless gesture. "There's not always a lot you can do for terminal patients while they're still ambulatory. It's more a matter of monitoring their progress, making sure they're comfortable."

"Did her state of mind seem out of the ordinary to you? Was there any evidence of depression? Nervousness?"

Felicity's smile held no humor. "Terminally ill patients are quite often depressed, Doctor. But no, I noticed nothing out of the ordinary that day. No indication that Jasmine might be contemplating taking her own life."

Unperturbed by Felicity's barb, Gordon continued his questioning. "And this was your normal routine? One daily visit?"

"Yes . . ." Felicity paused, her brow furrowing. "Although sometimes I would stop by on my way home in the evenings, if I'd had a case nearby. I told Jasmine I might be back that day. I'd forgotten."

"And did you stop by again?"

"No." She said it softly, regretfully. "It was too late by the time I'd finished my rounds."

"Miss Bellamy." Gordon transferred his sharp gaze to Meg, and Kincaid saw her hands jerk convulsively in her lap. "I understand Miss Dent discussed suicide with you."

"Yes, sir."

Gordon had to lean forward to hear her. "Did you understand the seriousness of what she asked you to do?"

Meg looked up at him, her face flushing blotchy red, her hands still. "She didn't actually ask me to *do* anything. She only wanted me to be with her. She didn't want to die alone. Can any of you understand that?" Meg looked at them all defiantly. No one held her gaze. After a moment she looked down, and said with her eyes fixed once again on her lap, "It doesn't matter. She was alone in the end, after all."

"You saw her last Thursday as well?" asked Gordon, a hint of sympathy in his voice.

"After work. I'd brought her a curry for

her supper. I knew she wouldn't eat much, but she usually made an effort if she thought I'd gone to any trouble." Meg looked up at the coroner and spoke as if they were the only ones in the room. "I'd never have left her if I'd thought . . . never. She seemed . . . You would have to have known Jasmine. Even when she talked about suicide, she did it so matter-of-factly. She never said, 'Meg, I'm scared,' or 'Meg, I don't want to be alone.' Even facing death, she never let you breach that reserve. But that day, last Thursday, she was different. I don't know how to explain it." Face scrunched up in concentration, hands poised as if she might pull the words out of the air, Meg stopped and took a deep breath. "Open. The walls were down. I could feel her affection for me so clearly. And she was happy. I could feel that, too."

"Miss Bellamy." Now Gordon's voice was actually gentle. Kincaid raised an eyebrow. He would have thought James Gordon impervious to appeals to his sympathy, but Margaret Bellamy seemed to inspire a protective response even in the most crusty of souls. "Miss Bellamy," Gordon began again, "Such behavior can be consistent with suicide. A decision made, the person feels relief, even euphoria."

Meg's chin came up. "So I've been told. But I don't believe it. Not Jasmine."

"Mr. Kincaid. You found no direct evidence indicating suicide?"

"No, sir. We found two vials of morphine in the refrigerator, but there was not enough missing from either to correlate with the amount found in Jasmine Dent's body, and no empty containers in the flat." Kincaid stopped and looked at Gordon while he organized his words. "She was quite weak. Stairs were difficult for her. I suppose it is within the realm of possibility that Jasmine could have given herself a lethal dose of morphine, disposed of the container outside the flat — perhaps by burying it in the garden — and put herself carefully back to bed to die. But I think it highly unlikely. And she was an organized and methodical person. I don't believe she would have killed herself without leaving some record, in case there were questions."

"Life insurance?" asked Gordon. "She might have gone to great lengths to make her death appear natural if it affected the validity of her policy."

"Suicide exclusion clause had expired. It didn't matter."

Gordon, his lips pursed, tapped the papers in front of him into a neat stack. "Well, Mr. Kincaid, in good conscience, I don't believe I can rule death by suicide. This inquest is therefore adjourned under section 20 of the

Coroners Act, so that the police may investigate further."

Kincaid nodded. "Thank you, Dr. Gordon."

As they all stood and moved toward the door, Gordon stopped Kincaid. He smiled for the first time, his formality dropping away like a shed cloak. "Might have made things easier for you if I *had* given a suicide verdict. I'd take a sociopath over one of these quiet domestic affairs any day — good forensic detail, blood spatters, DNA typing, psychological profiling. It's a bit of a hobby of mine," he added rather diffidently as he finished shuffling the papers into his briefcase. "Historic cases, too. Jack the Ripper. Crippen. Suppose I missed my calling. Should have gone into forensic pathology." Gordon buckled up his briefcase and sketched them a quick salute as he turned toward the door. "Well, ta. Best of British luck to you sorting this one out." The courtroom door creaked shut behind him.

Kincaid and Gemma looked at each other until they both started to laugh. "Who would have thought?" said Gemma.

"Bit like seeing Maggie Thatcher with her knickers down," Kincaid added, still grinning as they followed Gordon from the courtroom.

The corridor was empty, the only sound the squeak of their own shoes on the lino. Both

Margaret Bellamy and Felicity Howarth had disappeared. "They weren't inclined to hang around and chat, were they? Considering you've arranged to meet with them at —" Gemma glanced at her watch, "eleven o'clock."

"Not exactly a social occasion," he said, opening the door for Gemma as they stepped out into the gray London morning. Kincaid absently took her arm as a taxi roared past and sent up a spray of greasy water. "I feel like I'm stage-managing a bad farce with an unwilling cast. 'The Reading of the Will'," he intoned sepulchrally. "I think this may have been an absurd idea, but —" he paused as they reached the Midget and unlocked Gemma's door, "I do have power as Jasmine's executor to inform the beneficiaries any way I see fit. And if I'm going to go through with it, I'd like you to be there. You can watch them while I direct the action."

Sid made a beeline for Gemma, purring and twining his sleek black body around her ankles until she had to stand still to keep from falling over him. "Slut," Kincaid addressed him bitterly. "When I'm the one who's fed you."

"You *have* looked after him properly." Gemma knelt to stroke the cat. "He's certainly made a dramatic recovery."

Kincaid switched on Jasmine's lamps and

had just opened the blinds when the first knock sounded at the door. Theo Dent, the Major, and Felicity Howarth stood huddled together in the awkward silence common to strangers in a lift. Kincaid greeted them and had closed the door and taken their coats when a second knock announced more arrivals. He admitted Margaret Bellamy, who was out of breath and considerably more disheveled than she'd appeared at the inquest, and behind her, to Kincaid's delight, Roger Leveson-Gower. Kincaid met Gemma's eyes across the room and knew they shared the same thought — for five people to exhibit such promptness was decidedly unnatural. They must be very anxious indeed.

"Something wrong with Her Majesty's post," said Roger, immediately taking center-stage, "that you felt it necessary to cause everyone such inconvenience? Or do you just like to play petty dictator?"

Kincaid smiled. "I don't remember inviting you."

Roger draped a proprietary arm across Meg's shoulders, and she seemed to shrink into herself as he touched her. "Someone had to make sure Margaret wasn't bullied."

"And you were the obvious choice?"

"Well, of course," Roger said, the dig going over his head. Or rather past his ego,

Kincaid thought nastily.

Ignoring Roger, he turned to the rest of the group. Felicity had pulled out one of the dining chairs and sat in her usual erect posture, but something about the set of her head telegraphed weariness. The Major took a cue from her and sat as well, turning his cap in his hands, his blue eyes fixed on Kincaid's face. Theo stood alone, nervously popping his braces with his thumbs.

Kincaid spoke to them all. "This shouldn't take long. I'm sorry if I've inconvenienced you. I know you think this is a bit dramatic but it seemed the most practical way to go about things." He paused, making sure he had their full attention. "And it seemed right to me that Jasmine's intent should be conveyed to you in a more personal way. A letter comes in the post —" he shrugged, "you might as well have won the pools. These are not anonymous gifts. Jasmine thought very carefully about what she wanted to do for each of you. In a way, this is her last communication." Kincaid swallowed against a tightening in his throat. He hadn't rehearsed what he would say and his own words took him by surprise, as did the sense of finality they carried.

Meg's eyes filled with tears and she moved out of Roger's encircling arm. Kincaid started to speak to her, hesitated and turned to Theo instead. "Jasmine didn't make you a cash bequest, Theo, but she did arrange to pay off the mortgage on the shop. She also made you the beneficiary of a tidy life insurance policy." Emotions flitted across Theo's round face — disappointment, dawning relief, and finally consternation, as if he weren't sure whether he'd been patted or punished.

"Meg. Except for a couple of small bequests, Jasmine left you the bulk of her estate, which includes the equity in this flat and her stock and bond investments." Roger pressed his lips together and blinked, but he didn't quite manage to hide the flash of pleasure on his face. Meg simply looked more miserable than ever.

"Mrs. Howarth and Major Keith," Kincaid continued, "Jasmine left each of you a thousand pounds, in 'appreciation of your friendship', and she also made a donation to the RSPCA. That's it, I'm afraid. I have copies for each of you," he gestured at the neat stack he'd placed on the dining table. "If you'd just —"

"It's not right." Felicity's face had gone almost as pale as the white blouse she wore under her charcoal jacket, and she shook her head vehemently from side to side. "I can't accept that. It was my job to look after her, I never expected —"

"Nor I." The Major stood, crumpling his tweed cap between his blunt fingers. "Not fitting. Bad enough for her to be taken so soon, but to benefit by her death —" He stopped, looked round the room as if someone might give him the words to continue, then said, "Excuse me," turned abruptly and let himself out the door.

In the moment of silence that followed, Kincaid heard the vibration from the slam fade away.

Meg took a step toward the door. "Oh, can't someone do something? Talk to him? I'm sure Jasmine never meant for him to take it so . . . she only wanted to thank him for his kindness."

"Don't be daft." Roger's contempt was evident. "I'm sure he'll come to his senses soon enough."

Kincaid spoke to Felicity. "I don't know if you can legally refuse a bequest. You'll have to discuss it with Jasmine's solicitor. You would certainly have the prerogative of using the money as you pleased — donate it to a charity, perhaps, if that made you feel more comfortable."

"Nothing is going to make me feel comfortable about this. I simply will not accept it." Felicity's rising voice was the first crack Kincaid had seen in her professional demeanor.

Meg knelt before her chair and looked earnestly up into her face. "Jasmine talked so much about how good you were to her, how much she appreciated your honesty. 'No nonsense' was the way she put it." Smiling at the memory, Meg continued. "She liked that. You were the one person she could trust to play it straight with her. Most of us failed her. It's much easier to pretend it will just go away." Meg leaned back on her heels and looked away, picking at the fabric of her skirt. "Even when she talked about killing herself, I never quite believed in it — couldn't make it seem real. It was like something in a movie or a play." She looked around at all of them except Roger. "Do you see?"

"Yes," said Theo. He had stopped the nervous fiddling with his braces as he listened to Meg, and now he slid into a chair at the other end of the table and leaned forward on his elbows. "It was just the same for me. I should have known, when she said she was better but she wouldn't see me. I should have insisted, come to London and camped on the doorstep until she let me in, done what I could for her." He lifted his hands in a helpless shrug. "I'm sure she knew I'd take the easy way — I always have. Jasmine was always there — annoyed with me, more often than not," he smiled, "but there, and I didn't want to believe things would ever change." Theo paused and studied Meg. "I'm glad my sister knew you, Margaret. You didn't fail her."

"Didn't I?" asked Meg, meeting Theo's eyes.

Roger rolled his eyes in disgust. "This is all just too sweet for words. I think I'm going to be sick."

The spell shattered. Meg looked away from Theo, then down at herself, and Kincaid could see her self-consciousness flooding back as she became aware of her awkward position. As she tried to rise, her heel caught in the hem of her skirt with a ripping sound. She fell back to her knees, grimacing.

Felicity said, "Here, let me help you." She seemed to have regained some of her composure as she listened to Meg and Theo, and now she moved briskly back into her familiar role. Kneeling on the floor, she gently extricated Meg's heel from the torn hem. "All right, now? I'm afraid it will take a needle and thread to put you completely to rights."

Roger folded his arms and said with exaggerated patience, "If you're quite finished, Margaret?" but he made no move to help her up.

Felicity stood, held out a hand to Meg, then gathered her handbag off the chair. She turned to Kincaid and spoke slowly and deliberately, as if she'd been rehearsing her words. "Mr.

Kincaid. I'm sorry about all the fuss. It was unfair of me to lash out at you. I do realize it's not your responsibility, and I'll take whatever steps necessary to sort this out."

"You'll see Antony Thomas? Or perhaps your own solicitor?"

"Yes. Just as soon —"

"How long will it take?" Roger broke in. "Probate, I mean."

Kincaid raised an eyebrow. "Is Margaret in some particular hurry?"

"Will you all stop talking about me as if I weren't here?" Meg glared at them all. "No, I'm not in any hurry for Jasmine's money. I never wanted it in the first place and I don't care if I ever see a penny of it." She stopped, took a gulp of air, then delivered one last salvo. "And as far as I'm concerned, you can all just go to hell!" She stalked from the flat, her fury lending her a dignity even her trailing skirt hem couldn't spoil.

Roger gave a 'what can you do?' shrug and followed, scooping Meg's copy of the will off the table as he went.

To Kincaid's surprise, Theo recovered his tongue first. "She deserves better than that. What does she see in that miserable sod?" As soon as the words left his mouth he turned as red as his braces and muttered, "Sorry. Rude of me," to Gemma and Felicity, then

"I'd better be going as well." He did not, however, forget the will.

Felicity turned to Gemma and Kincaid. "You've been very kind," she said, the corners of her mouth lifting in a small smile, "although I'm not sure kindness figured in your motive. Mr. Kincaid, this investigation of yours is going to be very hard on Margaret and Theo — they have enough grief and guilt to deal with as it is — I don't suppose you're willing to drop it?"

Kincaid shook his head. "No. I'm sorry."

"I thought as much." Felicity sighed and glanced at her watch. "Well, I'll be off then. I've got patients waiting." She gathered her bag and coat and let herself out of the flat.

"And then there were none," Kincaid muttered under his breath. He sat on the edge of Jasmine's hospital bed. "Exit players. You faded admirably into the woodwork," he added as he looked at Gemma, who still stood with her back against the kitchen counter.

She stretched and moved to one of the dining room chairs. Sid, who had vanished like smoke with the first knock on the door, suddenly reappeared and jumped into her lap. Gemma stroked his head absently as she spoke. "I didn't expect darling Roger to be able to contain his glee, but Theo didn't kick up much protest either."

Kincaid raised an eyebrow. "And the others? Did they protest too much?"

Gemma's smile held a hint of mischief. "Your meek little Meg seems to be making an unexpected transformation into a tigress. Wouldn't you like to be a fly on the wall when she and Roger have a more private conversation?"

"Did it occur to you," said Kincaid, "that Meg seemed awfully well informed about Jasmine's intentions?"

Meg sat huddled on the edge of the bed, shivering. Even the remnants of last night's warmth had long since seeped away, and the room's single radiator felt icy to the touch. Mrs. Wilson's generosity did not extend to keeping her tenants' rooms warm during the day. She'd no patience with slug-a-beds, and she reiterated it often enough from the warm confines of her kitchen.

Of course, Meg wasn't ordinarily home in the middle of a working day. She'd taken a day of unpaid leave for personal business, and Mrs. Washburn's quick and silent acquiescence to her request left Meg little doubt that her days in the planning office were numbered. The prospect came almost as a relief.

On weekends when the room began to chill she left — to shop, to walk aimlessly in the streets, and in the last few months, to spend the days with Jasmine.

A crackle of paper drew her attention to Roger. He sat at the table, thoughtfully chewing the last of a meat-and-potato pasty — her pasty, in fact — he'd bought two at the bakery around the corner from the bedsit. Meg had taken one bite of the cold, greasy, onion-flavored meat and forced back the impulse to gag.

Roger finished crumpling the grease-proof paper into a wad and tossed it in the direction of the waste bin across the room. It missed. He shrugged and left it lying where it fell.

"Roger, couldn't you —" Meg began, then stopped, unable to find any words that might encourage him to go without incurring his temper.

"Want me to go, do you, sweetheart?" Roger said softly, crossing the room and sitting down beside her on the bed. Her stomach spasmed and her hands began to tremble. "Leave you all by yourself? I'd never do that, would I, Meg darling?" He ran his fingers lightly down her spine. "You know what this means, don't you, Meg? It won't take long for Jasmine's will to clear probate, and then we'll be set. A decent flat, maybe a holiday somewhere. Would you like to lie on the beach in Spain, Meg? Soak up the sun and drink pina coladas?" He'd been unbuttoning her blouse as he spoke, and now he traced a fingertip just under the edge of her bra.

Meg felt her nipples draw up, felt her stomach tighten in unwilling response. "Roger, we can't. Mrs. Wilson'll —"

"She'll be having her after-lunch kip in front of the telly. She won't hear a thing. Not if you're a good girl. And I want you to be a good girl. Not like this morning when you made such a scene. What was the Superintendent to think, darling, with you ranting and raving like a fishwife?" He pushed her back against the pillow and lifted her legs up on the bed. "It won't do, Meg. Do you hear me?" he asked, his voice even more gentle than before.

Meg nodded. In the cold, gray light from the window she could see the faint dusting of freckles on his skin and the flush beginning where the vee of his shirt exposed his chest. She clung to the memory of her defiance of him that morning, wrapping it about her like a second skin.

Roger pulled down his jeans and lifted her skirt, not bothering to finish undressing her. The rumpled bedspread made a lump beneath her shoulder blades and Meg focused on the discomfort, thinking that if she concentrated hard enough on that pinpoint she might block her body's traitorous rush of desire. Roger lowered himself onto her, his breath escaping in a soft grunt.

Meg turned her face to the wall.

CHAPTER
15

As soon as she felt Roger's breathing slow to the deep rhythm of sleep, Meg slid carefully from beneath him and stood up. She refastened her clothes and ran a hand through her tangled hair. Slipping into her shoes and lifting coat and handbag from the back of the armchair, she tiptoed toward the door. A loose board under the floor matting creaked and she stopped, her breath held, her heart thumping. Roger snorted and turned over, his bare buttocks exposed.

He can bloody well freeze, Meg thought spitefully as she turned the knob and let herself out of the room.

She walked, mindlessly, aimlessly, stopping to stare in shop windows at items she didn't see. The smell of hot grease and frying fish drifted from the open door of a chip shop and she hurried on, her stomach churning with nausea.

It was only when she found herself standing at an intersection on Finchley Road that she realized where her wandering feet had taken her. She shook herself, hesitated, then crossed with the light and began the long climb up Arkwright Road into Hampstead.

In spite of the cars lining both curbsides, Carlingford Road felt deserted, held in mid-afternoon repose before its occupants returned home from work. Meg climbed the stairs to Jasmine's flat and fished the key from the inside pocket of her handbag. She listened a moment, then unlocked the door and stepped inside. Sid regarded her from the bed, then curled himself back into a tight, black ball. "Wish I could do that," she said aloud. "Shut it out. Shut it all out."

Closing her eyes, she rested her back against the door and breathed — breathed in the stillness, the faint spicy scent that clung to Jasmine's things, the beginnings of the chill mustiness that signals an unused room.

Over the months the flat had become her safe haven, an inviolate space, and soon it would be lost to her forever. Meg pushed herself away from the door and walked slowly around the room, touching familiar things. She moved to the window, where Jasmine had often stood and caressed the carved wooden elephants as she watched the Major working in the garden. Today even the colors in the garden were subdued, the blaze of the tulips and forsythia muted by the moisture in the air. Her fingers traced the familiar pattern on the smallest elephant's back, the wood silky from much stroking. It brought no comfort. A sound from the hall caused her to start guiltily and drop the elephant back on the sill with shaking fingers. The doorknob turned, then someone tapped softly.

Panic closed Meg's throat, cramped her stomach. She forced it back, forced herself to think reasonably. It couldn't be Roger. The rapping knuckles had been much too tenuous. But whoever it was would have heard the elephant knocking against the windowsill.

She crossed the room, pulled back the latch and slowly opened the door. Theo Dent stood in the hall, looking as awkward as Meg felt.

"I'm sorry . . . I didn't realize," he said, the rest of his face coloring to match the end of his nose, which Meg assumed was pink from exposure to the chill wind. Damp beaded his curly hair. "I just came on the off chance . . . I didn't expect . . . I don't know why I came, really," he finished lamely. "I missed my train. There won't be another until the commuter rush."

Meg pulled the door open wider and stepped

back. "I didn't intend to come here, either," she said as Theo entered. She smiled at him, struck by a feeling of kinship. "I've no right to be here. It just seemed . . ."

"You do, you know." Theo wiped his hand under his nose and sniffed. "She left it to you."

Meg stared at him. Roger had talked of the flat in cash-in-hand terms so often — sell it and use the money for something else — that somehow the idea of ownership hadn't penetrated. She looked around the room, seeing it in a new perspective. She would actually possess this flat, be able to do with it as she pleased — sell it, lease it, even live here if she chose.

For a heady moment she imagined herself inhabiting these comfortable rooms, putting her own stamp on them, but the vision faded. She sensed that Jasmine's imprint was too strong for her own less assertive personality to take root. And Roger . . . she'd never escape from Roger here.

But the reminder of ownership gave her a new confidence. She knelt and turned on the radiator, then switched on a lamp and shed her coat. "I'll make us some tea."

Theo followed her into the kitchen area and watched her quietly for a while. "You must have spent a lot of time here with her. I envy you that. I suppose I thought that if I came here I could . . . I don't know . . . place her here more firmly."

"It's not fair, her leaving the flat to me instead of you." Meg turned from the kettle to regard him earnestly. "I argued with her about it, but she wouldn't —"

Theo held up a hand. "You mustn't say that. She did enough. All these years she did enough. More than she should." He took off his spectacles, looking blindly around for something to wipe them on. Meg handed him the tea towel. "You see, I've been a rotten failure all my life, and Jasmine always picked up the pieces." He hooked the spectacles back over his ears and pushed them up the bridge of his nose with a forefinger. "Everything always sounded so glorious at the start, and then somehow —" He shrugged and let the sentence hang.

Meg poured boiling water into two mugs, sloshed the tea bags around for a bit, then plopped them in the sink. "There's no milk. Sugar?" Theo nodded and she stirred in a spoonful before handing him the mug. They moved to the table and Meg sat in her usual chair. She rubbed at a smudge in the wood's dark gloss, marveling at this sudden surge of proprietary feeling. She'd never really possessed anything — a few bits and pieces bought for the furnished bedsit, her sister's

270

castoffs — never anything that inspired a sense of pride, of expanding the boundaries of her self past her own body.

"The table belonged to our Aunt May," Theo said, watching her. "I'm surprised Jasmine kept it."

"She never talked much about it. The years you lived in Dorset, I mean. I know you came to England to live with your aunt when your father died, but that's about all." Meg sipped her tea and studied Theo, searching for some resemblance to her friend. There was something, perhaps, in the set of his eyes, the oval shape of his face. He looked younger than his forty-five years, almost boyish — his face seemed curiously unmarked by experience.

Suddenly aware of how she must look, she ran her fingers through her hair. She'd left the bedsit without so much as a wash and a brush. "Jasmine talked about you, though," she continued a little hurriedly, covering her discomfort, "things you did as children. And she was pleased about your shop. She thought you'd finally found something that suited you."

Theo took his glasses off again and covered his face with his hands. "I couldn't tell her," he said, his voice muffled by his palms.

Meg waited a moment. When he didn't continue she said, "Tell her what?"

He raised his head. "It's just like the rest. A cock-up. I can't hang on much longer."

"But —"

"I thought that's why she wouldn't see me — that she just didn't want to hear it again. She'd told me this was the last time. 'No more free rides, Theo.' What was I to say?" He swallowed. "Then when she called and wanted to see me —"

"Would you have told her?"

Theo shrugged guilelessly. "I was never much good at lying."

"You must have been in a panic."

Theo nodded. "Didn't sleep that night, trying to work out what to say."

"She wouldn't have been angry with you."

"That would almost have been better." Theo's mug sat untouched on the table before him. He picked it up and drank thirstily, then licked his lips. "You don't understand what it's like to let someone down again and again. If she'd shouted at me, that I could have managed. Other people have done it often enough." He smiled. "But I'd wait for the flash of disappointment on her face — she could never quite conceal it — then she'd smile and make excuses for me. As if it were somehow her fault. I couldn't bear it."

Meg hesitated over the words forming on her lips, unsure of her right to ask them. "Will you be all right now? With the mortgage taken care of?"

Theo put his glasses on, pushing them up the bridge of his nose with the gesture Meg already found familiar. The light from the table lamp bounced off the lenses, shielding his eyes from her. "If probate doesn't drag on too long, if trade isn't too abysmal, I might scrape by. I know this is a terrible thing to say, but this happened just in the nick of time."

Kincaid stepped through the street door, then paused in the stairwell of his building, rotating his head to ease his aching neck and shoulder muscles and running a hand through his already rumpled hair. He'd spent the afternoon doing the kind of thing he most disliked, following up the vague and tenuous connections in Jasmine Dent's life. Former coworkers, employers, her doctor, her dentist, her insurance agent — anyone who might remember a name, an incident, provide a thread attaching past and present.

He came up blank, as he had suspected he would.

The murmur of voices came to him as he reached Jasmine's landing. Pausing, he cocked his head and listened, assuring himself that the sound issued from Jasmine's flat.

He fitted his key in the lock and quietly opened the door. Margaret Bellamy and Theo Dent sat at the dining table. They turned at the sound of the door, their faces frozen in that startled, guilty expression of children caught out at something forbidden.

"Mr. Kincaid?" Meg recovered first. She flushed and half rose from her chair.

"A tea party?" Kincaid said, and smiled at them. "Is anyone invited?"

Meg pushed her chair back. "Here. Let me —"

"No," Kincaid said as he turned toward the kitchen, "I'll get my own. I know my way around well enough."

They sat in awkward silence, their eyes fixed on Kincaid as he filled the electric kettle and put a tea bag in the pottery mug he'd begun to regard as his own. After a few moments, Meg turned to Theo and spoke with determined cheerfulness. "I know your village. I'm from Dorking, and I must have passed through it a hundred times on the way to my granny's in Guildford. Is your shop the one just at the crook in the road?"

Theo nodded, still watching Kincaid. "That's right. Across from the clock and the bell ringer."

"Must be lovely," Meg said rather wistfully, "all on your own like that."

Kincaid carried his cup to the table and sat down, then unbuttoned his collar and loosened the knot in his tie. "Which one of you," he said, smiling at them companionably, "has the key to this flat?"

Meg looked down at the table, twisting her cup in her hands. "I do. Jasmine had me make a copy, in case she couldn't get to the door when I came round."

"Why didn't you mention it before?"

"I didn't think of it." Meg met his eyes, her brow furrowed in entreaty. "Honestly. I was so upset it just never crossed my mind. Does it matter?"

"Tell me again what happened after you left Jasmine last Thursday afternoon."

She thought for a moment, her face relaxing as she remembered. "I walked home. I couldn't stand still, hadn't the patience to wait for the bus. I felt I might burst with the relief of not having to help Jasmine die. It was such a lovely day, do you remember?"

Kincaid nodded but didn't speak, not wanting to risk halting the flow of words.

"Everything seemed so clear and sharp; the lights coming on in the dusk, the crowds hurrying home from work. I felt a part of it all but lifted above it at the same time. I felt I could cope with anything." She looked from Kincaid to Theo, twin spots of color staining her cheeks. "It sounds absurd, doesn't it?"

"Not at all," said Theo quickly. "I know exactly —"

Kincaid interrupted him. "Then what happened, Meg?"

She shoved her hair behind her ear and looked down at her hands. "He was there, at the bedsit, waiting for me."

"Roger?" asked Kincaid. Meg nodded but didn't speak, and after a moment Kincaid prompted her. "And you told him what had happened, didn't you?"

She nodded again, her hair falling across her face, and this time she didn't push it back.

"What did Roger do?" The silence stretched. Theo opened his mouth to speak and Kincaid gave him a quick warning headshake.

"I thought he'd shout. That's what he does, usually." She rubbed the ball of one thumb against the nail of the other with great concentration.

Kincaid realized the daylight was fading, cut off by the buildings to the west, and the three of them sat illuminated in the pool of light cast by the single lamp.

Meg took a breath and laced her fingers together, as if to stop the compulsive rubbing. She glanced at Theo, then looked at Kincaid as she spoke. "He went silent. I've seen him that way once or twice before, when he was really angry. It doesn't sound much, but it's worse than words. It's almost like —" she frowned as she searched for the right description, "a physical force. A blow."

"He didn't say anything?" Kincaid asked, letting a hint of disbelief creep into his voice.

"Oh, he called me things at first," the corners of her mouth turned down in a grimace, "but it was like his mind wasn't really on it, if you know what I mean."

"Did he leave straight away?"

Meg shook her head. "No. I wanted him to go. All that elation I'd felt on the way home just vanished — like I'd been pricked with a pin. But I knew it was no use asking. It would just make him that much more difficult."

Kincaid remembered the emphatic quality of his wife's silences, and the discomfort of being confined in a small space with someone who used non-communication as a weapon. "You tried to talk to him, didn't you?" he said, pity making him more gentle than he intended. "To please him, to get some response?" She didn't answer, the shamed expression on her face more eloquent than words. After a moment she said, "I just curled up on the bed, finally, closed my eyes and pretended he wasn't there until he went away."

"Where were your keys, Meg?"

Her startled eyes met his. She reached for her handbag and patted it. "Here. Where they always are."

"Did you leave the room any time while Roger was there?"

"No, of course I —" she stopped, frowning. "Well, I did go to the loo."

"Did you go out again that night, or use your keys for any reason?"

"No." The word was a whisper.

"And when did he —"

"Look, Mr. Kincaid," Theo interrupted, "I don't know what you're getting at, but I think you're bullying Miss Bellamy unnecessarily. Don't you think —"

Kincaid held up a hand. "One more question, Theo, that's all." He found himself tempted to treat her as Roger did and take advantage of her conditioned response, but he also knew that crossing that line would damage his own integrity beyond repair. "Meg, when did Roger come back?"

"Late. After midnight. He made a copy of the front door key, even though I told him that Mrs. Wilson would throw me out if she caught him sneaking in late at night that way."

"Were you asleep?"

She nodded. "It was only when he got in bed that I —" She glanced at Theo and stopped, her quick color rising. "I mean . . ."

Kincaid thought it was time he let her off the hook. "Theo," he said conversationally, "are you sure you had no idea how Jasmine intended to leave her money? You could use it, couldn't you? Something gives me the impression that the antique business isn't going all that well." A look passed between Theo and Meg that Kincaid could have sworn was conspiratorial. If so, they'd made a quick alliance.

"I'll be honest with you, Mr. Kincaid." Theo leaned forward, forearms on the table. "I've told Margaret that things were pretty desperate. I needed the money, all right. But I didn't intend to tell Jasmine, even after she called last Thursday and said she wanted to see me."

"Very noble of you, I'm sure," Kincaid said, and Theo pressed his lips together at the sarcasm.

"You can believe what you like, Mr. Kincaid. I've no proof of anything. But I loved my sister and I thought she'd suffered over me enough." He looked at his watch, then stood and carried his cup to the sink. "And if I don't go I'll miss my train. You know where to reach me if you want anything further from me, although I can't imagine how I could help you." Leaning across the table,

Theo held out a hand to Meg. "Margaret. Thanks."

The smile stayed on Meg's face until the door closed behind him.

"The party's over, I guess, Meg." Kincaid rose and took her cup and his own to the sink. She stayed at the table, hands locked tightly in her lap, while he did the washing up and spooned tinned food into Sid's bowl.

He finished his chores and stood studying her downcast face, sensing her reluctance. "You know, I don't see any reason you shouldn't stay here for a bit if you want."

She looked up at him, her expression more tentative than hopeful, as if letting herself want something too badly automatically meant it would be snatched away. "Honestly? Do you think it would be all right? I could look after things —" Her smile vanished as quickly as it had come. "No. He'd find me, and I don't want him here again, in these rooms."

"You wouldn't have to let him in, or let him stay."

She was already shaking her head before he'd finished the sentence. "You don't understand. Until today I'd managed to keep him away from here. Nothing would have been the same." She gestured around the room and Kincaid saw it through her eyes, familiar and secure in the lamplight. "You don't know

Roger. He spoils everything he touches."

Having insisted on walking Meg to her bus, Kincaid stood, hands in pockets against the chill, at the top of Hampstead High Street. This growing sense of responsibility toward Margaret Bellamy might be disastrous if she proved to have been involved in Jasmine's death, yet every time he encountered her, the temptation to act *in loco parentis* became stronger. He thought suddenly of Gemma and smiled. Although the two women must be near the same age, Gemma never inspired the least bit of parental feeling.

A sliver of moon hung above the fading pink in the western sky. People pushed past, hurrying home to their suppers in the gathering dusk. Kincaid looked east and west along Heath Street at the array of restaurants — Italian, Mexican, Indian, Greek, Thai, Japanese, even Cajun. If one wanted traditional British fare, Hampstead was not the place to be.

Although hungry, he felt too restless to settle down to a restaurant dinner, whatever its persuasion, on his own. He walked the short half-block west on Heath Street to the top of Fitzjohn Avenue and pushed open the door of the Italian deli. The smells of garlic and olive oil poured out into the street, tempting other passers-by. Inside, the counter beneath the window held pottery bowls filled with dark purple olives and multi-colored pastas, seafood marinating in olive oil, peppers and aubergine mixed with sliced garlic. Overwhelmed by the profusion, Kincaid bought his usual, a ready-to-cook pizza made with roasted sweet peppers and fresh mozzarella.

He stopped in the off-license across the street for a bottle of red wine, then started down the hill toward home, thinking that he might almost be going to some long-awaited assignation.

In a sense, he supposed he was, although the faded blue copy-books kept no account of time.

The wind scoured the streets today, shredding scraps of paper and hurling grit into the air, stinging skin and eyes like nettles. Punishment.

Waiting in the bus queue, huddled behind the Plexiglas partition, suddenly I thought of long-ago evenings spent sitting on the veranda in Mohur Street. There was a stillness to things then, an almost melancholy anticipation. Something exciting seemed always waiting just round the corner if I could only see it.

Did I ever imagine that days could be lived with such numbing repetition?

Seems odd leaving Bayswater after so many years. At least I knew the shopkeepers, even the neighbors' cats. Carlingford Road radiates quiet and respectability in comparison, all the things I used to find least appealing. Have I grown old without noticing?

I feel more at home in this flat than anywhere I've lived since childhood. I don't know why. It fits me somehow, or I fit it. The furniture looks as though it's been here for years; my things seemed naturally to find their appointed spots. When I wake at night I know exactly where I am and I can find my way around the flat in the dark.

Met my downstairs neighbor, Major Keith. What a funny old bird, so formal and polite, yet something about him seems familiar. He lifts his cap to me, calls me Miss Dent. It's the Major who keeps the garden looking so lovely. Now that the air's warming a bit he's out every day, tidying this and that, but really I think he's watching for the first buds, the first green shoots to push through the earth. Even though he doesn't speak to me much, I don't think he minds my sitting on my steps while he works.

This cough is worrying me. I thought it was a spring cold, but it's lingered now for months.

Suppose I'll have to see someone about it if it doesn't clear up soon.

My poor Theo. What am I to do if this doesn't work out? Surely he can manage this little shop with some semblance of competence? But then he's never done so — why should things suddenly change? Wishful thinking on my part, I'm afraid.

It's funny how much we depend on our bodies without ever really thinking about it. Cells and organs chug away, blood runs, heart pumps. We worry endlessly about accidents and falls and catching things. Betrayal from within is the last thing we expect.

And cancer is the most insidious enemy, the body turning on itself like some secret cannibal. How could this happen and I not know it? Not feel it? Not sense a spot of decay stretching fingers outward?

Radiation and chemotherapy, the consultant says. Will I poison my body's hideous child?

Dear god, I feel so bloody helpless.

Sometimes I go hours without thinking of it. I manage to pretend I'm like the others, whole and healthy, manage to pretend that the decision to grant planning permission on some project is of earth-shaking importance,

284

pretend I care whether the new cafe has better chips than the old, pretend anything other than my own body matters.

It comes out in tufts, in handfuls, like plucking a bird. Decorates the bottom of the tub with long, dark swirls, fills combs and brushes with thick mats. I've thought of putting it out in the garden for the birds to use in their nests. How absurd.

May would laugh, tell me I'd got my comeuppance. She berated me often enough for my vanity. I've taken to wearing caps, a beret mostly, like a travesty of a French peasant. Can't bear to see Theo.

New clerk at the office while I was away for the last course of treatment. Such a lame duck, with her missing buttons and terribly fair skin that flushes whenever anyone speaks to her. She watches me when she thinks I'm not looking, her expression one of . . . what? Not pity, I've seen that often enough. Concern? It's very odd.

They've washed their hands of me, abandoned me to Morpheus. So sorry, can't do any more for you, let us get on to someone who will feel properly grateful.

Too weak now to work, left without much fanfare. What did I expect?

Meg Bellamy's come, first bringing cards and flowers from the office, then on her own when the rest of staff's communal guilt began to fade.

Reading Eliot again. These long, golden autumn afternoons do seem to have an almost physical presence, an existence separate from my experience.

I've been rereading all my favorites, folding the stories around me like the comfort of old friends.

The Major and I have developed a routine. We don't speak of it, of course, that would be somehow stepping beyond the bounds of propriety, but we observe it faithfully nonetheless. On fine afternoons I sit on the steps and watch him work in the garden, then when he begins to clean his tools I make tea. Sometimes we talk, sometimes not, comfortable either way. On one of his most loquacious days he volunteered a little history: he served in India, in Calcutta, during and after the war. Must have been the colonial manner that struck a chord when I first met him. He would have been a young officer when I was a child, might even have known my parents, considering the incestuous nature of the compound.

Since they stopped the treatments my hair's

come in again, thick and short, like a child's, and as I've lost weight my breasts have shrunk to almost nothing. I've become androgynous, a fragile shell of skin and muscle wrapped around memories.

I shall need a nurse soon.

CHAPTER
16

"You didn't know he served in India?" Gemma swiveled in Kincaid's chair, having usurped it when she arrived before him at the Yard.

"Until Jasmine died I'd hardly passed the time of day with him," Kincaid said rather defensively from the visitor's chair on the other side of his desk. "Why would I have thought to ask him that? And if you're going to take over my office," he added, "make yourself useful and put out a request for his service records."

The phone rang as Gemma reached for it, the distinctive double-burr stilling her hand for a moment in mid-air. Lifting the receiver, she said, "Superintendent Kincaid's office" in her most efficient manner, then pulling pad and pen toward her began to write. "I'll pass it along. Ta." She reread her scribbled notes, then looked at Kincaid. "A Mrs. Alice Finney left a message for you with the switchboard. Said there was no need for you to call her back, she just wanted to tell you she remembered his name. It was Timothy Franklin."

"That's it?"

Gemma raised an eyebrow. "What's that all about?"

"A boy that Jasmine seems to have been involved with just before she cleared out of Dorset like the hounds of hell were after her. Give Dorset Constabulary a ring and see if they can trace him. And while you're at it," he continued before she could protest, "get on to the Constable at Abinger Hammer. Theo Dent doesn't have a driver's license — I checked — but I'd like to know if he bought a ticket at the local station last Thursday night, or if he called a taxi, or if anyone else might have driven him to a different station or loaned him a car." He stopped, waiting for Gemma's pen to catch up. "And find out if he owns a bicycle."

"I don't think —"

"I know you don't, but I'd like to check it out anyway. Theo Dent may be as innocent as Mother Teresa, but Jasmine's death bailed him out too bloody conveniently for my liking. Don't worry," he added with a grin, "we'll get on to our Roger. This morning, in fact.

We've an appointment with the head at his old school before lunch. It was the best I could do. No college or university, and he never seems to have held a steady job."

"Somehow that doesn't surprise me," Gemma said acidly.

"Did you drive this morning?"

"No. You?"

He shook his head. "We'll sign a car out, the sooner the better. There's one stop I'd like to make along the way."

Kincaid watched Gemma's obvious enjoyment as she eased the Rover through traffic. "Makes a nice change, doesn't it?"

"A covered wagon would be an improvement over my Escort," she said as she slipped into a parking space along Tottenham Court Road. "Not bad for a Thursday morning. I expected to have to queue for it. And thank heavens the rain's stopped." The thin haze covering the morning sun showed promise of burning off in the course of the day.

Martha Trevellyan answered the door almost before the sound of the buzzer had died away, showing not the least surprise at finding coppers on her doorstep. Kincaid wondered if she'd seen them crossing the road from the flat's front window.

"Sergeant James." She smiled at Gemma

and motioned them in. "I hope I look a bit more business-like than the last time you dropped by," she said, gesturing to her sweater and skirt. "I've even managed make-up. What can I do for you?"

Kincaid introduced himself, then said, "Just a quick question — won't take up more than a moment of your time." He looked around at the neat living/office area, thinking that the lack of personal clutter matched Martha Trevellyan's brisk manner. He sensed, though, that some of the briskness might be manufactured, and that Martha Trevellyan was a bit more wary of them than she'd like to admit. "I assume you had references for Felicity Howarth. You hadn't any indication of problems with terminal patients? No carelessness in administering drugs, anything of that nature?"

She stared at Kincaid, mouth open in shock. "Of course not! I'd never take on someone without a clean record. My business depends on the quality of the care. And Felicity wasn't only experienced — she had special training."

"What sort of special training?" Gemma asked, pulling out her notebook and pen. "I didn't know there was such a thing."

"There's a training course just for the care of the terminally ill. Felicity was a graduate. It's in Winchester or Exeter, something like that." She moved toward her desk, then pulled her hand back and folded her arms tightly across her chest. "I'd like for more of my nurses to be as well qualified, but it's difficult. The demand becomes greater all the time."

"You've quit smoking again, haven't you?" Gemma said, nodding toward the clean and polished ashtray on the desk.

"I'm still reaching for them. Hand's faster than the brain." Martha smiled apologetically. "My resolution won't last long, though, if my morning keeps on like this."

"Can you remember exactly where Felicity took this training?" Kincaid asked, content to let Gemma diffuse the tension he'd generated. It had served its purpose. Martha's initial reaction to his question had been unguarded enough to convince him of its sincerity.

"I don't need to remember. I've got it right here in my file." Pulling open a drawer, she flipped through the brightly colored files with practiced ease. "Here it is. Not Winchester. Dorchester. I always get those two confused." She handed a piece of paper to Gemma. "Copy the address if you need it, but as far as I know it's a very reputable course. Do you need the references from physicians as well?"

"Please."

"I'd stake my reputation on Felicity Howarth's competence," Martha said slowly.

"I feel that strongly about it. In fact," she added a bit ruefully, "I suppose I already have."

"I don't think you've any cause to worry, Ms. Trevellyan." Kincaid smiled at her, paving the way for a graceful exit. "We're just tidying up loose ends."

By the time they reached Richmond the haze had dissipated and pale sunlight filtered through the fringe of leaves overhanging the road. Kincaid checked the map. "Petersham's just a bit further on, and according to the directions they gave me over the phone, the school's just off the main road."

"I've heard that one before. Your navigational skills leave something to be desired."

He looked up at her profile. Although her gaze was fixed intently on the road, the corner of her mouth turned up in a hint of a smile. "You can't drive and navigate both, so you'll just have to live with my deficiencies, won't you?"

Shortly after they entered Petersham, a high, red-brick wall began to run alongside the road on their right. "Slow down, Gemma. The entrance should be along here." A sharp right turn through an open gate revealed an expanse of green lawns, symmetrically laid out red-brick buildings, and beyond the school, shining in the sun, the Thames.

"Oh my," said Gemma as she parked the car, "our Roger did have a difficult time of things, didn't he?"

A secretary showed them to a book-lined study with long French windows overlooking the river. They waited in silence. Gemma stood watching the swans moving languidly on the water, and Kincaid noticed that the black jersey she wore made the contrast more evident between her bright hair and pale skin.

The door swung open and the head charged into the room, black gown flapping like crow's wings. About Kincaid's age, with thinning hair, glasses and an incipient paunch, he radiated gale-force energy. "I'm Martin Farrow." He shook their hands in turn with a quick, firm grip. "What can I do for you?"

Kincaid decided this man wouldn't appreciate wasted words. "One of your former students, Roger Leveson-Gower — do you remember him? I'm afraid it's been a good ten years."

Martin Farrow didn't ask them to sit. Kincaid thought the omission was probably not due to a lack of courtesy, but that it simply didn't occur to Farrow that anyone would not prefer to stand.

Farrow limited himself to rocking on the balls of his feet while he thought about the question. "Oh, I remember him, all right. I was assistant head then, so most of the discipline problems came to me. What's Roger gone in for? A career in forgery? Insurance fraud? Conning little old ladies out of their life savings?"

"Nothing so glamorous. I take it Roger showed criminal promise early. Why didn't you chuck him?"

"Would have if it'd been up to me." Farrow began to move around the room as he talked, straightening sofa cushions, adjusting chairs by a millimeter, so that Kincaid and Gemma had to turn like tops to follow him. "We run a good school here, progressive, none of that medieval boy-bashing and gruel for supper nonsense, and turning out students like Roger Leveson-Gower does nothing for one's reputation."

Kincaid, accustomed to their usual give-and-take in an interview, looked expectantly at Gemma. Her face was expressionless, her gaze fixed somewhere beyond the back of Martin Farrow's head. "Uh," he said, before the gap in the conversation lengthened, "so what was his ace in the hole?"

Farrow came to rest with his hands on the back of a wingback chair, and Kincaid suddenly saw him behind a lectern, his perpetual motion stilled by a physical anchor. "His father contributed generously to our building fund." He shrugged. "The usual thing. And as thorough a rotter as Leveson-Gower was, he was too sly to get caught at anything really serious. But I was certainly glad to see the back of him."

"Either his father's funds or his generosity have dried up, because these days Roger seems to be scrounging a living off a woman who probably doesn't make much more than minimum wage."

Farrow smiled. "Sounds right up his alley. He bullied the junior boys — they were terrified of him, and he always managed things so that they took the fall for his schemes."

"Did you ever see any indication that he might be violent?"

"No." Farrow shook his head. "Too bloody calculating by half, too concerned with his own skin." He thought for a moment. "If Roger Leveson-Gower ever took to violence, I'd say he'd make very sure he couldn't be found out."

"Satisfied?" Kincaid asked, when Farrow had swept them out the door and seen them into their car with a cheerful wave.

"He was a bright boy," had been Farrow's last comment. "Always hate to see a good mind go to waste."

"You were expecting him to have been Best Boy?" Gemma said as she put the Rover in gear and pulled out into the road.

"Would Jasmine's death have been fool-proof enough to tempt him, do you suppose? Would he have felt safe?"

Gemma shrugged, her eyes on the road. "He wouldn't have counted on you. You were the unforeseen ingredient, the spanner in the works. Without you Jasmine's death would have gone unremarked."

He waited for her to push home her point, take advantage of every tempting possibility to make her case against Roger, but she remained silent. As they entered Richmond again, he spoke. "Gemma, what's wrong? I thought you'd got lockjaw during that interview, and now you're shutting me out. Come to think of it, you haven't been quite right all day."

She glanced at him, then back at the traffic. "Bloody hell." The second's distraction had left her no room to maneuver into the right-hand lane, and the left shunted them off the main road and into a narrow one-way side street. "Now what?"

Kincaid smiled. "Not much choice is there? Follow it and see where it goes."

The street twisted and turned, narrowing into a cobbled alleyway that snaked between rows of warehouses. Suddenly, they shot out into the sun. The Thames lay before them, beyond a wide expanse of brick paving and a post-and-chain railing. "Pull up there." Kincaid pointed to a spot near the railing. "Let's get out for a bit." Up to their right traffic sped busily across the hump-backed bridge they had crossed just before they'd derailed.

The sun felt warm on their faces, and the air moved just enough to ruffle their hair. Across the water, budding willows trailed lazy fronds in the water. A moored houseboat bobbed against its gaudy reflection in the current, and a pelican stood dreaming one-legged on a post. Even the sound of the traffic seemed muted by the river's peaceful sway.

"That was a fortuitous wrong-turning. Come on." Kincaid turned and began walking along the railing. "Too bad fate doesn't prepare you for these little gifts. We should have brought a picnic." He paused as Gemma stopped and turned her face up to the sun, her eyes half closed. "So what's up?"

Sighing, she answered without looking at him. "Privilege. The place reeked of privilege. Generations of it, progressive or not. I don't expect you to understand." She faced him, arms folded across her chest, and in the light he could see gold flecks in the hazel irises of her eyes. "Money by itself doesn't faze me. The Leveson-Gowers, for instance — they may be rolling in the stuff but they're trash. They've no taste, and I can beat them at their own game. It's the in-bred assurance that makes my skin crawl — that instinctive knowledge of the right thing to say, the right thing to do. And it's as natural to you as breathing."

"I'm no public school product. You know that, Gemma. My parents considered themselves much too liberal to send their children to such a bastion of conservatism, even if they could have afforded it. They thought the local comprehensive was good enough for us, and I dare say it was." He put his hands in his pockets and moved on. Gemma fell in step with him again, and when she didn't respond he continued. "There's something else, isn't there? You usually take on the ranks of male privilege without turning a hair. I've seen you hold your own at the Yard, and stomp on a few toes while you're at it."

"That's different," she shot back at him. "I know the rules." Then she smiled a little sheepishly. "I suppose I am a bit on the defensive today. Sorry. Shouldn't take it out on you just because you fit the general description."

"Is it Rob?" Kincaid asked noncommittally.

He had gathered from her occasional dropped comments that her ex-husband showed little interest in Toby or in maintaining a cordial relationship, and he hadn't liked to pry further.

The pavement narrowed to a single-file width on the bank's edge. Gemma stopped and looked out across the river, resting her hands on the railing's last iron post. "I think he's skipped out on me. No checks, no phone, no forwarding address. Brilliant deduction."

"Have you tried to trace him?"

"As much as I could without raising eyebrows in the department. I've called in some favors." She paused, her knuckles white where she gripped the post. "The bastard! I try not to feel angry but sometimes it seeps through the cracks. How could he do this to us?"

Kincaid waited until she blew out her breath in a gusty sigh and her hands relaxed their stranglehold on the post. "Except he didn't," she said. "I did. I chose to marry Rob James against my better judgement and now I'm reaping the consequences. Complaining about it doesn't do a bloody bit of good, and besides, we can't spend our lives second-guessing every decision. We just do the best we can at the time."

"And there's Toby," Kincaid said gently.

"Yes. I can't imagine my life without Toby.

But that brings me right back to the starting point — how am I going to manage?"

"Surely —"

"Toby's care is eating me up. It's bad enough even under ordinary circumstances, but when I work long hours on a case . . . I just barely made ends meet as it was."

"Can you cut corners anywhere else?" He kept his tone as casual as he could, sensing that if he displayed the sympathy he felt, Gemma wouldn't feel comfortable later with having confided in him.

"Rob insisted on buying the house when interest was high, an investment for our future." Her smile was bitter. "A bloody great millstone around my neck is more like it, and a tatty one at that. Rob was full of ideas for all these do-it-yourself projects — of course they never got —" Stopping, she rubbed her face with both hands. "Oh god, just listen to me. And I said I wouldn't take it out on you. I'm sorry." She smiled, this time ruefully. "I've seen enough people pour out their life stories to you without any encouragement. I should be more wary."

"What are you going to do, Gemma?"

"I don't know. My mum's offered to help out with Toby —"

"That's great. That would —"

She was already shaking her head. "I don't

want to be obligated to them. I've managed on my own since I left school and I don't intend —"

"So who suffers for your stubbornness? Toby? Don't you think refusing help in a really rough spot is a kind of false pride?"

"It's not just that. It's . . . They don't really approve of what I do." A cloud covered the sun and Gemma hugged her arms against her chest. The wind had risen, driving tiny ripples along the surface of the water. "I'm afraid they'll pass that along to Toby, not deliberately, but that he'll pick it up in insidious little ways. *Good mums don't work nights and weekends. Good mums stay married. Good mums don't do men's jobs.*"

Kincaid put his hand on her elbow and turned her toward the car. "Let's go back." Through the soft flesh of her arm he felt firm, delicate bone, and a faint shiver as the wind whipped into their faces. He dropped his hand. "Give yourself credit, Gemma. He's your son, and your influence is stronger than that." He smiled a little wickedly at her doubtful expression. "And you might give them a little credit as well — after all, they raised you and you didn't turn out too badly."

CHAPTER
17

Kincaid woke before dawn on Friday morning. He'd not drawn his curtains the night before, and he lay in bed watching the faint gray light steal into the eastern sky. The days of the past week ran through his mind, each one toppling the next like falling dominoes, and he felt no nearer to solving the riddle of Jasmine's death than he'd been a week ago. Frustration finally drove him to throw off the covers, but shower, toast and coffee didn't take the edge off his nagging sense of failure.

It would be easy enough to nominate Roger Leveson-Gower as the most likely candidate, but he had not one smidgen of hard evidence. And no matter how well Roger might fit the emotional profile of a murderer, it didn't feel right. The idea of Jasmine complacently letting someone she didn't know and wouldn't have been at all likely to trust give her a fatal dose of morphine was a logical stumbling block Kincaid couldn't get over.

He dawdled over shaving and dressing, but when he reached the street the milk float was just making its silent rounds and no sounds of slamming doors and starting cars marred Carlingford Road's early morning repose. The sky was clear, the air still, and on impulse he pulled the tarp from the Midget. He loved driving through London late at night or early in the morning, when the traffic was at its ebb. It gave him a sense of being at peace with the city, of being a part of it rather than at war with it.

A stack of slick, flimsy fax paper filled his in-tray. Kincaid took possession of his own chair, having arrived well before Gemma, and began to read.

Major Harley Keith had indeed been posted to India just after the War, in 1945, sporting a new commission and a new bride. He'd been stationed in Calcutta during the outbreak of 1946, and had lost both wife and baby daughter in the rioting. From what Kincaid could deduce from the unfamiliar military jargon, Keith's promotion had been minimal after that time, a once promising career stalled in mediocrity. Posted back to Britain in 1948, the Major seemed to have spent the remainder of his career pushing paper for senior officers.

Kincaid sighed and reached for the next sheet in the pile. A brief report from Dorset Constabulary informed him that one Timothy Franklin had been institutionalized twenty-five years previously in the Farrington Center for Mental Health, or as it had previously been known, the Farrington Asylum. Committal papers had been signed by Althea Franklin, the patient's mother. Franklin's condition had been listed upon admittance as schizophrenic, and he had never been released. Althea Franklin had died in Bladen Valley in 1977.

A handwritten note added by the officer compiling the report informed Kincaid that the Farrington Center was two miles north of Dorchester and a bit hard to find.

Gemma came in as he was finishing the report and his second cup of coffee. Disappointment flashed across her face before she smiled and said, "You're bright-eyed and bushy-tailed this morning, Sir."

"Beat you to it, didn't I?" A silly game of one-upmanship, but he enjoyed it, and he contrived to lose more often than he won because he knew Gemma liked the sense of power conferred by a few minutes alone in his office.

"Anything interesting?" she asked as she sat down across from him.

He handed her the reports and waited si-

305

lently while she read. Her brow creased as she read Major Keith's, and when she finished she looked up, shaking her head. "It looks as though he never recovered from the deaths of his wife and daughter. It's frightening, isn't it, that someone who seems as ordinary and commonplace as the Major could have suffered such a tragedy?"

Kincaid understood what she meant — in some way it made one's own life seem less immune. *If it could happen to someone as unremarkable as the Major it could happen to me.* "I'll have to ask him about it." Without quite intending it, he found himself confiding his discomfort to Gemma. "It's awkward — I can't leave it alone, yet I have to go on being neighbors with him after I've pried into the most painful part of his life. And it's more difficult because he seems such an intensely private person." He thought for a moment. "Jasmine gave the same impression. You wouldn't have dreamed of asking her anything about her life she hadn't volunteered. She and the Major must have formed an odd sort of bond."

"Will you see him today?"

Kincaid hesitated, then made another spur-of-the-moment decision even though he knew it was partly fueled by reluctance to confront the Major. "I'm going to Dorset."

306

"Again?" Gemma's tone was distinctly critical. "I think you're wasting your time. There's enough here in London to concentrate on without chasing wild hares in some little god-forsaken west-country village. What about Roger?"

He grinned. "I'm glad to see you're back in fine argumentative fettle. Since you're so keen on the lovely Roger, you can handle things yourself. See if you can find anyone other than his mum and Jimmy Dawson who'll vouch for his whereabouts on Thursday evening. We'll see if Roger's managed to inspire any loyalty other than Meg's."

The motorway took him as far as the New Forest. Although according to his map the motorway designation ended where the forest began, a divided highway still cut a straight swath across the irregular patch of mottled green on the page. He crossed the theoretical line demarcating the forest on the map, and any anticipation he might have had of primeval trunks and leafy, green tunnels was quickly put to rest. A wide expanse of moorland stretched away on either side of the road, broken only by gorse and distant shaggy shapes he thought might be New Forest wild ponies. He decided he'd just as soon they stayed in the distance — he'd hate to suffer a further disappointment by discovering that they were only small, hairy cows.

Halfway between Wimbourne Minster and Dorchester he passed the turning for Briantspuddle. The village lay tucked away behind the folds of the hills, invisible from the main road, and the lane leading to it dived down between the high hedges like a secret shaft. In a moment's idle fancy he entered the village and found time turned back, saw himself meeting a twenty-year-old Jasmine as she walked out the door of her cottage. What would he say to her, and how would she answer him?

He shook his head, laughing at the absurdity of it, and thought that if he didn't sort this out soon he would go right round the bend.

"A bit hard to find" turned out to be an accurate description of Farrington Center. He'd stopped for a sandwich in Dorchester, at a tatty teashop at the top of the High Street, then blithely taken the road north.

A half-dozen wrong turnings and three stops for directions later, he drove slowly down a farm lane. The last helpful pedestrian, an old woman in an oiled jacket and heavy brogues, out walking her terrier, had assured him "this wurrit be," so he kept on in good faith. A high chain-link fence appeared at the top of the bank on his right, and rounding a curve he caught a brief glimpse of red brick before it was again hidden by trees.

The fence continued until it angled back upon itself at an unmarked junction. An asphalt drive led up the hill in the direction from which he'd come, and a faded sign informed him he'd reached the visitor's entrance of the Farrington Mental Health Center. He followed the drive through the trees and parked the Midget in the small, empty carpark at its top. Before him spread a vast, Victorian pile of red masonry. The place had an almost tactile air of neglect and decay. Chipboard-covered windows gave the buildings a blank, abandoned look, and the grounds were overgrown with a thicket of rank vegetation. Apart from the main complex of buildings stood a chapel built of the same orange-red brick, but its windows were broken out and the door hung from its hinges.

Kincaid locked the car and walked toward the only visible sign of habitation, a small wood and plaster annex attached to the front of the nearest building. He pushed through the double glass-doors and found himself in a lino-floored hallway. Doors stood open along the corridor and he could hear the soft clicking of electronic keyboards and an occasional voice.

A young woman hurried from the first door on his left, a sheaf of papers clutched in her hand. She stopped when she saw him, a startled expression on her face. Apparently casual visitors didn't make a habit of dropping in at Farrington Center. "Can I help you?"

He showed her his warrant card and smiled. "I'm Duncan Kincaid. I'd like to see a patient here, a Timothy Franklin."

"Tim?" She seemed even more nonplussed than before. "I can't imagine anyone wanting to see Tim," she said, then seemed to collect herself. Shaking his hand, she said, "I'm sorry. I'm Melanie Abbot. The Director's not in the facility today but I'm his personal assistant." She looked both confident and capable in her brown sweater and slacks, her glossy, brown chin-length hair framing a round cheerful face. "Why do you want to see Tim, if you don't mind me asking? It won't upset him, will it?"

"Just some routine inquiries about someone he might have known a long time ago." Kincaid gestured around him. "What's happened to this place? It looks like it's barely survived a bombing."

"Nothing so drastic. County policy's changed over the last few years. Most of the patients have been farmed out, so to speak. Halfway houses, foster homes, supervised independent living," she said earnestly, seemingly unaware of the contradiction in the last terms. "We help them become functional, self-actualizing members of the community. This facility," she repeated Kincaid's circular gesture, "is used mainly for administrative purposes now."

"But you still care for some patients?"

"Yes," said Melanie Abbot, holding her forgotten papers against her chest with one arm. Kincaid sensed a slight reluctance in her reply as if she had somehow failed to live up to expectations. "There are a few who are simply unplaceable, for various reasons."

"Like Timothy Franklin?"

Nodding, she said, "We've made tremendous progress treating schizophrenia in the last decade, but Tim is one of the rare schizophrenics who does not respond to medication." She looked down at the papers still clutched to her chest and glanced at her watch. "Look, I've got to use the fax. Let me show you to the patients' sitting room and I'll ring a nurse to bring Tim down."

The floor in the patients' sitting room was covered in lino even more stained and yellowed than that in the annex's corridor. Straight-backed chairs, cushioned in cracked orange vinyl, sat haphazardly pushed against the walls. A fuzzy picture flickered on a television in one corner, and a rubber plant drooped dispiritedly in the other. In a wheelchair parked in front of the telly sat a woman wearing a green cotton hospital gown and felt slippers. Her head listed to one side like a sinking ship, and spittle oozed from the corner of her open mouth. Kincaid could not bring himself to sit down.

The door opened and a man came into the room, followed by a white-uniformed nurse. "Here's the gentleman to see you, Timmy." To Kincaid she added brightly, "He's having a good day today. I'll be just up the corridor if you need me."

Kincaid knew that the man who stood staring so placidly at him must be near fifty, but his physical beauty gave the impression of a much younger man. Timothy Franklin's dark hair held no gray and the skin around his dark eyes was unmarred by lines. He was about Kincaid's height and build, but the fit of the baggy cardigan and corduroys he wore made Kincaid think he might recently have lost weight.

"Hello, Tim." Kincaid held out his hand. "My name's Duncan Kincaid."

"Hullo." Tim allowed his hand to be grasped but returned no pressure, and his tone, while not unfriendly, held no interest at all.

"Can we sit down?"

Instead of answering, Tim shuffled over to the nearest orange chair and sat, resting his hands on the scarred wooden arms.

Kincaid pulled a chair around so that he could face him and tried again. "Do you mind if I call you Tim?"

A blink, and after a long pause, "Timmy."

"Okay, Timmy." Kincaid cursed himself for the false heartiness he heard in his own voice. "I want to ask you about someone you knew a long time ago." Timmy's eyes had strayed to the soundless television. "Timmy," Kincaid said again, as normally as he could. "Do you remember Jasmine?"

The dark eyes left the television and focused on Kincaid, then a smile lit Tim's face and transformed it. " 'Course I remember Jasmine."

It was a few seconds before Kincaid realized that the expected *How is she? What's she doing?* responses were not going to follow. "You were friends, weren't you?" he asked, wishing he had more knowledge of how Tim Franklin's mental disorder affected his thought processes. Was his memory intact?

"We're mates, Jasmine and me."

"You went around together, didn't you, in the village?"

Tim nodded, his gaze drifting back to the television.

Kincaid tried a little more aggressive tack. "But your mum and Jasmine's Aunt May didn't like your being friends. They tried to stop you from being together, didn't they?"

Tim made no response and Kincaid grimaced in frustration. "Do you remember Jasmine leaving, Tim? Did that upset you?"

Although Tim's eyes remained fixed on the telly, one of the hands which had been resting loosely on the chair arm clenched convulsively. Under his breath he muttered, "Pretty hair. Pretty hair. Pretty hair."

The woman in the wheelchair moaned. Kincaid looked around, startled. He had forgotten about her as completely as if she'd been a piece of furniture. She moaned again more loudly and Kincaid felt the hair on the back of his neck rise. The sound carried primitive pain, more animal than human.

Tim Franklin began to shake his head, although his eyes never left the television. The back-and-forth motion grew faster, more agitated, as the woman's moans increased in frequency.

Kincaid stood up. "Tim. Timmy!"

"No-no-no-no-no," Timmy said, head still moving, both fists now clenched and pounding on the chair arms.

Fearing that the situation would soon be completely out of control, Kincaid rushed to the door and called out into the corridor, "Nurse. Nurse!"

Her white-uniformed figure appeared around the corner. She smiled cheerfully at him. "Things getting a bit out of hand, are they? First thing to do is to get Mrs. Mason back to her bed." Kincaid stepped aside as she entered the room, still talking. "It's all right, dear, we'll just have a little nap now," she said soothingly as she wheeled the woman's chair to the door. "Be hours now before we get that one settled down," she added, nodding her head toward Tim. "You'll not get anything else out of him."

Kincaid looked back as he followed her from the room. Tim Franklin was still pounding and chanting, his head jerking to a rhythm Kincaid couldn't hear.

CHAPTER
18

The hands on the Midget's dash clock read straight-up six o'clock when Kincaid pulled up to the curb in Carlingford Road. He killed the engine and sat in the silent car, unable to shake the depression that had ridden him all the way back from Dorset. If he'd listened to Gemma he wouldn't have wasted a day on a fool's errand and still be facing what he'd dreaded in the first place. Telling himself there was no point in putting it off any longer, he still stalled, taking his time locking the car and fastening the tarp over its cherry-red paint.

There was no answer to his knock on the Major's door. He waited a moment, then climbed the stairs and let himself into Jasmine's flat. A sleek, black body wrapped around his ankles as he turned on the lamps. "Hullo, Sid. You doing okay, mate?" Reaching down, he stroked Sid's head until the cat's green eyes closed to contented slits. "Be patient, you'll get your supper."

Kincaid unlocked the French doors and stepped outside. The Major knelt before the roses he'd bought in Jasmine's memory. Only the pale fabric of his trousers across his buttocks and the rhythmic motion of the hand holding the trowel made him visible in the dusk. Kincaid descended the steps and crossed the square of garden, then squatted beside him. "You're working late. The light's almost gone."

The Major gave one last dig with the trowel and sat back, hands on his knees. "Weeds. Can't keep up with 'em this time of year. They'll take over like the Day of the bloody Triffids if you give 'em an inch."

Kincaid smiled. Maybe the Major had another secret occupation even less likely than choral singing — an addiction to watching late-night B movies on the telly. "I wondered if I might have a word with you."

The Major looked at him for the first time. "Of course. Let me just wash up." He stood up, his knees popping audibly. Kincaid trailed behind him as he cleaned his trowel in the work area under the steps, then followed him into the kitchen as he washed his hands and scrubbed his nails.

The small kitchen was spotlessly clean, the countertops bare except for a marked-down bag of potatoes and an unopened carton of beer. "Like one?" the Major asked as he wiped his hands on a tea towel, and when Kincaid nodded he twisted two tops off and stowed them neatly in the bin under the sink. "Pensioner's luxury," he said after he'd taken a swallow and smacked his lips. "Pinch pennies on necessities in order to buy good beer once or twice a week." He smiled, his teeth still strong and white under the toothbrush mustache. "Worth it, though."

They went through into the spartan sitting room. The Major switched on a lamp and motioned Kincaid to a seat on the sofa while he took the armchair himself. The brown, nubby fabric on the arms of the chair had patches rubbed shiny with wear and its seat cushion bore a permanent indentation. Kincaid imagined the Major sitting there evening after solitary evening with his bottle of beer and the telly for company, and he was more loath than ever to say what he knew he must. "Major, I understand you served in India after the war."

The Major regarded him quizzically. "Understand from whom, Mr. Kincaid? I don't believe I've ever mentioned it."

Kincaid, feeling as though he'd been caught

out in a distasteful act of voyeurism, fought the urge to apologize. "I'm conducting a murder investigation, Major, and as unpleasant as I may personally find it, I've had to check background on everyone who had even the slightest connection with Jasmine. We called up your service records. You were stationed in Calcutta during the time that Jasmine's family lived there." He waited for the explosion, but none came.

After a moment the Major took another swallow from his beer and sighed. "Aye, well, I'd have mentioned it myself if I'd known it was of any importance to you. It was all a very long time ago."

"But you told Jasmine?"

"Aye, and wished I had not."

"Why was that, Major?" Kincaid asked quietly, setting his beer on the end table and leaning forward. For the first time he noticed the age spots patterning the Major's callused hands.

"Because I couldn't tell her the whole truth and it created a falseness between us. She might not have noticed, but I could never feel as comfortable with her after that." He paused, and when Kincaid didn't speak he went on after a moment. "I'm a god-fearing man, Mr. Kincaid, but I don't believe the sins of the fathers are visited upon the children.

319

To my mind, God wouldn't be so bloody unfair. But Jasmine now, I thought she would see it differently, would take it upon herself, and she'd had her share of suffering, poor lass." Taking a final pull on his beer, he held up the empty bottle and raised an eyebrow at Kincaid.

Kincaid shook his head. "No, thanks." He waited until the Major returned from the kitchen with a fresh bottle, then said, "What would Jasmine have taken upon herself, Major?"

The Major stared at the beer bottle as he rotated it delicately between his fingertips. "Do you have any idea what happened in Calcutta in 1946, Mr. Kincaid?" He looked up, and Kincaid saw that his pale blue eyes were bloodshot. "Muslims seeking partition attacked and killed Hindus, and the rioting that followed spread through the city like wildfire. The history books refer to it as the Calcutta Killings." He gave a snort of derision. "Makes it sound like a bank robbery, or some idiot gunning people down in a supermarket." Shaking his head in disgust, he said, "They've no idea. You see horrors enough in your job, I dare say, but I hope you never see the likes of those days. Six thousand bodies in the streets by the time it was all over. Six thousand bodies rotting, or burning in the fires that smoldered for days. You could never forget the smell. It clung to your skin, the roof of your mouth, the inside of your nose." He drank deeply, as if the beer might wash the memory of the taste from his mouth.

"Jasmine would have been only a child," Kincaid said, doing some mental arithmetic. "Why should she have felt guilty?"

"Jasmine's father was a minor civil servant, a paper pusher, with a reputation for not being particularly competent. He was in charge of evacuating a small residential area, a sort of civil defense sergeant." The Major drank again, and Kincaid fancied he heard the edges of his words beginning to slur. "He bungled it. Only a few families got out before the mob poured through the streets. I've wondered since if he put his own family first, or if he just turned tail to save his own skin."

Kincaid waited silently for what he now guessed was coming. He felt the rough, brown fabric of the sofa under his fingertips, smelled a faint spicy scent that might have been the Major's aftershave, overlaid with the odor of beer.

"It took me three days to find my wife and daughter, and then I only recognized them by their clothes. I won't tell you what had been done to them before they died — it doesn't bear thinking of, even now." The rims of the

Major's eyes were as red now as if they'd been lined with a pencil, but he still spoke slowly, reflectively. "I thought nothing of it when Jasmine first moved here, Dent's a common enough name, after all. It was only when she began to tell me about her childhood that I realized who she must be." He smiled. "Thought someone up there," he raised his eyes heavenward, "was playing some kind of practical joke on me, at first. Then the more I came to know her the more I wondered if she'd been sent me as a replacement for my own daughter. Silly old bugger," he added, the words definitely slurring now. Then he looked directly into Kincaid's eyes and said more distinctly, "You see I couldn't have told Jasmine, don't you, Mr. Kincaid? I wouldn't have hurt her for the world."

Kincaid finished his beer and stood up. "Thank you, Major. I'm sorry." Letting himself out the back way, he climbed the steps to Jasmine's flat and stood a moment at the top, looking down into the garden. The Major's roses were only visible as dark shapes in the light from the flat's windows. Roses as tribute to Jasmine, and perhaps to his long-dead wife and daughter as well. Kincaid felt sure that the Major had carried their deaths inside himself for most of a lifetime, a tightly wrapped nugget of sorrow. Perhaps his contact with Jasmine had begun a much-needed release.

Lights came on in the house behind the garden. Through the windows the illuminated rooms were as sharp and clear as stage sets, and Kincaid wondered what secret despair their inhabitants hid under their everyday personas. Someone drew the curtains, the glimpse into those unknown lives vanishing as quickly as it had appeared. Kincaid shivered and went in.

I've spent my life waiting for things that never happened, and now I find I can't wait for the one thing that will finally, inevitably come.

I'm afraid. Felicity says the tumor's growth could break my ribs, and then even the morphine may not protect me from the pain. As it is, swallowing solid food becomes more difficult every day, and I can't bear the idea of a feeding tube, or of being utterly helpless, bathed and cleaned like a baby.

Life has an odd way of coming full circle. It's rather ironic that Felicity is the one person who's been unfailingly honest with me. Although Meg's adopted my disease like a stepchild, fascinated with its every aspect, she still tries to shield me from what's to come. Can I count on her to help me?

Don't need Meg's help, that's just weakness. It won't keep me from being alone, but at least I'll be prepared, meet death face-to-face rather than have it take me unawares.

Poor Meg. What will she do without looking after me, or without me to look after her?

Should I say good-bye to Theo? No. That's weakness on my part again. Better for him to remember me as I was. And I find I don't want to know if the business is going well — I'd know in an instant from his face if it's not, and this last reprieve is all I can give him. From now on he'll have to manage the best he can.

It's odd how my world has shrunk to the walls of the flat and the view from the garden steps, and what importance those who come through my door have assumed. Their visits are the clock of my days: Felicity's morning briskness, Meg's lunchtime breathless disarray, the Major's comforting teatime silence, and Duncan — Duncan is dessert, I suppose. No matter how I've been, if he stops by in the evening I find the strength to talk, to listen, to laugh. He can't know what a difference he's made in my life, yet if I tell him I'm afraid it will spoil the ease between us.

Sidhi watches me as I write, puts a paw up occasionally to touch the moving pen. One of those ridiculous human occupations, I'm sure he thinks, as incomprehensible and fascinating as the turning pages of a book. I think how much I'll miss him before I can stop myself. How absurd. I shan't miss anything at all.

He closed the last journal slowly and returned it to the shoebox. A glass of wine stood half-drunk on the coffee table — he'd become so absorbed in reading that he'd forgotten it.

The final journal entry was dated the week before Jasmine's death and occupied the last page in the book.

Kincaid stood and stretched, finishing his wine and carrying his crepe wrappers into the kitchen. After leaving Jasmine's flat he'd changed into jeans and sweater and walked up Rosslyn Hill to the crepe stand. The young man in the open booth poured batter and wielded his spatula with the dexterity of an artist, his arms bare against the evening chill. "Ham? Cheese? Mushrooms? Bell peppers? Fancy anything else, then?" he'd asked, the questions not interrupting his concentration or the smoothness of his movements. Kincaid had watched, his back turned deliberately to the Häagen-Dazs shop, determined not to think of Jasmine and rum-raisin ice cream.

Now he washed out his glass and stood irresolutely in his kitchen, tired from the day's driving, too restless and unsettled to contemplate sleep. After a long moment he picked up his keys from the counter and went downstairs to Jasmine's flat.

He'd left a lamp on earlier for the cat, chiding himself for being a fool. Weren't cats supposed to see in the dark? And he doubted very much whether Sid found comfort in the familiar light.

Everything looked just as he had left it, looked just as it had looked a week ago when he and Gemma had searched the flat from top to bottom. Nevertheless, he started again, lifting the mattress on the hospital bed, feeling under the armchair cushion, running his hands behind the rows of the books on the shelves. He moved to the secretary, examining each nook and slot as carefully as he had the first time.

People's lives accumulated the oddest detritus, he thought, staring at the items littering the top drawer. Stubs of old theater tickets, aged and yellowed business cards, receipts for things bought and forgotten long ago, all mixed with a jumble of pens, pencil stubs and scraps of paper.

What would he leave behind in his flat if he were to walk in front of a bus tomorrow? What would some anonymous searcher make of his dusty collection of paperback science fiction, or the sixties' and seventies' records he couldn't bear to give away even though he no longer owned a turntable?

What would they make of the wedding photos stuck in the back of his bureau drawer? Of Vic, with her Alice-in-Wonderland hair and pale, innocent face — Vic, who had sabotaged much of his trust and naive faith in human nature? He should thank her, he supposed — neither quality would have proved advantageous to a rising career copper.

The school reports and drawings, term papers and rugby trophies his mother had boxed away in her Cheshire attic with other childish souvenirs. What had Jasmine done with the mementos of her childhood? He'd found no snapshots or letters, nothing from the years in India or Dorset except the journals.

He moved into the bedroom. Jasmine's silky caftans brushed against his fingers as he felt along the back of the wardrobe. To one side hung business suits and dresses, their shoulders covered with a film of dust, as were the stylish pumps neatly arranged in the wardrobe's floor.

Finding nothing there, he sat down on the small stool before the dressing table and stared at his reflection in the mirror. The light from the lamp on the table's right side cast shadows that rendered unfamiliar the planes and angles of his face and left his eyes dark. He blinked and pushed the hair off his brow with his fingers, then pulled open the middle drawer. Women's cosmetics never ceased to amaze him. Even women like Jasmine, who in all other respects were relatively orderly, seemed unable to do more than confine the mess to a specific area. And they never seemed to throw the used bits and pieces away. Jasmine's drawer proved no exception. Half-empty pots of eye shadow and rouge, lipsticks used down to the metal inner casing, brushes and sponges, all covered with a fine dusting of face powder. He sniffed. From somewhere came the scent he associated with Jasmine. Exotically floral with a hint of musk, it almost reminded him of incense.

He was lifting the slips and nightgowns in a bottom drawer when his hand struck something hard. His pulse quickened, then sank as he lifted the object out and realized it was not a journal but a framed photograph. He turned it over curiously.

She was instantly recognizable. When he'd passed Briantspuddle the day before and imagined a twenty-year-old Jasmine walking out her cottage door, he'd seen her exactly like this — the long, dark hair, the smooth, olive skin and delicate oval of her face. Her expression was relaxed, serious except for the hint of a smile at the corners of her mouth and in the dark eyes that gazed directly into his.

Carefully, he set the photo on the dresser-top, Jasmine's face next to his mirrored reflection. Gemma had searched this room carefully — she must have seen the photo. He wondered briefly why she hadn't shown it to him.

He finished with the dresser and the chest of drawers, looked under the bed and in the drawer of the nightstand, but found nothing else.

Returning to the sitting room, he found Sid curled up on the hospital bed's bright cotton spread. He'd seen the cat so often in the same spot, tucked into a tight, black ball against Jasmine's hip or thigh.

Kincaid sat on the edge of the bed and pushed the button to raise its head, then leaned back against the pillows. His chest ached suddenly, fiercely. He squeezed his eyes shut and buried his fingers in Sid's thick coat.

CHAPTER
19

Meg took the baggage claim ticket from the attendant and tucked it away inside her handbag. Eighteen months of her life were contained in one battered leather suitcase and a dufflebag, now locked securely away in the railway station baggage claim. It had surprised her how large and bare the bedsit looked, stripped of her meager belongings.

On her way to the station she had taken great satisfaction in posting a letter to the planning office giving her notice, but telling her landlady she was leaving hadn't quite lived up to her expectations. In fact, an expression Meg might almost have described as regret flashed across Mrs. Wilson's fleshy face before she said, "I'll not be sorry to see the back of that Roger, I can tell you. You mind my words, girl, you'll be better off without him."

Meg had come to the same conclusion herself some time ago, but doing something about it was a more difficult matter. She'd lain awake all night in the narrow bed, thinking, planning, daring to imagine a future in which she controlled her own destiny.

By morning she'd reached a decision, if only she had the courage to see it through. She knew she couldn't confront Roger alone, but face him she must. So she compromised, burning her other bridges first, making sure there could be no going back.

From the station she took the bus to Shepherd's Bush roundabout and walked the last few blocks to The Blue Angel. Roger's mate Jimmy worked in a nearby garage and Roger could often be found in the pub at Saturday lunchtime. She was counting on his pride in front of his mates keeping him from following her when she'd finished what she had to say.

Still, she hesitated outside the door of the pub, her stomach in knots, her breath coming fast. Two men barrelled out the door, nearly knocking her down. Meg stepped back, then ran her fingers through her hair and pulled open the door.

The air was thick with smoke, the noise level raucously high. Holding on to her position in the scrum near the door, she stood on tiptoe as she searched the crowded tables. She spotted Jimmy first, then Matt with his fluffy blond hair and drooping mustache, then Roger, with his back to her. The crowd didn't part like the Red Sea as she pushed her way across the room — she almost laughed as the biblical analogy flew through her mind, wondering at the strange sense of exhilaration she felt. Matt saw her before she reached the table, said in his sneering way, "Hey, Rog, here's your bird come looking for you," but for once that didn't bother her. Jimmy smiled at her — he wasn't a bad sort, really — and Roger turned to face her, expressionless.

"Roger. Can I have a word?" Her voice was steadier than she expected.

"What's stopping you?"

She looked at Jimmy and Matt. "I meant alone."

Roger rolled his eyes in exasperation. There were no free tables, and every available bench and stool was jammed with bodies. He looked at his friends and jerked his head toward the bar. "Get us another one, will you, lads?"

They went, Jimmy with better grace than Matt, and Meg wedged herself past a heavy woman at the next table and sat on the bench they'd vacated.

Roger started before she could draw a breath, pushing his pint aside to lean across the table and hiss at her. "What do you mean, coming here and making a fool of me in front of my mates, you silly bi—"

"Roger, I'm leaving. I —"

"— should bloody well hope so. And don't —"

"Roger. I mean it's finished. You and me. I've given notice at work. I've left the bedsit. I've written to Superintendent Kincaid, letting him know how to reach me. I'm telling you good-bye."

For the first time she could remember she'd left him speechless — not sulking in deliberate silence, but mouth open, bereft of words.

He closed his mouth, opened it again and said, "What do you mean, you're leaving? You can't."

Meg could feel her body starting to tremble, but she hung on to the feeling of power that had flooded through her. "I can."

"What about the money," he said, leaning forward again and lowering his voice. "We agreed —"

Meg didn't bother to lower hers. "I never agreed to anything. And you'll not see a penny of it. You wanted her dead. Did you make sure, Roger? I don't know what you've done, but I'm finished covering up for you."

His eyes widened in astonishment. "You'd grass on me, wouldn't you? You bitch. You —" He stopped, took a breath and closed his eyes, and when he opened them again he was back in control. "Think about it, Meg. Think about how much you'll miss me." He raised his hand and ran a finger down her cheek.

She jerked her head back, turning her face away from him.

"So that's how it is," he said, the venom fully evident again. "Run home to Mummy and Daddy, then. You've got no place else to go. Work in your dad's garage, let every filthy old bastard that comes in pinch your bum; change your sister's brats' dirty nappies — you're welcome to it. And you can tell your precious Superintendent Kincaid whatever you bloody well like, because they'll not pin anything on me." There was nothing pleasant about Roger's smile. "You fancy the Superintendent, don't you, Meg? I've seen the way you look at him. Well, he's way out of your league, darling, and you're a bigger fool than I thought."

Meg felt the hot rush of color stain her face, but she refused to let him bait her. Standing, she squeezed her way clear of the table and stood close enough to Roger for his arm to brush her thighs when he moved. She looked down into his face, noted the way his eyelashes fanned against his cheek when he blinked, and she sensed the fear beneath his bravado. "So are you," she said, and turned away. She didn't look back.

"Ta, Charlie," Meg said to the driver as the bus groaned to a halt beneath the Abinger Hammer clock. It was the daily Dorking to Guildford run, and the driver one of her father's regular customers. She waved as the doors swished shut behind her, then watched the bus until it disappeared around the bend in the road.

The shop was across the road, unmistakable, just the way she remembered it. She brushed her hands down the front of her coat, discovering a stain where she must have spilled the pop she'd drunk on the train from London to Dorking. The stop at her parents' had been brief — she'd put her bags in her old room, refused her mother's offer of tea, and refused to answer any questions. "Not now, Mum. There's somebody I have to see."

The thought of the astonished expression on her mum's face made her smile. No one in her family ever expected little Margaret to be uncooperative, or to have plans of her own.

She crossed the street slowly, pausing again outside the shop. Lights shone through the French panes of the windows, but there was no movement inside. Her heart thumped against her chest and her fingers trembled as she touched the door handle. A bell tinkled briefly somewhere in the back of the shop as she stepped inside. Her heart sank as she looked around at the jumble of rubbish that passed for a display. Old farm implements, china, a rocking horse, moldy books, nothing arranged with a semblance of balance or order, and over everything lay an aura of neglect.

But as she moved carefully through the cluttered aisle, looking, touching, possibilities began to emerge. She had knelt to dip her hand into a basket of antique buttons when a door opened and she heard Theo's voice. "Can I help — Margaret?"

She stood, a silver-gilt button still clasped in her fingers. "Hullo, Theo. Why don't you call me Meg. Jasmine did, you know."

"What are you doing . . . I mean, it's nice to see you. I just didn't expect —"

"I've come to make you a proposition." Although her voice felt shaky, it seemed to sound all right, so she took a breath and plowed on. "Is there someplace we can talk?"

Theo seemed to collect himself. "Of course. We can go upstairs.

"I'm afraid it's not much," he said as he led the way. "I suppose I've got used to living out of boxes over the years. The bare necessities."

Meg surveyed the armchair and camp bed,

336

the packing crates and hot-plate. "I know," she said, thinking of her bedsit, "but you've made it cozy enough."

"Here, have a seat," he directed her to the armchair, "and I'll make us some tea."

She watched him fill an electric kettle in the little alcove that served as a kitchen, her tongue suddenly too frozen to make small talk. Dear god, what ever had possessed her to invent such a harebrained scheme? He'd laugh at her, at the very least, at worst reject her with well-deserved scorn — and then where would she be? No worse off than she'd been before, she told herself firmly, and still with the means to start a new life for herself.

Theo brought the tea on a lacquered tray, with china cups and matching cream and sugar. "Sometimes I do pinch nice things for myself," he said, seeing her expression. "Coalport. I've always had a fondness for this pattern, and it's common enough not to be terribly valuable."

The china seemed to focus the light in the bare room, and its cobalt-and-rust, intertwining leaf-and-dragon pattern made Meg think of Jasmine. "Jasmine never lost her taste for the exotic, either."

Theo didn't speak until he had poured her tea and pulled up a seat for himself, then he said, "No, and it was in part an affectation, a vanity. It made her different." He smiled. "I, on the other hand, never wanted to be different, but I suppose I find things that remind me of my childhood comforting."

"You never knew your mother, did you?"

"No. Only Jasmine." Cup in mid-air, he gazed at some point behind Meg's head. "It's odd to look back on one's childhood from an adult's perspective. Jasmine was only five when Mummy died having me. I see now that taking complete responsibility for me must have been her childish way of dealing with her own grief and loss, but to me it seemed the most natural thing in the world. I thought all families were like ours." He sipped his tea and returned his cup to the saucer.

Meg gathered her courage. "Theo, it's Jasmine I've come about." Seeing his lips purse to form a question, she hurried on. "Or rather, it's Jasmine's money. You see, I want to help with the shop."

He was shaking his head before she'd finished. "I couldn't let you do that. It wouldn't be right. Jasmine did what she thought best for both of us —"

"Theo, I'm not talking about a loan. I want to come in as a working partner. I'll have capital to invest from the sale of the flat, and I'm good with figures. I think we could —" She stopped herself, feeling an idiot. Theo's mouth had formed a perfect round 'o' of astonishment, making his resemblance to a teddy-bear more marked than ever. "I'm sorry. It was stupid of me." She finished her tea and stood up, glad she hadn't taken off her coat. The awkwardness of getting into it again would have delayed her exit. "Thanks for the —"

"Wait, Meg," Theo said, standing so quickly he sloshed his tea into the saucer as he tried to set it down. He touched her arm. "You're quite serious, aren't you?"

She nodded, not trusting herself to speak.

"I thought you were joking at first. You'd really be interested in this place?" His tone expressed his disbelief, and when she nodded again he said, "Why? What about your job? Your life in London?"

He meant Roger, she thought, but was too tactful to say it. "I quit my job. And Jasmine was the only thing in my life that really mattered." She struggled to find words that would make him understand what she wasn't sure she understood herself. They both sat down again without quite realizing it, Meg on the edge of her chair, Theo leaning forward on his stool. "I didn't count, Theo. Anyone could have done my job, rented my room — and Roger will find a better prospect soon enough. My family complained when I left because it left more work for them, but they didn't miss me.

"I want . . ." She looked down at her hands, extended toward him palm upwards, then balled them into fists again and tucked them into her lap. "I can't . . ."

"You don't have to explain." Theo smiled, and she read in it understanding, but not pity. "I'll make us some more tea, shall I? I forgot the biscuits before." He gathered up the tea things, and as he started toward the kitchen alcove a thought seemed to strike him. He paused, turning back to her. "I say, Meg. You don't happen to like old films, do you?"

He'd done all the Saturday chores — cleaned the flat, trundled the laundry down to the service laundromat on East Heath Road, brought in some groceries, even carried bucket and sponges downstairs and washed the Midget where it stood at the curb. A more glorious spring day couldn't be imagined — a day for drives in the country, sipping lemonade at cricket matches, picnics by the Serpentine — yet Kincaid stood in his clean sitting room, staring at the shoebox that still stood accusingly on his coffee table. Beneath the grief that had dogged his morning like a hangover lay the knowledge that he had missed something yesterday. A connection, a word, a

340

memory slumbered in his brain, awaiting the cue that would allow it to make the synaptic leap into his consciousness. He knew he couldn't force it, yet he couldn't rest.

He went downstairs, folded back the Midget's top, and drove to the Yard.

The corridor was quiet, lacking the weekday hum of voices and keyboards. He waved a greeting into the few occupied offices, then absently pushed open his own door. A familiar figure sat at his desk, copper head bent over a file. "Gemma!"

"Hullo. Didn't expect to see you in today." She smiled at him and he thought she looked tired and a little pale.

"What are you doing here?" He sat on his desk, taking in her jeans and trainers, and the bright blue pullover that made the color of her hair shine like a new penny.

Gesturing at the file, she said, "Hunting for needles in haystacks, I suppose." She pushed back the chair, propping her feet on the handle of his bottom drawer. "I spent yesterday learning more about Roger Leveson-Gower, and his friends, and his habits than I or anyone else ever wanted to know, and I came up with nothing. A big, fat zero. A couple of his yobbo friends swear he was drinking with them until the wee hours of the morning, when he supposedly fell into bed with Meg. And I turned up corroborating witnesses." Sighing, she rubbed her face with her hands, stretching the skin over her cheekbones. "How did you get on?"

"Dorset was a wash-out." He acknowledged her I-told-you-so expression with a grin. "And I talked to the Major," he added more seriously, finding himself reluctant to recount the Major's tale even to Gemma. "I don't think he could have killed Jasmine. Of course, he hasn't an alibi, but there is no physical evidence to indicate him, either."

"But didn't he leave practice early, an unusual occurrence for him?"

Kincaid shrugged. "I suppose he really didn't feel well. A coincidence."

Gemma raised an eyebrow. "You didn't ask him?"

"Somehow I didn't feel I could, after what he'd told me. And coincidences do happen, inconvenient as they may be," he added a little defensively.

"We're not getting anywhere, and you know the Guv isn't going to let us slide any longer. Our caseload has suffered this past week." She righted the chair. "The odd thing is that I've suddenly found I care in more than the ordinary way — I feel I've come to know Jasmine, through you, through Meg and the others, and I hate to think of her death going in the unsolved file."

"Anything useful come in overnight?" He tapped the open file with a forefinger.

Gemma shook her head. "Only for elimination purposes. There's not a breath of evidence that Theo Dent left Abinger Hammer by car, train, horse, bus, or bicycle on the night Jasmine died. And . . ." she hunted through the loose pages, "a reply came from the nursing school in Dorchester where Felicity Howarth did her specialized training. A clean bill of health, an 'exceptional student,' according to a note from the dean. They included her transcripts." Gemma frowned as she read. "She must have been married twice. She applied to her initial training college as Felicity Jane Heggerty, nee Atkins, giving an address in Blandford Forum." Gemma looked up at Kincaid, puzzled. "Isn't that where . . ."

Kincaid didn't hear the rest. The pieces snicked into place in his mind with blinding clarity. "Gemma, call Martha Trevellyan and find out if Felicity's scheduled to work today." Gemma raised an eyebrow, but looked the number up in the file and complied without question. She replaced the receiver and said, "Felicity called in ill. Martha's just now found someone to cover for her, and she sounded very put out — said it was not like Felicity at all."

"I think I'll pay Felicity a visit, ill or not."

"Do you want me to call her first?"

He shook his head. "No, best not."

"I'll come with you." She stood and shrugged into a cardigan she'd hung over the back of his chair.

Kincaid stopped her with a hand on her arm as she came around the desk. "Go home, Gemma. You've done more than necessary already. Spend your Saturday properly, with Toby." He smiled. "And it would be discreet on your part not to be associated with this, because it's quite likely I've just lost every marble I ever possessed."

CHAPTER
20

The April sun lent an air of industrious festivity even to Felicity Howarth's run-down street. The uncollected rubbish had disappeared, a few residents washed cars or worked in their tiny front gardens.

Kincaid rang Felicity's bell and waited, hands in pockets, until the echoes died away, then rang again. He had reached for the bell for the third time when the door opened. "Mr. Kincaid."

"Hello, Felicity. Can you spare me a few minutes?" She did indeed look unwell, wrapped in an old, pink dressing gown that clashed with the faded red-gold of her hair, her face scrubbed free of make-up and lined with exhaustion.

She stepped aside without speaking and he followed her into the sitting room. Pulling the dressing gown more tightly around her body, she sank into a chair, the crisp authority that he associated with her missing entirely.

"I called the service. Martha said you weren't well."

After a moment in which he thought she wouldn't respond, she said, "No. Poor Martha. She doesn't expect me to let her down."

Kincaid looked around the neat sitting room, checking details against his memory. There were no photographs among the ornaments and knick-knacks. "Felicity, how old is your son?"

"My son?" she said blankly.

"I understand from Martha Trevellyan that you have a son in a nursing home."

"Barry. His name is Barry." A trace of anger came through her lethargy. "He's twenty-nine."

"Why didn't you tell us you came from Dorset? You and Jasmine must have shared a common bond."

"I didn't think of it. I've lived in London for years, and Jasmine and I never spoke of it."

"But you were aware that Jasmine had lived in Dorset, even though you never discussed it."

Felicity pleated a fold of her dressing gown between her fingers. "She must have mentioned it, but I can't remember that we ever actually talked about it. I have a lot of patients, Mr. Kincaid. I can't be expected to keep the details of their life stories straight in my mind."

A little progress, he thought, pleased to have moved her from apathy to a more revealing defensive posture. "But surely the parallel was unusual enough to be remarked upon? After all, during the time you lived in Blandford Forum, Jasmine worked in the solicitor's office on the market square. Do you know the one, next to the bank? It's still there."

He left the sofa and shifted the chair from Felicity's desk around so that he could sit facing her, their knees almost touching. "Tell me exactly what's wrong with your son, Felicity. Why is he kept in a nursing home?" Kincaid held his breath, knowing he had not a shred of evidence, only a wild surmise that had blossomed suddenly in his brain.

Felicity studied the fold of dressing gown now scrunched in both hands. After a moment she looked up and met Kincaid's eyes. "He's almost completely blind and deaf. He responds to very little stimulus, but he does know me."

"Martha Trevellyan said something about a childhood injury. What happened to Barry, Felicity?"

Her hands became still in her lap. "Now they call it DAI, diffuse axonal injury, but when Barry was a baby so little was known about profound head injuries that they were often misdiagnosed."

Kincaid sighed and sat back. "I think," he said slowly, "that you didn't need to be told that Jasmine came from Dorset because you remembered her very well. What I don't understand is Jasmine not mentioning in her journals that she knew you."

Felicity stood up and went to the window. Since Kincaid's last visit, clusters of pale green leaves had burst out along the bramble shoots and a few late daffodils had pushed their heads through the grass. "I always mean to do something with the garden," she said, her back to him. "Then I work extra shifts and visit Barry on my days off, and somehow I never get around to it."

Kincaid waited. After a moment he saw her shoulders relax, and he knew she had made up her mind. She continued as if she hadn't interrupted the thread of the conversation. "Perhaps she saw it as a judgement. Retribution. And at first I think she wasn't sure, didn't trust her own memory. My name was different." She turned to face him, but with the light behind her he couldn't read her eyes. "I went by Janey in those days — my first husband thought Felicity too Victorian, and I humored him — and I later remarried, so my last name changed as well. It was almost thirty years ago, after all, and people do change physically, as hard as we try to prevent it." The corners of her mouth turned up.

"How did you come to know Jasmine then?"

Felicity smiled again. "I considered myself very lucky to have found her to look after Barry. She was only a couple of years younger than I, responsible, ambitious, wanted to get on in the world. Evenings and weekends when she wasn't working in old Mr. Rawlinson's office she liked to pick up a bit extra."

She moved back to the chair, her dressing gown falling open at the knees to reveal a sliver of nylon nightdress as she sat, carelessly now. "It was an ordinary Saturday. I'd gone shopping. Jasmine met me at the door, her face white and stiff with fright. She said she'd called for the doctor, she thought Barry was having some kind of a seizure. I remember putting my parcels down carefully before I went to him. He lay rigid in his cot, his face contorted, making little circles around his head with his fists." She fell silent, her gaze fixed on her fingers intertwined in her lap.

"Felicity —"

"There was never any proof. Small town doctors . . . no one was sure what had happened to him. One doctor said he'd seen damage like that when a child had been shaken, but he wouldn't swear to it. But I played detective." She looked up and smiled at him. "You would have been proud of me. A neighbor said she'd seen Jasmine let a young man into the flat, and that Jasmine had later left for a few minutes. I checked round all the shops in the street. She'd bought something at the chemist to rub in the baby's gums — he was teething and had been horribly fussy.

"I rode the bus to Jasmine's village and made some excuse to gossip with the post mistress. There was talk of Jasmine going around with a boy who wasn't quite right in the head."

"Timmy Franklin?"

Felicity nodded. "I never believed Jasmine knew he would hurt Barry. But she was responsible for him, wasn't she?" For the first time Felicity seemed to lose confidence. "She should never have left him alone."

"What happened then?"

"Nothing." She lifted her hands in a gesture of defeat. "For a while we thought Barry might get better. When it became obvious that there would be no change my husband began to drift even further away — he'd never wanted a baby anyway and he couldn't cope. He stayed just long enough for me to finish my nurse's training. At first I managed to have Barry cared for at home, but it became more and more difficult, and when we moved to

London I had to place him in a nursing home."

"And Jasmine?" Kincaid asked. "What happened to Jasmine?"

"She disappeared. Didn't even come back for her aunt's funeral. I never thought to see her again."

"You didn't look for her?"

Felicity shook her head. "I thought I'd stopped hating her, over the years. I didn't even think of her often. I couldn't believe it when I saw her name in Martha's case files. And dying of cancer — how suitable. I had to see her, I couldn't rest until I did."

"She must have become certain who you were, after a time."

"But I didn't speak of it, so she didn't either. I thought it would torment her, make her doubt her sanity." Felicity shivered and rubbed her hands over her upper arms. "The absurd thing was that she seemed to trust me, to depend on me. My job is comforting and reassuring the dying, yet I told her how much she would hurt, how pitiful her existence would become. And she accepted it.

"When I saw the suicide literature I didn't discourage her. It seemed fitting that she should take her own life."

"But she didn't, did she? What happened the day Jasmine died?"

Closing her eyes, she spoke slowly, as if

351

reliving events in her mind. "She'd been very quiet for a few days. I thought she was working herself up to suicide. But when I arrived that Thursday morning she seemed different. Calm, with a brightness about her. Sometimes the dying acquire a certain grace. You can't predict it, and it doesn't always happen, but it had happened for Jasmine. She told me she felt she could face anything." Felicity looked at Kincaid, imploring. "I couldn't bear it. Do you understand? I couldn't bear it."

"What did you do?" Kincaid asked gently.

"Oh, the ordinary things. Helped her with her bath, changed her bed. Made her comfortable." Felicity gave a ghost of a laugh at the irony of it. "The rest of the day was a nightmare. I must have seen my other patients, but I don't remember doing it."

"But you went back."

"Yes."

Kincaid heard a clock ticking somewhere in the house, and it seemed to counterpoint the rise and fall of his own breath.

"I didn't know until I walked in and she smiled at me from the bed what I intended to do. And then it seemed so right, so simple. It was time for her evening medication and I offered to fix it for her. I used her own supply and put the empty vials in my bag. I never thought anyone would question that she'd slipped away in her sleep." Looking out into the garden, she said after a moment, "After I'd given her the morphine she took my hand and thanked me for my kindness to her."

Felicity leaned forward, clasping her knees, and the top of her dressing gown gapped enough to reveal the pale swell of her breast. The exposure made her seem even more vulnerable, and pity warred with necessity in his heart. "You stayed, didn't you?"

"Until she lost consciousness. I found I couldn't leave her."

He watched her as she sat lost in her thoughts, and he knew he could not escape his obligation to his job, or to Jasmine. "Felicity, you know I'm going to have to ask you to come with me."

"Let me put on something a little more suitable."

Felicity returned from the bedroom wearing the navy suit in which he'd first seen her. In her hand she held a blue composition book. "Jasmine kept this under her pillow. I took it as an afterthought, only because I thought it might contain some reference to me." She collected her handbag and keys, then paused with her hand on the door. "And once I'd read it I knew I'd never be able to live with what I'd done."

CHAPTER 21

Kincaid saw her as he turned the corner into Carlingford Road. She sat on his front step, elbows on knees, chin in hands. The street lay in shadow, and the air was fast losing the day's warmth. The process of charging Felicity Howarth with the murder of Jasmine Dent had taken most of the afternoon and what remained of his energy.

When he had parked the car and come to sit beside her, Gemma said, "I thought you might like some company."

"The duty sergeant said you'd called." Although she had moved over to make room for him on the narrow step, their shoulders and thighs still touched, and he was surprised at the warmth generated by such a small area of contact.

"You'll have to tell me, you know. Was it very bad?"

354

He leaned against the doorjamb and closed his eyes for a moment, then rubbed his face with his hands. "From the beginning I felt Jasmine must have trusted whoever gave her the morphine, and Felicity was the obvious choice, but for my life I couldn't see why. Now I think I'd have been happier not knowing." He related the story as he had pieced it together. "Schizophrenia is a progressive disease. Timmy Franklin must have appeared almost normal unless something triggered a violent episode. Jasmine couldn't have known. I imagine he shook the baby to stop him crying."

"And Jasmine loved him enough to protect him?"

Kincaid brushed at a spot on the knee of his jeans. "Partly that. Partly guilt. I think she suffered all her life for that moment's well-meant negligence."

Gemma glanced at him, then said slowly, "So did Felicity Howarth and her son."

"Yes." He looked more carefully at her, noting consciously what had been only a vague impression. The past few weeks' tension was gone from the set of her shoulders, the tiny crease missing from her forehead, her hands lay still and relaxed in her lap. "What's happened, Gemma? It's not just the case, is it? You've made a decision."

She smiled. "The great detective displays his amazing powers of deduction. I called an estate agent this morning. I'm selling the house. There are some nice flats in Wanstead, near the Common, that would do for Toby and me. It occurred to me that keeping the house was my way of holding on to Rob — that was his idea of what a family should do, should be. Perhaps if he'd been able to see other alternatives, it wouldn't have frightened him so much."

"And Toby?"

"We'll still be close enough for my mum to help out a bit more. Only a bit, mind you." Laughing, she looked up at him, and he felt an unaccountable release, as if Jasmine and Felicity's lives no longer weighed quite so heavily upon his own.

"I promised you a walk on the Heath."

"So you did." She stood and stepped lightly down to the pavement, and he followed.

Kincaid held the squirming cat against his chest with one hand as he unlocked the door to his flat with the other. As soon as he'd maneuvered through the door he relaxed his grip and Sid leaped for the floor, leaving parallel lines of blood welling on the back of his hand.

"That's bloody grateful for you," Kincaid

said, sucking his hand. "It'll take a bit of getting used to for both of us, mate." All but the tip of Sid's tail disappeared under the sofa, and Kincaid left him to adjust in his own time. He had moved the cat's things upstairs after Gemma had gone, tidying Jasmine's flat with a sense of finality.

One thing remained. He'd not felt it necessary to enter the blue composition book as evidence, as Felicity had made a full confession. Now he rescued it from the car and set it on the coffee table while he drew the blinds and poured himself a drink. "Glenfiddich, Sid. Reserved for special occasions." He sat, feeling the whiskey warm his empty stomach, watching the cat emerge and begin a delicate exploration.

Setting aside his glass, he picked up the book and leafed carefully through pages filled with neat, familiar script. The last entry was dated the day of Jasmine's death.

I realized today had not been such a bad day, nor the one before, nor the one before that. If I had lived every moment of my life with the same awareness and intensity as these last weeks, it would have been rich beyond measuring.

As it is, I seem to have been blessed with a peculiar sense of time slowing down and open-

ing up, allowing experience and reflection si-multaneously. A quirk of physics, an alteration in consciousness — whatever its origin, it is a gift I shall not refuse.

The employees of THORNDIKE PRESS hope you have enjoyed this Large Print book. All our Large Print books are designed for easy reading — and they're made to last.

Other Thorndike Large Print books are available at your library, through selected bookstores, or directly from us. Suggestions for books you would like to see in Large Print are always welcome.

For more information about current and upcoming titles, please call or mail your name and address to:

THORNDIKE PRESS
PO Box 159
Thorndike, Maine 04986
800/223-6121
207/948-2962